Whose Death Is It, Anyway?

Whose Death Is It, Anyway?

Elizabeth Daniels Squire

WHEELER
PUBLISHING

This Large Print edition is published by Wheeler Publishing, Waterville, Maine USA and by BBC Audiobooks, Ltd, Bath, England.

Published in 2004 in the U.S. by arrangement with C. B. Squire, Squire Editorial Consultants.

Published in 2005 in the U.K. by arrangement with the Author's Estate.

U.S. Softcover 1-58724-866-2 (Softcover)
U.K. Hardcover 1-4056-3212-7 (Chivers Large Print)
U.K. Softcover 1-4056-3213-5 (Camden Large Print)

A Peaches Dann Mystery.

The text of this Large Print edition is unabridged.
Other aspects of the book may vary from the original edition.

Set in 16 pt. Plantin by Christina S. Huff.

Printed in the United States on permanent paper.

British Library Cataloguing-in-Publication Data available

ISBN 1-58724-866-2 (lg. print : sc : alk. paper)

Whose Death Is It, Anyway?

Acknowledgments

I would like to thank all the wonderful bookshops and libraries where I've had the pleasure of meeting readers, who often share their interesting and colorful memory-coping skills. Peaches is indebted to them all.

Robert H. Haggard made legal suggestions, but if any legal mistakes crept in, they are mine, not his.

Also, thanks for tips from Donna Miguel of Pisgah Legal Services and Betsy Bolton of Guardian Ad Litem.

Thanks to the False Memory Syndrome Foundation for material about false memory and how that can work.

Suel Anglin of the Richmond Hill Inn in Asheville, who lent a hand with scenes in that establishment, thank you.

Thanks to Cheiro and some of the fascinating early writers on hand reading whose work piqued my interest in that subject back in the days when I wrote a syndicated newspaper feature on how to read character and inclinations from the hands.

My writing group members — Dershie McDevitt, Peggy Parris, Geraldine Powell, and Florence Wallin — gave great suggestions as always, and Elizabeth Franklin, Bonnie Blue, and Linda March were invaluable in their aid.

My editors, Laura Anne Gilman and Judith Stern Palais, and my agent, Luna Carne-Ross, have helped in making this a better book.

And most of all I am grateful to my husband, C. B. Squire, for moral support, good ideas, and putting up with me in the throes of creation!

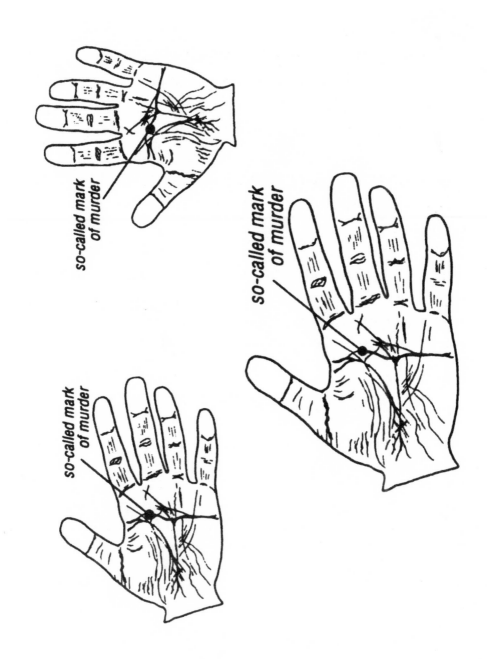

Chapter

1

Saturday, August 26

Only my father would decide to have our family reunion next to the fishpond where his sister had drowned! Right there among the water lilies in his garden. And not by natural causes, either — she'd been murdered.

"But, Peaches, that was two years ago," Pop said when I objected, "and we have to be mature about this. Nobody lives forever." By mature, he means like him. Eighty-five and as uninhibited as a newborn babe.

Frail as he is, he can be dignified, sitting at his favorite table in his living room, near the sliding glass doors to the garden. The white-haired ruler of his own world. And totally unpredictable.

A large tear rolled down his cheek as he turned his faded blue eyes and stared out toward the water lilies. He's too blind to see more than outlines now, but his memory fills in details. He smiled proudly. "This is the best damned garden in the whole family."

As I sat there at the table with Pop, my eyes agreed. It *is* lovely. His yard is cut into the side of the mountain, with the green lawn and the roses my mother planted and the little pond and the view beyond of the next range of blue-green mountains.

"But, Pop," I said, "the family won't like it. That pond will make us all uncomfortable. And you know perfectly well we're at our very worst when we're uncomfortable."

Unfortunately, as it turned out, the rest of the family was happy for Pop to have the reunion anyplace he wanted as long as he'd take care of all the details. That left the job to me, with help from my husband, Ted.

Worse yet, the reunion would be just before the publication date of my new book, *How to Survive Without a Memory*, written for my friends and others who don't remember as well as they used to. (I never did remember as well as they used to.) I should be setting up promotion for my book, not finding tents and borrowing chairs.

"We can't rent the tent from West's Funeral Home, Pop," I said firmly when we conferred further. "They buried Aunt Nancy."

"They have the cheapest tent that's big enough in case it rains," Pop retorted. "All those people will not fit in my house. And besides, since the family always rents a funeral tent for reunions, people would notice and talk if we didn't."

I made up my mind to think positive. Hope springs eternal.

And that's why, on Saturday afternoon, August 26, we found ourselves at long tables under the discreetly labeled West's Funeral Home tent, 131 of us, not counting small children. And if the lily pond worried any of us, you couldn't tell.

At least not until Cousin Fern Allen from California brought up the Mark of Murder.

I should have known things were going too well. "We don't need anything else, do we?" asked Ted, in his lively plaid picnic shirt. He'd been off, making sure we had enough tables and chairs.

"We have what we need and more," Pop crowed, head held high, white shock of hair tossed back. Like a skinny rooster, even to the big beak. He sat at the table next to ours in his wheelchair, happily ensconced between a pretty young thing in pink and Cousin Arthur, who's a baby doctor. "At my age," Pop trumpeted, "you never know when this will be your last year, boys and girls, so, by gosh, I've made sure this get-together at my house is going to be a lulu! Unforgettable! With all you great folks here!"

Only one more thing was needed to make the reunion perfect, I told myself. If only my daughter, Eve, could have come home from Hong Kong to be with us. She's my daughter from my first marriage. Ted plucked me from widowhood, God bless him. I don't worry about Eve because she's so independent. She exports Oriental art, and she's happy doing it. But with all these relatives on hand, I missed my daughter.

Still, I was pleased to have Ted on one side of me and Cousin Fern — who is never dull — on the other. The Mars family, all ages, filled up the rest of the table. They are a laid-back farm family with one exception: pink-cheeked daughter Janet, who has sparkling, hopeful eyes, curly yellow hair, and is full of what-next wiggles.

Between bites of barbecue, Fern said, "Peaches, you ought to learn to read hands."

That didn't alarm me, since I know Fern likes to be dramatic. Always has, since she grew up down the road from us here in the mountains. She used to scare all the kids to death with ghost stories. Sometimes she'd scare herself, too. Moving to California hasn't toned Fern down. She has bleached-blond hair and favors large earrings and bright colors. She's a real-estate broker — and good at it, I hear, but she's sure not good at avoiding subjects that stir people up.

"You're a people watcher like me," Fern said, "and it's interesting to know, for instance, that at least three people here have the old-fashioned

14

Mark of Murder on their palms." She swept her eyes around the tent. "I was looking at hands before we sat down."

Oh, brother! This was no place to talk about a Mark of Murder. I mean, aside from Nancy and the fishpond, somebody had once even tried to kill my father.[1]

I tried to change the subject. "I would expect our hands to show determination," I said. The truth is, most of us in this family are like our mountains: we may be lovely on the surface, but there's flint underneath.

"The Mark of Murder!" squealed Janet Mars. I call her Janet the Planet. She goes into orbit. A few name tricks, along with rhymes and such, help me remember who's who.

"What's this about the Mark of Murder?" Pop called out — more like shouted — from the next table. His eyesight may be weak, but his ears are sharp. Trust Pop to hear anything that might make life more exciting. My heart sank. He'd never let this subject drop.

Heads turned when he yelled, and that was fine with Fern. She has a husky voice that carries.

"The Mark of Murder," Fern announced to one and all, "is the old name for a single line

[1] Those problems are explained in earlier Peaches Dann books — Nancy's death in *Who Killed What's-Her-Name?* and the threat to Pop in *Remember the Alibi.*

across your palm. Most folks have a lower line we call the head line and an upper line we call the heart line. When one line goes up and joins the other, that's the mark." Fern took a sip of her iced tea, charm bracelets jangling.

I looked at my hands. I couldn't help it. Yes, I had two horizontal lines, no way merged.

The folks near us held out their palms in front of them, too — quite an assortment of kin, from young Janet the Planet to Cousin Toto (rhymes with photo) Small, the photographer.

Cousin Arthur, the baby doctor, chirped up next to Pop. "One horizontal line instead of two is a sign of Down's syndrome." Arthur is not known for tact.

Pop sat up ramrod straight in his wheelchair and glared at him. "Not in our family!"

Janet screamed. "I've got it! I've got the Mark of Murder! But I never — and I certainly wouldn't . . . !" She glanced toward the fishpond. Oh, brother!

"Of course not," Fern said calmly but plainly, savoring the furor she was causing. And I admit I didn't do a thing to stop it. Even Ted seemed to be frozen. It was horrible but fascinating. Like a car wreck happening.

"What that mark actually means, in the opinion of modern hand readers, is *not* that the person might be tempted to commit murder, as the old books say." Fern paused to let us digest that. "It simply means a strong streak of originality. In fact, depending on the other marks in

16

the hand, it might be on the hand of an inventor. Henry Wallace, who developed hybrid corn and was once vice president, had a mark kind of like that." Fern was being her factual broker self, full of details. "Henry Miller, the novelist, had a line like that." She paused and looked thoughtful. "Though his line wasn't exactly the same."

Janet preened. "Hey, I never heard of them, but it sounds like they did okay."

"The so-called Mark of Murder must be quite common," I said to Fern, noticing the waves of nervous conversation sweeping through the tent, not to mention heads turned toward the fishpond. I tried to tone things down. "You say you've already found three palms with that mark, right here at this reunion. And you haven't studied all the hands here," I added, glancing at the sea of folding tables on the wide lawn. Then I got curious. "How many of our hands have you looked at?"

Pop had deserted his supper and scooted his wheelchair over next to Fern. "Of course that mark isn't common, Peaches," he interrupted proudly. "Nothing in our family is common."

"I've looked at the hands of about thirty of us," Fern announced. "We'd find more Marks of Murder, no doubt, if we looked at more. Just like you have Great Uncle John's eagle nose," she said to Pop, "or your Grandma Bessie's twinkly eyes," she said to me, "hand markings run in families, too. And even if we weren't all related, whenever a group of people get together

17

with a common interest, you'll find a lot of the same marks." She spoke in a theatrical voice which carried across the lawn. I'd almost forgotten Fern had wanted to be an actress when she was younger.

She's one of the Show-Off Allens. You see, we all have nicknames for each other. We act as if it's in fun, but the truth is, those nicknames fit: the Pig-Headed Joneses, the Swell-Headed Baylors, the Show-Off Allens, the Self-Righteous Morrisons. The wags in the family call my branch the Tight-Fisted Smiths. But never mind, blood draws us together.

I knew I needed to squelch Fern before our cousin John Baylor heard her. He's a lawyer here in Buncombe County. (He keeps folks away from the jailer, which rhymes with Baylor.) He's a wildly logical lawyer. Anything mystical or occult or such sets him off.

Too late. I saw John rising from his chair. His round face was red and shining with sweat. And no wonder he was hot. In our sea of T-shirts and shorts, Cousin John had on a suit, white shirt, and tie.

"I'd like to object," John thundered. "A family reunion is no place for silly superstitions."

A broad happy smile spread over Pop's face. He turned in his wheelchair, nodded like a wise chairman of the board, and said, "You're good for us, Cousin John. You make us think."

When Pop says he's thinking, watch out. But I couldn't just gag him. After all, he is my father.

"Let's find out if this mark shows something special about our family." Pop waved his arm grandly to take in all of us. "If it does, then we will find many more of these marks in the hands of the members here. Isn't that right, Fern?"

Fern nodded her blond curls. "Absolutely," she said. "You wait and see!" Fern has never been one to back down. Ted got up, went over, and whispered something in her ear. His hair was standing out at odd angles. He'd been running his fingers through it, which is what my good-looking husband tends to do when something worries him. But if he hoped to shut Fern up, he was an optimist.

By this time the little alarm bells in my head were going flat out. The whole crowd seemed tuned in to the hand reading talk, for better or for worse. At a table in a far corner, I saw tears began to run down the face of Mary Mary-Sue (who is named after her two grandmothers, Mary on her mother's side and Mary-Sue on her father's). Mary Mary-Sue never cries in public. That's why I noticed. That, and because she's six feet tall. Her husband, Ward, sat there by her side, ignoring her tears. He's a kind of handsome hunk who can't seem to hold a job. He hunts and hikes while other people toe the line. But Mary Mary-Sue is smart enough to have a good job running our senator's mountain office. She manages to look noble, like the Statue of Liberty without a torch. Except now.

Was she that upset by the hand-reading talk? How odd. What was going on?

"Pop," I said, "maybe this isn't the time . . ."

But the president of the United States couldn't have stopped Pop. "I will take bets," he announced triumphantly. "Each of you estimate how many of us have the Mark of Murder on our hands and write the number on a slip of paper with your name. Peaches and Fern will look at all the hands and collect the slips of paper. I'll put up a prize of a hundred dollars for the one who makes the closest guess. You two girls stand up." Boy, Pop was really outdoing himself. He is stingy, even if he did pay for the barbecue. Offering a hundred dollars meant he truly wanted to know.

Cousin John Baylor rushed over to us, almost bursting out of his lawyer suit and tie. He pulled me aside. "Is there any way we can stop this?" he begged. He had turned from red to gray.

All around us was a sea of conversation and laughter — people comparing their hands. "Better to get it over with," I sighed. "When Pop gets something in his head, it's hard to stop him. And now everybody wants the hundred dollars."

Cousin Truthful Birdsong, self-righteous branch, came charging over and almost rescued John. She's a gospel singer. "Hand reading and all kinds of prophesying the future are a sin." She quivered with purpose in her white satin T-shirt, which said I.O.U. GOD in

20

rose-colored glitter across the front. She glared a challenge at Pop.

Pop turned to Fern, who just laughed. "Oh, I don't read the future," she shrugged. "I only read character and prospects."

"Character!" said Janet the Planet with a pout. "What fun is that?"

"My Lord," said a gangly, gray-haired woman in a black T-shirt (one of the Joneses?). "I've been putting up with my character for fifty-three years. The less said about that the better!"

"We won't look at hands until we finish eating," I said firmly. I was still hungry, and that gave time for some miracle to divert Pop and his hundred dollars. I glanced back at Mary Mary-Sue (double cousin: mother, self-righteous branch; father, pig-headed branch). The tears were still on her face, but she wasn't producing more. She looked angry. I'd heard she was unhappy because her daughter Kim had left home. Kim was adopted and the apple of her mother's eye. I'd accepted my Eve's leaving because it made her happy. Mary Mary-Sue did not look accepting. But then again, maybe she was mad at something else. But why now?

I went to get some dessert, which was all laid out with the other good things on a long table, and was trying to decide between the black-walnut pound cake and the lemon-meringue pie — and about to take a little of both, to calm my nerves — when John Baylor pulled me aside again. He was still sweating more than the suit and tie should have accounted for, I thought.

"Listen," he said, "this is more serious than you think." His I-am-an-important-lawyer voice was ominous. "Cousin Mary Mary-Sue is terribly upset."

"Yes," I said, "I noticed. In a minute I'll go ask her what's wrong."

"For God's sake, don't do that!" he whispered. "I know what's wrong. And she'd love an excuse to tell you what a martyr she is."

Mary Mary-Sue? She didn't strike me as a martyr.

John pulled me even farther away from the dessert table, out of anyone's earshot. "Mary Mary-Sue gets strange ideas," he said, "and this hand-reading foolishness is going to make it worse by riling her up more about murder. Because she has decided that because her daughter Kim doesn't write home, the girl is dead. And since Kim wouldn't just die for no good reason, that fool woman has jumped to the conclusion that the girl was murdered." His voice rose in amazement. He stood straight, like the counsel for the defense. "And Mary Mary-Sue is blaming it on me."

I wasn't alarmed. You see, our family takes a dim view of anyone who leaves home in a huff, even if all our clannishness sometimes inspires departure. Like with Cousin What's-His-Name, swell-headed branch, who was presumed dead until he returned after ten anonymous years, flaunting his all-by-myself success as a real-estate man in Omaha. Or John Charles Jones, pig-headed branch, who went off back in the 1970s, leaving an angry note about how his father read his diary. He announced he'd resigned from the family. Only boy I ever knew who kept a diary.

But suppose something really had happened to Kim? I suddenly saw her vividly in my mind's eye: pretty, with wide-set, violet eyes and vibrant brown-black hair. She had style and a good sense of humor. She could be moody and her practical jokes were sometimes a little much, but I liked her.

"I think you'd better tell me the whole story about Kim," I told John Baylor firmly. "And in return I'll do what I can to keep Pop quiet."

"Not now," he said, as Cousin Elvira, the family super-gossip, bore down on us. *Elvira* always looks for something dire or preferably *direr*. On her the family eagle nose was always quivering with curiosity.

"Come by my office at ten o'clock Monday morning, and I'll tell you all about it," he whispered in his most legal manner. He stalked off. But why his office? That was odd. I went back to contemplating the cakes and pies.

Ted appeared, pretending to case desserts. "What's up?" he asked, looking like a friendly porcupine — hair-wise, at least. We drifted away from the table.

I told him about John and Mary Mary-Sue. "I'm praying that nothing is really wrong with Kim."

"John tends to exaggerate trouble," Ted said. "He sees the dark side."

But I was exasperated. "I could deal with just John," I said, "but when Fern gets dramatic and Pop won't shut up and John gets on his high horse and Mary Mary-Sue actually cries and Kim may be in danger — or she may just want to get away from family, for which I wouldn't blame her — and everybody here looks greedy to win one hundred dollars quick — well, it's getting to me.

"Why is it," I went on, "that the things our family members have in common — the stubbornness and pride, the exact things that draw them together because they are alike — can be the very same things that make big trouble?"

"You mean," Ted said, "that Mary Mary-Sue and John Baylor are both strong-willed and proud. And it's got them on some kind of collision course, and you're afraid they're going to get the rest of us — especially you and me — mixed up in it." Sometimes I think Ted is psychic.

"I may be the only one in this family," I said angrily, "who isn't hell-bent on having her way."

Would you believe Ted laughed?

"Ha!" he snorted. "You never give up, Peaches. That's hell-bent — though maybe in a good way. You're determined not to let anything

24

that gets in your way stay in your way. I mean, how many people turn being absentminded into an asset by writing a book about how to get around it?"

He was trying to calm me down by appealing to my pride in *How to Survive Without a Memory* by Peaches Dann. Out in the stores in two weeks. Thinking about my book always makes me cheerful.

"Okay," I said, "you've made a point. So let them all stew in their own juices. Let them sit under this funeral-parlor tent, near the place where Nancy died, and look for Marks of Murder in their hands and think all the negative thoughts they please. Or let them be in denial about it all. I don't care which. Because there's one thing I can tell you for sure: Whatever is going wrong, I do not intend to get in the middle of it. Not this time. I am going to be out promoting my book instead. No matter what."

Chapter

2

1:50 P.M.

By the time I finished my dessert, Pop was beaming. "Mary Mary-Sue has agreed to help with the Mark of Murder census," he informed me, "and Ted has gone in the house to get paper and pencils." Pop had even roped Ted in! My husband, the traitor.

Mary Mary-Sue looked pale. No tears now, but her mouth was in a hard straight line, making everything in her square face parallel: straight mouth, straight eyebrows, straight worry line right across her brow. Before I could say a word, Pop went on: "Mary Mary-Sue, you've done political polls. How wonderful of you to offer to help! You can record the results. You are just what we need!" Ted handed her a yellow legal pad and a pen, and she was set to go. But what was she up to? Upsetting Cousin

John Baylor, for sure. John had stalked off, yanking wife and daughter with him. His car left fast.

I stood there between Mary Mary-Sue and Fern and looked around at the crowd. People sat at their tables staring at their hands. So many! I mean, hands have been in front of me all my life, and I notice if they are clenched in anguish or languidly waved without direction or sure and artful because the owner is a good storyteller. But beyond that I have never truly looked into hands. So, in spite of myself, I was fascinated with what we might find out.

"In hand reading the shape is important as well as the lines," Fern said to me in her real-estate tone of voice. "You're more likely to find the Mark of Murder in the broad hand of action than in the long, narrow hand of the introvert. Later I'll tell you more about what the shape of the fingers means if you're interested. Hand reading could be useful to you in solving mysteries, Peaches," she said. "It was once an important tool for spies. Sleuthing is a lot like spying, don't you think?"

I started to say, *No, of course not!* But it's true that sleuths and spies are both trying to find out what's going on and also what's gone wrong.

"Now, each time one of you finds the Mark of Murder," Pop said to Fern and me, "you raise your hand and call out, and Mary Mary-Sue will record it. Hey, maybe we can find out if each of us who has that line is really an inventor!

I like what Fern said about the line really meaning that. Maybe we are such a remarkable family because we are such brilliant inventors." Pop luxuriated like a pleased cat. "Janet, here, invents unusual stories."

Actually, when she was younger, Janet the Planet told the most outrageous and creative lies. Luckily, in the second grade she had a teacher who showed her how to turn those lies into stories, and now she mostly told the truth on ordinary occasions.

"Now, get to work," Pop ordered, and it did seem to me that the best thing was to get this over with as fast as possible, especially now that John Baylor had left anyway. Mary Mary-Sue held her pencil so tightly her fingertips were white. If this poll upset her so, why had she agreed to help?

But Fern was enjoying herself. Whenever she came to a line even a little bit like the special mark, she'd beam with pleasure, outline the hand in pencil on a piece of paper, draw in the line, and get the person to sign the paper. Fern explained she'd tell them more about their hands later if they liked. Each time I found the line, she did the same thing.

At the first table I tackled, I found two narrow hands on women who seemed relieved not to have an unusual mark, and two broad hands — the ones that Fern said were a better bet to have the line — on men who seemed a little disappointed not to be marked. They were all out-of-town cousins whose names I couldn't remember, so it was a good thing I didn't have to tell Mary Mary-Sue who they were.

At the next table I came to Cousin Gloria, one of Pop's favorites, who ran a doll hospital over in Madison County. She had what Fern called the broad hands of a doer. Nothing unusual in her right hand, but in the left was one line across, plainly formed where the lower line ran up and merged with the upper line. A shiver waved over me involuntarily. Cousin Gloria had the mark. She is mostly a dear, but she does have a nasty temper. "She might kill *me*," her husband said cheerfully.

Lots of nervous laughter all over the place about who might be inspired to kill, and why, particularly with spouses.

I kept looking at hands and found seven with the special line. Fern found ten.

Fern made outlines of the seventeen hands that had the mark and sketched the mark in. Not all exactly the traditional Mark of Murder, she said, but some almost the same. Mary Mary-Sue recorded them all. Toto (as in photo) Small won the prize for the closest guess as to how many. He had guessed eighteen.

Then we all mingled and talked. The sun was under a cloud, and a breeze suggested we might have rain. But not yet. Most of us had wandered out from under the tent and stood around the garden. I moved from one group to another. Fern, meanwhile, went around and read more from some of the palms of the people whose hands she'd outlined. Mary Mary-Sue followed her closely and listened. I heard laughter and upbeat conversation. Nobody seemed upset at what Fern said their hands revealed. I listened as Fern told Janet she had that "murder" line for inventiveness. Fern said her hand also showed she thought big. That was usually true of people with hands that were small in proportion to their bodies. And Janet was a natural-born gambler, Fern said. "Look at that ring finger, longer than the index, and those short, smooth, pointed fingers. You're spoiled," Fern added, "because you often win. Look at the high padding on your palm. You tend to be lucky."

I looked at my own hands. The padding wasn't as high. Oh, well. But, I told myself, I work for what I get, so I'm not spoiled.

Fern told Cousin Gloria she had big hands in proportion to her body, which usually meant patience with details, and since Gloria restores antique dolls, that must be true. Mary Mary-Sue was still at Fern's side, listening.

"I want to hear what my sister's hand tells!" Gloria cried. "She thinks she's not interesting. I'll bet her hands prove she is! You remember my big sister," she said to me and pointed to a gal about my age who stood quietly by her side.

Oh, bother. I never could dredge up this gal's name. There were no handles on Gloria's sister. She had a bland face and short, brown hair like mine.

"It's Gertrude!" Gloria cried, laughing at me. "You must have a trick, Peaches, to remember Gertrude."

Fern was busy reading Gertrude's hand. She said Gertrude was a very private person. Fern could tell by the way Cousin Gertrude naturally held her fingers close together and her hand curled closed. "There are mysteries about you that no one knows," Fern said and winked at Gloria. The only mystery I knew about Gertrude was that she almost always wore a white shirtwaist blouse and a navy-blue skirt. She wore her uniform for the reunion, except she had on navy-blue shorts. Ger*true blued.* I could think of her that way, though it wouldn't allow for the white blouse. Naturally she didn't have the Mark of Murder. She would never have the spark to kill. Nothing colorful was ever likely to happen to Cousin Gertrude, I told myself.

Fern hurried on to read the hand of Cousin Truthful Birdsong. Aha! She might sing gospel like a saint, but she was too extravagant. "Look at that double-jointed thumb. That's what it means," Fern said. "Extravagant. But you are always generous." The family nightingale had the head and heart lines combined in her hand, and was pleased to hear how that meant she was original. She disapproved of reading the future but not the present.

With every single hand Cousin Mary Mary-Sue stuck around, never straying too far from Fern.

The breeze was getting downright cool. I expected rain soon.

Finally Fern said she was going to leave us for a minute and headed through the sliding glass doors into the house — to the bathroom, I figured. Mary Mary-Sue followed. I meandered after. I'd begun to suspect Mary Mary-Sue was trying to find a chance to speak to Fern in private. About what? I was curious.

When I was inside, Fern and Mary Mary-Sue had vanished beyond the living room into the hall that led to Pop's room and, of course, the bathroom. I stood by the table where Pop likes to sit and listened. They must have stopped to talk in the hallway. I heard Mary Mary-Sue say, "I have a palm print of my daughter Kim back at my house. She's left home, and I'm worried. In fact I don't even know where she is." I could hardly believe that Mary Mary-Sue had a palm print of her daughter. How convenient.

"Kim and Janet were playing around with a copy machine years ago, and they made copies of their own hands," she added. "And somehow I kept the things. I put Kim's up on the bulletin board with family pictures, and it's still there. It's not a recent print, but would you look at it?" Her voice was anxious.

"Of course," Fern said. "You know I've always been fond of Kim." There was a kind of pregnant pause. Rain started outside. I saw my family running back under the tent, Ted pushing Pop's wheelchair fast.

"Kim's hand contains that line, right?" Fern asked. There was something odd about her voice, almost smug. "The one that's called the Mark of Murder? And you're worried about that."

She what? But Kim was adopted! And yet I remembered that Cousin Elvira once said Kim was of our blood — that there was something secret or tragic about her adoption. Elvira must have been guessing, since she'd stopped right there. Cousin Elvira always tells absolutely everything she knows — and a great deal she doesn't know besides.

Fern had said that, even though a lot of our family members had the line in their hands, in the population at large, it was quite rare. So what did it mean if Kim had the so-called Mark of Murder?

"You mustn't be worried, Mary Mary-Sue," Fern said. "Even in the old books that mark doesn't denote danger to the owner of the hand except by his or her own acts."

"But please look at the handprint." Mary Mary-Sue still sounded frightened. "Kim's been gone a whole week with no word."

"I'll come to your house first thing Monday morning when all this reunion whoop-de-do is over," Fern was saying. "I always love to ride out your way, Mary Mary-Sue. Then I'll tell you what Kim's hand reveals."

Chapter

3

Monday, August 28, 7 to 9 A.M.

Sunday's reunion events had included a church service with Cousin Edgar Beecher preaching the sermon. Cousin Truthful Birdsong and several others sang some old hymns, and Pop thanked everybody for coming. Later on Sunday we dispersed, somewhat exhausted.

Early Monday morning — about seven — while I sat at the kitchen table, having coffee with Ted and looking out the window at puffy white clouds in an electric-blue sky, Mary Mary-Sue called. She used her best political voice. "I know how busy you are, Peaches. You're in demand because you have such a good head on your shoulders."

"Yes," I said before she could finish buttering me up, "whenever I remember to bring it with me."

Ted regarded me wryly over the top of his newspaper. He has a kind of sixth sense about which people are calling to ask for my help. He sat there in his college-professor corduroy jacket and tortoiseshell glasses, looking wise.

Mary Mary-Sue ignored my disclaimer. "I need your advice, Peaches, and I'd appreciate it so much if you'd come over to my house this morning. I've persuaded Fern to come, too, at eight. I hope you'll give me the advantage of your wonderful common sense. I need you to look at a missing person's handprint."

Obviously she meant Kim's. John Baylor had said Mary Mary-Sue believed Kim had been killed and that it was his fault. And Kim might be of our blood, although she was adopted. How did all that fit in? But did I want to get mixed up in a feud between one of the most successful lawyers in the county and our senator's hand-maiden? No, I didn't.

"I'd love to come," I said, "but I'm just swamped doing things for Pop." I hung up and congratulated myself for saying "no." "That was Mary Mary-Sue," I told Ted and ex-plained. He raised one eyebrow in that here-we-go-again expression. "I am not going to do it!" I said firmly.

The phone rang again — Fern, sounding hurt. "Peaches," she said, "Mary Mary-Sue tells me you won't come to our meeting." Aha. This was Mary Mary-Sue's way of not taking "no" for an answer, unleashing Fern on me. "Listen,

Peaches, I had to talk her into asking you. Then you blew it. This is important."

"Why?" I asked. "A young girl wants to be off on her own. Her mother jumps to the conclusion she must be dead. Why get mixed up in that?"

"It's important for you to see this handprint," Fern said, "as part of your hand-reading education." Now she sounded patient. I hate it when people are patient. "Here you have a chance to learn one of the oldest information-gathering techniques in the world, and this is related to memory, you know. And you're the author of a book about memory. You need to know about this." More buttering up.

"Fern," I said, "you're trying to con me. Why do you want me to come?"

"For moral support," she said. "Mary Mary-Sue is a steamroller, which makes me nervous. I don't know why I agreed to go to her house, except I'm curious. And maybe I'm sorry for her."

That seemed honest, but Fern kept on in a cajoling voice. "Hand reading really is a kind of memory — it's folk memory. People have been handing it down and adding to it like a rolling snowball since as far back as history goes." She was on a roll herself. "I mean, it's not like astrology, which was part of ancient religions, an elitist thing. Plain and fancy folks read hands. It's a part of our human memory, existing for ages, all over the world. Like certain folk tales. Why, there are handprints even on prehistoric cave walls. I'm telling you, you need to know about this. And now you have a chance to look at the hand map of the character of a girl who may be either wonderfully independent or a victim. We don't know which. Aren't you intrigued by that?"

I was. My lips tried hard to form "no." I took a deep breath to gather strength. Suppose Kim was in some kind of trouble? Ted winked at me, as if he knew I'd give in. The stinker. My resolve cracked. "Okay. I'll be there," I said. Curiosity killed the cat, my grandmother used to tell me. So far it hadn't killed me.

"And could you give me a ride?" Fern asked. "I'm right along your way, and my rent-a-car has a flat tire."

So I said I'd give her a ride to Mary Mary-Sue's to study Kim's handprint.

Ted laughed. "Fern never lacks nerve."

"So why did you encourage me to go?" I asked him.

"Me?" he said, all innocence, putting down his paper. "I was sure you were going to do it all along. You're fond of Kim. You can't resist a mystery. Besides, Mary Mary-Sue always gets her way. She'd even have enlisted Pop on her side if she had to. So you might as well go look at that handprint gracefully. Just tell her that her daughter Kim has the hand of a survivor. That's what Mary Mary-Sue wants to hear."

"After I see her, I said I'd stop by John Baylor's office and hear some warning about the same situation." I sighed. "I'd like it if you came, too, if that fits your schedule. I feel like he's so slick it takes two people to know what he's up to. He's such a male chauvinist, he'll figure it's only normal for you to come along. Not like Mary Mary-Sue who would resent it if you weren't asked and came anyway."

"And she didn't invite me," Ted said. "You're allowed to see more of the family dirty linen than I am. Be sure to take notes. And take your new camera. You never know what may come up that you'd like to record. It's been my experience," he joked, "that where you go, things happen."

Ted had given me the camera for my fifty-sixth birthday in July. After all, it's another memory trick, he'd explained. It remembers what you see better than anybody but a genius could. And it's small and easy to stick in a pocketbook. So, okay, why not? I reached up to the top of the bookcase where it lives and put it in my shoulder bag. I also took the little tape recorder that is sound-activated so it doesn't run if nobody is talking. Forget that see-no-evil, hear-no-evil stuff. I was ready to record evil two ways — and hoping not to find either.

I set forth with speed but some trepidation. I picked up Fern from her motel and listened to her rehash the reunion. "So what does it mean," I asked, "that Kim has a rare mark that's common in our family?"

"That," said Fern, smoothing the skirt of her

red sundress, "is one of the things we want to find out more about."

I will say Mary Mary-Sue lives in a marvelous house — bright white and wildly Victorian with porches all over, even on the second floor, and turrets above. She came to the door as soon as I knocked and let us in to the shadowy front hall. Down the hall I could see Ward totally relaxed at the kitchen table in an old plaid shirt and jeans, sipping a cup of something, and I could hear the television going. He was pouting as usual, which somehow made me feel less good.

"Won't you have some coffee?" Mary Mary-Sue asked. Her tone of voice said she was just being polite. We both told her we'd just eaten, and I told myself not to feel looked down on. Somehow, in the house she looked even taller than her six feet, with those power-beam eyes directed right at me.

Fern stopped to admire the big, old grandfather clock that said 12:45 — and had for the last twenty years. Mary Mary-Sue always said 12:45 was the time her father died, but I suspect she stayed so busy with other things she never got the clock fixed.

"This way," she directed, and led us into a small room fixed up with file cabinets, a computer on a stand, and pictures on the wall of Mary Mary-Sue with assorted politicians: her home office to supplement the senator's official one. A table along one wall was bare except for two pictures of a hand. Maybe "pictures" is not the right word. A copy machine had picked up the main features of a right hand in black and white. "One of these is a copy of the handprint for you, Fern," Mary Mary-Sue said, handing a print to her. "You can study it at home and let me know if you see even more in it later than you do on the spot." Fern thanked her and put it in her purse.

Mary Mary-Sue indicated we should sit down in two chairs, alongside the table and settled herself in a chair at the end. "Tell me everything you see in Kim's hand," she asked Fern. Her smile seemed forced and her eyes too large, and I thought: she is truly afraid.

Fern sat down in the chair right in front of the remaining picture, and I sat down next to her. I could see that the picture on the table was reminiscent of Janet the Planet's small, plump hand. So were they kin? Janet's hand had made quite an impression on me because she was so excited about having the Mark of Murder in it.

"Interesting," Fern said, studying the picture. "Kim is impulsive, and yet she has a strong will. You see," Fern said to me, "this hand is small with tapered fingers. Kim has the short, smooth fingers that tend to show impulsiveness. But she also has large thumbs, which is one sign of strong determination, a balancing factor."

I glanced beyond Fern at Mary Mary-Sue's thumbs and back at my own. "How big is large?" I asked.

"The thumb is large if it comes higher than

the mid point of the segment of the index finger closest to the palm when all of the fingers are held together."

I held my fingers flat and together and stared at my hand. My thumb came all the way up to the second joint of my index finger. Wow!

"Exactly," Fern said. "You have big thumbs. So does Kim. The good side of that is that, if the rest of the hand shows harmony, you are wonderfully determined. If the rest of the hand shows problems, you may be just plain willful."

She didn't say what the rest of my hand showed, but she frowned as she stared at Kim's. I stared at Mary Mary-Sue's. She held her hands flat on the table, palms down. Her thumbs were almost bigger than mine.

"Kim has tremendous intuition," Fern said. "Those smooth fingers plus the bowed intuition line up the side of the palm away from the thumb tell me that." Her tone of voice had a "but" in it.

"I think Kim was confused," Fern said, "at least back when she made this handprint. Though she never seemed too much that way on the surface. But see how the lines waver and some of them are not simple straight lines but more like chains."

Mary Mary-Sue lit up with alarm. "Chains!" she gasped, as if that were a sentence to the chain gang.

"But lines change," Fern said calmly. "Most people don't know that. When we're under

41

stress, they can get like lines in this hand." She tapped the handprint. "And later they can gradually become straighter and surer and even longer. That's why I don't predict the future from lines."

"Yes, chains," Mary Mary-Sue repeated. She straightened the collar of her blouse. "Of course, Kim was confused. She wouldn't have run away from home if she weren't confused. She was happy here. I know she was. We did everything for her. We loved her so much. And now she's gone." Tears filled her eyes. She got up and took down a head-and-shoulders photograph from the wall by the computer. "Kim had confused eyes, didn't she? Somebody saw that and took advantage of my poor lamb! That's what I think."

Kim was wild-orchid pretty with lustrous dark hair so curly, I wondered how she combed it. Also smart and fun, but maybe a little bit naive. And moody sometimes. She had a small willful toss of the head. And, yes, there was something about her eyes. Hard to decipher in a picture. I let the picture lead me back to how she looked in person. Her eyes were asking for approval, or was it help? Yes, but at the same time they were gambler's eyes. Did I imagine that? Perhaps not.

"Listen," said Fern firmly to Mary Mary-Sue, "you wanted to know whether Kim is likely to take reckless chances, right?"

Mary Mary-Sue gulped, and the tears froze on her face. "Or if she'd be likely to be influenced by the wrong people," Mary Mary-Sue said. She paused and looked thoughtful, and I had the least little feeling that she was shaping the next sentence for some agenda of her own. Political animals are like that. "I can't believe Kim would have run away all by herself."

"I could tell better," Fern said, "if I knew if her hand was firm or flabby and whether it was dead white or pink or unhealthy red the last time you saw her."

Just the mention of dead white and unhealthy red made Mary Mary-Sue pale. "I should have noticed," she moaned, "but I'm sure there weren't any extremes, or I would have been aware." Behind her a signed picture of the senator hung on the wall. He looked deadly earnest. He wanted my vote.

"A dead-white hand in a warm room suggests depression or bad health," Fern said to me, obviously not wanting to neglect my education. "And if a hand is flabby and lacks strength, you'd give much less weight to signs of determination." I hoped for Kim's sake that hers was firm.

"So what can you tell me?" Mary Mary-Sue asked impatiently. "What do you think has happened to the girl who made this handprint? Is she dead or alive?"

"I'd guess alive," Fern said, and Mary Mary-Sue let out a relieved sigh. "But that's a guess based on what her hand shows she's like. She probably hasn't been led off by a con artist because she thinks for herself. She hasn't drifted into trouble for the same reason. But she may have decided to do something highly unconventional. She's a gambler. Look at the long ring finger." (Aha. I was right.)

Fern said, "People with ring fingers like that — noticeably longer than the index finger — take chances, and that may have gotten her in trouble. Or not."

Mary Mary-Sue nodded. "She did tend to surprise us," she said dryly.

"I hope you won't take this wrong," I said, "but speaking of unconventional and taking chances, I've always heard that Kim liked practical jokes. I don't suppose —"

At that, Mary Mary-Sue managed a smile. "Oh, yes," she said, "Kim didn't like to be bored — or for us to be bored. One day we were all sitting around and Ward and his sister, Sandra, were talking about the house they lived in as little kids — actually a great big, ugly house — and I guess the talk was getting boring, and Kim stood up and let out a bloodcurdling scream. And we all jumped up and began looking around for a man with a gun or a rattlesnake at our feet or God knows what, and finally we asked her what was wrong, and she said she just wanted to see how we'd all act if somebody screamed. And first we were mad, but we all got to laughing." Mary Mary-Sue's smile twisted into a sob.

I was not sure I would have laughed.

Mary Mary-Sue swallowed her sob. "But she wouldn't scare me this badly. This is no joke." She turned to Fern. "What else does her hand say?"

Fern nodded wisely, as if to say we'd come to the good part, and tapped the handprint. "Notice exactly how the lower line across the palm — the head line — rises and joins the upper line — the heart line — so they are like one line across the palm, but with a branch that rises between the index and long middle finger. That branch is all that is left of the heart line. The head and heart lines would normally run more or less parallel." Fern pointed to the line in the picture, and I looked at my palms, although I already knew I didn't have that single line. Yep, I had two horizontal lines across, God bless their hearts.

"As you know," Fern said to me, "the Mark of Murder suggests a streak of originality and inventiveness in a good hand. That's what I find. Throw in those short, smooth, impulsive fingers and the ring finger long in comparison to the others, and there's no telling what this girl might do. Actually, she is torn two ways. Her fingers say 'gambler,' and her thumb says 'plan ahead.' Her intuition may save her. Combinations are the important thing in hand reading, Peaches. That's what you need to learn." Actually, the more I learned, the more confused I became.

Mary Mary-Sue kept listening to Fern with a

worried frown. "But Kim is loving, isn't she? So she wouldn't run away without telling me and not write home. I know she wouldn't do that. Something is terribly wrong." She began to cry again. "She was a good student," she said through her sobs. "She was planning on going to Mars Hill College this fall. The boys liked her. In fact, there was one who liked her too much. But she was happy. I know she was happy."

"Didn't you fight?" Fern asked, challenging those power-driven eyes. "Two strong-willed women under the same roof?"

Mary Mary-Sue blinked as if Fern had slapped her. "Oh, not to speak of," she said quickly. "We disagreed sometimes, but that's normal with a teenager, don't you think? Kim just disappeared for no reason." Did she protest too much?

Mary Mary-Sue jumped up, grabbed Fern's hand, and pulled. "Come look at this." She led us down the hall to the kitchen, where a big section of the wall was covered with family pictures. Kim was in almost every one. Baby Kim and Mary Mary-Sue at a reunion, ribbons in Kim's hair. Small Kim being licked on her nose by a black-and-white puppy. Kim and Ward hiking along. Kim in a play, maybe junior-high vintage. And many more. "You see," said Mary Mary-Sue triumphantly, "she was always smiling." But in one picture there was no Kim, and Mary Mary-Sue was crying.

Tears were on her cheeks as she hugged a pretty bride.

Mary Mary-Sue saw me staring. "Kim's in that picture, too, in a way," she said. "That's Ward's sister at her wedding, the same day I was married only five years later. And that's the day I found out I could never have a baby." Tears came to her eyes in the here and now. "But Kim came to us, and that made it all right. We have a child. God willing, we still do."

"When did you see her last?" I asked, just what I always asked with anything lost. Where is the last place you saw it?

"Right here," she said, "right in this house. I got up to find her already dressed, and we had coffee together, and she said she was going to Asheville early to have breakfast with a friend. She had a summer job at The Compleat Naturalist shop in Asheville. But what I didn't know was that she had already quit. That was on Friday, the nineteenth, nine days ago, the day my child vanished."

"Mary Mary-Sue," I said, "there's a rumor that at least one of Kim's parents was related to us. Could that be true? Could that have anything to do with why or where she's gone?"

"I've heard that rumor," she said. "I don't know who her parents were. The records are sealed. But people like to gossip. They don't care who they hurt!"

Was she telling all she knew? She was plainly in real anguish — face white, blue circles under her eyes. "What I do know is: she's gone. I know she had help," Mary Mary-Sue said bitterly. "John Baylor, our big-shot lawyer cousin, egged her on."

"But why would he do that?" Fern asked and shook her head in disapproval.

"He gave Kim money so she could leave." A shiver made a little earthquake in Mary Mary-Sue's shoulders. "I've no idea why. Kim had no reason to leave." She clenched her fists. "And that stinker won't tell me where she might have gone." She frowned as if she were trying to read fine print while she stared into space. "That man has always taken an interest in my Kim. He arranged the adoption, you know. But that doesn't give John some kind of power over my daughter, does it? It doesn't give him a right to keep secrets from me! I know something has happened to that girl." Mary Mary-Sue's voice shook. "I know." She hugged herself as if the temperature had dropped.

She seemed so distraught, I had to say something. "Listen," I said, "you need to go back over the time just before she left and look for clues about what was on her mind. You need to talk to her friends and find out what she told them. You need to find out if any travel agent helped to get her a ticket to anywhere. You need . . ." I stopped dead. Mary Mary-Sue was throwing her arms around me.

"Oh, Peaches," she cried, "I knew you'd help!"

Chapter

4

Monday Morning, 9:30

"Where are you going next?" Fern asked as we thumped down the wooden steps from the white-railed porch and headed for the car. Next I was going to drop her off at her motel. She must have meant after that. Her eyes shone with curiosity.

The day was beginning to heat up. The air was steamy, which was unusual in the mountains. I was literally hot under the collar. Thank goodness, I'd parked the car under a tree.

"Don't look peevish," Fern said, running her fingers impatiently through her yellow curls, as if to untangle life. "I know you can't help looking into this disappearance. And I can help you. This is my vacation. I can do what I please. In fact, I'm so intrigued, I'm going to stay on a few days." She paused with her hand on my car's passenger door, obviously waiting for me to approve.

I was noncommittal. In fact, I felt the need for space.

"I bet you're going to see John Baylor, aren't you?" She smiled at me across the top of the car as though she wanted a favor. "I heard John try to stop the Mark of Murder contest. I saw you two confer as thick as thieves. And nosy Elvira got in the way." She ducked into the car, and I got in my side. At least the car was cool.

"Elvira is a pain in the ass," Fern said as I fished for my keys in my pocketbook. Usually I put the keys right on their key snap as I should. It was worth getting a special pocketbook that had one of those. But today I'd had my mind so entirely on Kim's handprint when I got out of the car that I hadn't done it. My fingers had stashed the keys while my mind was out to lunch.

"Mary Mary-Sue says John's mixed up in this. I bet you already knew that, right?" I glanced up from the pocketbook jungle to see Fern wink. "I swear, you're a homing pigeon, Peaches, drawn to mystery."

I thought: California has increased that gal's love of the weird.

I'd had enough weird already for one lifetime. I was late and in bad humor. I pulled three tissues and a sales slip out of the pocketbook to improve visibility. Ha! My fingers touched the keys.

"It's like magic," Fern said, "the way you can't do easy things like keeping track of stuff, but you can do hard things like solving crimes. It's a miracle!" Her voice vibrated with drama.

"Magic," I said firmly, "means something you don't understand!" I put the key in the ignition. "And I keep a card on my bulletin board which says: MIRACLES ARE NATURAL. WHEN THEY DO NOT HAPPEN, SOMETHING IS WRONG."

I turned the key in the ignition and put my foot on the gas pedal. Something *was* wrong. The car got the dry heaves. Normally it never did that.

I looked down at the gas gauge: dead empty. My heart sank. *Dern,* I said to myself. *Double dern. This is not the day when I need to be out of gas.* And I was already late to see John Baylor.

Fern did not seem to notice. "At least you must agree," she said, "that this has been a very fruitful trip."

"Fruitful?" I asked. "First I agreed to help Mary Mary-Sue when I should get out and promote my book, and now I'm out of gas, and it sure isn't fruitful for me to be stuck here."

She laughed. "You see! You can't remember to get gas, but I bet you'll find Kim."

Words rose in my throat. *If you're so dern smart, Fern, and you've read my hand so you know my character, why weren't you smart enough to remind me to check the gas?* That's what I wanted to yell. I said it in my head. Then I visualized a bright red stop sign. I took a deep breath. Like it says in my chapter "The Great Importance of Judicious Pauses," I stopped and pulled myself together. And thereby reconsidered. Because if you're mad at yourself for what you forgot, it doesn't help to get other people mad at you by blaming them.

Most memory books ignore what to do *after* memory lapses, but that's like flying without a parachute. I believe in parachutes, so I stayed calm.

"I'll go and see if Mary Mary-Sue has an emergency can or some gas for the lawn mower." That's all I said. I did kind of breathe fire around the words, but not at Fern. "You wait here, please," I said. "If we both go back in, we'll never get away." And, wonder of wonders, Fern agreed.

Mary Mary-Sue met me at the door, just inside the screen, hovering. She must have been waiting there to see us leave.

"You remembered!" she enthused as she opened the screen door. Perhaps she'd been there to call me back for something. But what?

I was glad I'd been reminded of "Judicious Pauses." Works in all sorts of ways. As it says in my twelfth chapter, if someone says, "You remembered," or "You guessed," or anything to suggest you're cleverer than you are, for God's sake pause. Nine times out of ten, he'll tell you what it is that he assumes you know, but actually you've forgotten. And then you will know. There's more than one way to be smart!

I made eye contact and waited. The pause lengthened. Most folks can't stand that, so they fill it. Mary Mary-Sue was no exception. "You remembered that you need to look at Kim's room," she said, "because a person's room tells who they are, don't you think? You knew Kim over the years, but not really well. And maybe that's even an advantage. Because when you look at her things, something that we take for granted may strike you as a clue to where she's gone. I hope it does." Tears sprang into her eyes, but she stopped them with a quick little shake of her head.

I gave her my best wise smile. "Actually there were two reasons I came back," I said. "Do you happen to have a can of gas? I'm out."

Also it was getting late. I'd have to zip through Kim's room as fast as a tornado.

Then I thought of my camera. Hoorah! With that I could, in effect, take Kim's room with me and study it when I had time. God, as they say, takes care of fools, drunks, and the United States of America. Also me. Although in this case it was Ted who had suggested the camera, wasn't it? Well, actually, Ted was one of the best things God ever did. I called and alerted Ted to let John know we'd be late.

"And while we're looking at Kim's room, I'll get Ward to put gas in your car because we do have a can in the garage," Mary Mary-Sue promised. She hallooed for Ward, who came in with a gun he was cleaning. I don't know gun makes, but it was a long one which I associate with hunting. He was still pouting. I think the pout was tattooed on his face. Ward trudged off to see about the gas.

We walked down the corridor past the clock and up creaking steps to a second-story central hall. Kim's room was on the right with the door open, so I could see in to ruffled curtains. Once inside I could see it was a room of many facets. A collection of dolls and a few stuffed animals which Kim must have loved as a little child were perched on a shelf to the left of the door. A stuffed octopus with a red bow leaned on the pillow on her bed. On the wall were a picture of a hugely oversized, very arty flower and a poster of a rock star. Bare-chested. Long-haired. Very sexy.

The old-fashioned ruffled curtains and bed-spread with a print of small flowers didn't go with the rugged rock star caught in violent motion. A dressing table with a mirror and bottles of cologne seemed very grown-up and ladylike, but next to the colognes I saw an envelope clearly marked RATTLESNAKE EGGS. Honest.

A pile of books on a small desk included a high-school math book and one called *How to Find Almost Anyone, Anywhere*. On top of the pile was one Indian arrowhead. And next to the pile was a photograph of Kim.

"Nice picture," I said to Mary Mary-Sue, who had come in and was peering at the picture. "Makes Kim look more mature somehow."

"I don't remember that picture," she said. "And Kim has on somebody else's SAVE THE WHALES T-shirt. Isn't that strange?"

I didn't answer. I was carefully photographing the four sides of the room, with close-ups of interesting areas like the desk. I could go over this room with Ted later. He has a good eye for important details.

I didn't ask questions. No time, though Mary Mary-Sue obviously wanted to linger and tell me anecdotes about Kim. She picked up the most battered baby doll, hugged it against her shoulder, and stood between me and the door. "Kim wasn't a child anymore, so of course she had her own private thoughts." She swallowed and squeezed her eyes shut. She opened those eyes and turned them full force on me. "I felt she had secrets. I knew. But I didn't know of any way to find out what."

I hugged Mary Mary-Sue and explained I had to hurry. But I wanted to hear more later. I'd call. I thanked Ward, who came in to say my car now had enough gas to get to the Exxon station down the road. I hurried out and slipped into the car next to Fern. I told her about Kim's room as we started back to town, stopping, of course, for gas. Then we rode in silence. I needed that.

At Fern's motel she jumped out of the car and came around to my window. "Thank you," she said, adding, "You see how quiet I can be when you are thinking something out? I make a good partner." So that was a demonstration! Or maybe propaganda.

Fern drew herself up to her full red-dressed, blond-curled height. "You may not believe in magic," she said, "but you do believe in 'just knowing.' And I just know you are going to see John Baylor. Are you going now?"

My face must have shown she had gotten that right.

"I'll meet you afterward, outside his office," she said with satisfaction. "I'll walk over from my motel in about an hour, and if you aren't outside his building, I'll come up and wait in his outer office. I have a book I can read." She started to leave and then came back. "Be sure to watch our sneaky cousin's hands." She winked. "If he holds them curled up closed so you can't see the palms that can mean he's hiding something. Unless they're in fists 'cause he's mad." She nodded, pleased with herself. "Then we'll confer about what to do next."

Chapter

5

Monday Morning, 10 O'clock

John Baylor's office is on Market Street, one of the last streets in Asheville paved with bricks. The bricks, though pretty uneven, are still going strong, and the longtime citizens of Asheville, with their Scots-Irish background, would never pay to replace anything that still works. And the newcomers would never replace anything that is quaint enough to be a tourist attraction.

Market Street is even famous in a small way. On the street a building that was once a garage appears in a very early Robert Mitchum movie about mountain moonshine-runners, called *Thunder Road*. The movie is a cult classic, and folks around here like to watch it and play Spot the Landmarks. John's office is in sight of the landmark, but I was sure he hadn't picked it for that. He doesn't want to be reminded that he's descended from moonshiners.

Ted was waiting for me by the entrance to the office building. "Whew," he said, "I wouldn't expect Asheville to be this hot. At least John Baylor's office has airconditioning."

Baylor's velvet-voiced receptionist took us past several very annoyed-looking people right in to him. A sour-looking woman with red hair said to a man in a red checked shirt, "By the time we get in, we'll be ready to sue this lawyer, too."

John met us in a conference room with chairs around an oval table and a portrait of the firm's founder in a gold-leaf frame, frowning down on us. It was that kind of firm. John wore the expression I was sure he used for reading wills, the corners of his mouth gently sloping down, eyes earnest, white shirt gleaming beneath his dark suit. To show his purity?

"Thank you for coming," John said soberly, taking Ted's presence for granted, just as I thought he would. "Won't you sit down?" He waved a hand at chairs. It was not curled shut, not in the position Fern said meant hiding something. "Would you like some coffee?" he asked.

He sat at the head of the oval mahogany table; I sat on his right, and Ted sat on his left. We said "yes" to coffee. I had a feeling this meeting was going to be heavy and we were going to need to be fortified with any stimulant we could get. He sent his secretary off to get our brew, with sugar for Ted, cream for me.

John clutched a manila folder of papers in front of him. So what did clutching mean? "You are aware," he said ponderously, "that Kim is adopted." He stressed the present tense. *Kim is.* I noticed he was wearing gold cuff links. There was something old-fashioned about John. And he wanted to impress. "I arranged the adoption," he said. I knew that.

Before he even said another word, my radar beeped: This is a snow job. This is a snow job. You see, that's one of the odd things about my Swiss-cheese memory full of holes: it makes me look at people hard. I mean, if there are times when you can't exactly remember what happened and you have to ask somebody, you'd better be able to judge who on earth to ask. I'm pretty good at that.

"I can't tell you who the real parents were," John said. "I have to keep that confidential. I am sworn to do so, and the laws about confidentiality in this state are very strict. Kim herself has begged for information, and I can't give it. There is no legal way for her to find out who her birth parents were."

He was telling us more than we'd asked. Solemn as an owl. Warning us off.

"And that's that?" Ted asked. "No exceptions to confidentiality when a kid's life could be in danger?"

John laughed — a condescending laugh. "Oh,

come now," he said, "the girl just wants some privacy. The police are not worried, though they are trying to keep Mary Mary-Sue calmed down." He played with his pencil. "The only exception to confidentiality is some real emergency like a life-threatening medical condition when family medical records might help save an adopted child's life. And even then, the medical records are all an adopted child can get."

Why did I feel he was hiding more than he had to hide by law? And me so curious, I almost couldn't stand it. "You must know there's a rumor that Kim's related to us by blood," I said. His only reaction was to blink. "And just to prove it," I continued, "her hands are like the hands of some of our family. One hand has that rare line that a lot of us have. Which is inherited."

He frowned, exactly like the founder of the firm over his head.

"I can't tell you anything related to the parents," he said. "Aside from legal issues, I was sworn to secrecy by the one who gave her up for adoption."

"So one of the parents was dead?" Ted asked.

John pressed his lips together. He put the folder down and straightened his tie. Nervously? He didn't need to be so cold.

"Kim's pretty closely related to her adopted parents, isn't she?" I asked that just to see if I could get a rise.

His face stayed stony, but luckily I was

watching his hands. He curled them into fists. Did that mean I'd guessed right? Or was he mad I'd asked?

"I will absolutely not comment on heredity in any way," he said, "but there is one fact on the record." Diversionary tactics? "I can tell you that a trust fund was put aside, administered by me, to go to Kim at the age of twenty-one or to provide funds for any emergency before that time."

"If a trust fund was set up, either her father or mother had money," Ted said.

John did not answer. He went back to clutching the folder.

Still, if Kim was from our family and one parent had enough money to set up a trust, that narrowed it down. Who would have that kind of money? John Baylor himself? Or Pop? Heaven forbid. Of course, one parent might not be from our blood, and that could be the wealthy one. The only spouse I could think of born very rich is Lorna Jones, whose father runs a mail-order funny-toy company. Could she have set up a trust fund for Kim? I doubted it. And Lorna was not likely to be Kim's secret birth mother. She was plump and blond. Kim was slender and dark.

"Does Mary Mary-Sue know all about the trust fund and the blood relationship?" Ted asked.

John Baylor turned a shade pinker. "She knew as much as I was allowed to tell her." He kept

61

his voice avuncular and fatherly. "As much as I've told you." He turned pinker yet. "And God knows, since Kim left, Mary Mary-Sue has called me constantly, demanding to know where Kim is." He began to breathe harder. "She drives me crazy."

"And where is Kim?" I asked.

"I don't know." He looked off into space sadly. "I had to obey *mortmain*." He sighed. "The dead hand."

"What?" Ted and I asked in chorus. I half expected Cousin Fern to pop up and tell us to read the dead hand, whatever that meant.

"The one who left the trust for Kim is dead," John explained. "But through the will and the trust, the dead one's hand still tries to guide Kim's fate." He relaxed, glad to change the subject slightly. "We call that situation the dead hand. The trust provides that, in an emergency that I agree is legitimate, I have to give Kim the money she asks for, up to a certain limit. Then Kim alone can decide what to do. I have no say. Mary Mary-Sue and Ward agreed to that in the adoption papers. The relationship between the beneficiary and the trustee is a direct one. It does not have to involve the adopting parents, though God knows that's not a comfortable arrangement."

"What was the emergency?" Ted asked.

John looked us over as if still deciding how much we could be trusted. "Kim is a lovely girl," he said, "and she's young and not yet always wise about how that affects other people." He looked self-conscious. So he was attracted to Kim. But he was old enough to be her father, and furthermore, he'd sent her away. Or at least helped her leave.

"There's a young man who has a fixation on her." John now sounded like the prosecution lawyer. "He's been in trouble, getting drunk, accused of burning a barn but without enough proof to get him arrested. Abner Hale."

I nodded. "I've met him. He did some yard work for us. Kim suggested him." For once I agreed with John. "Abner has reckless eyes," I said. "He makes you feel he can't see anything but what he wants. He made me feel like he might steal my sundial. But he didn't."

Our coffee arrived in thin china cups. I took a sip.

John was smiling. "Yes," he said. "He cleaned out my garage. Kim suggested him for the job. And he wanted an old bicycle that belonged to Lucy. I said, 'No,' and somehow the wheels got bent. That boy can look at you like you're his oyster and he's searching for an oyster knife."

I laughed. John so rarely shows a sense of humor.

"I met Abner a while back, before Peaches and I were married. He's scary," Ted chimed in. "I advertised a car for sale, an old convertible. He arrived reeking of alcohol and wanted to buy it for half of what I was willing to sell it for. So I said, 'No.' Later I found the tires slashed."

John smiled broadly. "Typical. And yet, as I said, he's never been arrested. So Kim came to me and said she'd been wanting to get off on her own anyway. And I figured Abner must be looking at her, like — well, like she was his oyster and he was looking for a knife." He regarded his tented hands and smiled. He really liked that phrase. "She didn't mention Abner's name. She refused to name names, only said she felt she was in danger from someone. She wanted to disappear for a while. I knew Kim was scared."

Abner was good-looking, with the gracefulness of a racehorse. He was also passionate to have his way, as with Ted's car. Maybe Kim flirted with him and then saw her mistake and panicked — saw he was dangerous to anyone who said no.

"A little over a week ago, I arranged for Kim to have ten thousand dollars to go find a new life. Ten thousand was the maximum she could demand under the trust," John said importantly. He waited for us to applaud him. We waited for whatever he'd say next. "And under the terms of the trust, I had no choice."

Ten thousand dollars! I almost whistled.

Suddenly John was restless in his seat, twitching. "Unfortunately I was in the middle of a tricky estate case with all the beneficiaries in town for a meeting," he said, holding his head at a proud angle. "Kim said she'd spend the night at the Best Western and we'd meet for breakfast and talk about her plans. I gave her five hundred cash because she needed motel money and such, and made her promise to meet me." He bowed his head and studied his manicured thumbnails.

I thought, she didn't need motel money. She'd spent the night at home. That seventeen-year-old girl could twist this man around her little finger. Well, she was mortally pretty. And he must get tired of hearing his wife, Maureen, describe the neighbors' ailments. Maureen was a do-gooder, visiting and caring for the sick, and she liked to talk about their ailments as much as some people liked to talk about their own.

"And when I walked over to the Best Western to meet Kim," John added, "all I found was a note at the front desk."

John said "note" as if he'd said "bomb." Then he looked me straight in the eye, terribly earnest. "In the note she said she didn't want anybody to know where she was. She said good-bye and thanks and she'd get in touch. That is absolutely all." He opened the folder in front of him and took out a handwritten note on Best Western stationery. He handed it to us to examine.

He lowered his eyes as if he felt guilty. Well, he should feel guilty if he gave her the cash before he found out all he needed to know. Had he invited us here to convince us of his ignorance? His innocence?

"And Mary Mary-Sue wouldn't believe you didn't know more?" I asked.

"Of course not," he said, forgetting to be impressive. "That damn woman won't ever believe you can't do what she wants." Now his hands were in fists of anger.

"In what form did you give Kim the money?" Ted asked.

John hurried to tell that. It must be a safe subject. "I gave her the five hundred dollars in cash and put the rest in a bank account in Atlanta for her. That's what she asked me to do. But I've checked, and she hasn't tried to draw any money from the bank account. She must be staying with a friend somewhere. These young people help each other out."

"So," Ted said, "you're saying that, if nobody has heard from Kim, that may not be such a bad sign."

I could tell Ted was being sarcastic, but John Baylor took him at his word and included Ted in a hopeful smile. "Exactly. And after all, it's been only nine days."

"But," I said, "there's more to this than you've told us, isn't there? What else?"

John shot me a glance that would have frozen whiskey. I thought I should whip out my camera and record that self-righteous, angry look on his mug, but of course I didn't.

Ignoring my question, John said, "I hope, now that you understand, you won't stir up trouble and gossip about Kim. That wouldn't be fruitful."

"I will certainly look into all the gossip if you

don't at least tell us whether Kim is actually of our blood," I said angrily.

He looked me over carefully, considering. "I can't confirm it," he said, "but you've seen for yourself that her hand markings make it likely." Hoity-toity for "yes."

"And furthermore, if Abner was the problem, where is Abner now?" I asked.

"I can't be expected to keep track of Abner," he said haughtily, "but I have tried. And while the police would not get too upset about Kim's disappearance, they have made inquiries about Abner. And haven't found him."

"So you don't know where he is," Ted said. "For all you know, he could be off tracking down Kim to slash her tires or God knows what."

"Who were Kim's good friends?" I asked. It seemed to me that I'd remembered seeing her with a studious girl with pink plastic glasses. Opposites drawn together? But I hadn't really paid attention. I turned the page in my note-book to jot down what he said.

"Everybody liked Kim, but I urge you to drop this and not ask questions and stir up rumors," he said, tapping the closed file folder with his black pen.

"You can be sure," Ted said, "that Mary Mary-Sue will have someone looking into this. You must know her that well. At least if it's Peaches doing the asking, this may not have to go outside the family."

John Baylor wasn't dumb. He caught that "may not have to go outside the family." In other words, there was a chance it would. He began to sweat in a fascinating way. Tiny droplets popped out all over his forehead like wet polka dots. I would have liked to photograph that, too, but it would not have been tactful.

"If by any wild chance it does turn out that Kim was murdered," I said, "then it would be out of our hands."

He still seemed more upset than I'd expect, even with the possibility of foul play.

"Come back to my office," he said. "I have Janet Mars's number. I know Kim used to be good friends with her."

Offices tell a lot, whereas conference rooms don't. John's office had a big mahogany desk with one neat pile of papers and Maureen's photograph in a fussy frame with pink roses around it — the kind of frame she must have picked out herself. She was standing by a van marked MEALS ON WHEELS and smiling a good Samaritan smile. And John had a bust of Teddy Roosevelt on his bookcase. There was a slight resemblance, though John didn't have a mustache. He saw me looking. "Belonged to my grandfather," he said. "Not on your side of the family. He was a state senator."

The bookcase was full of leather-bound books with gold lettering. Several framed pictures were there, too. There was one of John with his arm wrapped protectively around a studious, gangly young girl with braces. An odd picture. He looked mildly apprehensive, as if he were afraid somebody might take a potshot at that girl. "That's Lucy, isn't it?" I asked.

John smiled. "Yes, that's Lucy." But his eyes registered worry. Had he hoped we'd forget Lucy?

"I remember seeing her with Kim," I said. "They used to giggle together at family reunions when they were younger." Kim and Lucy and Janet the Planet.

"They used to be good friends," he admitted grudgingly, "but then Lucy decided Kim was boy crazy. My Lucy is a late bloomer. She's still more interested in good grades than in boys."

"But she might be able to help with insights about Kim," I said. I could see him struggling with himself. His hands quivered as if they wanted to do something but weren't sure what. His lips compressed. His eyes blinked.

"Well, you're certainly free to talk to her," he said finally. I guess he'd figured he'd make us more eager if he said "no."

We thanked him for his help. We made our way to the elevator and began to wheeze down.

"Oh, dern," I said as we hit bottom. "I left my notes." I looked in my pocketbook to be sure. Yes, I'd left them. "I'll go back and get them. You stay down here and intercept Fern so she won't go up to John's office."

The elevator wheezed back up. The velvet-voiced receptionist was not at her desk and

John's office was just down the hall, so I hurried toward it. The door was open a crack. Good. I could be sure nobody was inside with him. I stopped. He was talking, so he must have had a client in there already. I listened. Well, he should shut the door if he wants privacy!

"Listen, Maureen," John was saying, "just try to see that Lucy doesn't talk to her. I know. Just do that and don't worry." Silence. Then: "Well, if she's not home now and you don't know where she is, catch her as soon as you can. Of course we don't want this blown up into a hulla-baloo." I heard a click. He must have been on the phone, now he'd hung up. I waited a minute and then knocked.

He was startled to see me. Was he afraid of what I'd heard? He rushed over and handed me my notebook. "Now, do you have everything?" he asked rather caustically. Yes, I did — I had more than I'd come for. I thanked him sweetly and departed.

Chapter

6

Monday Morning, 11:15

Fern and Ted were waiting outside, chatting.

"Listen," I said, "I have an eavesdrop report." I looked both ways to be sure nobody was near us on the sidewalk. Across the street a sign on an Italian restaurant sported a picture of an old-fashioned count (or someone fancy) with a cat. Other than that and the passing cars, the red-brick street was empty.

"The receptionist wasn't at her desk," I said breathlessly. "I walked right to John's office. He was on the phone. I overheard him tell Maureen to try to stop us from talking to Lucy. What do you think of that?"

"Where is Lucy now?" Ted asked. "Were you able to find that out?"

"Her father and mother don't know where she is, but they're going to tell her to shut up as

71

soon as she appears."

"We should get there fast and talk to that girl before her mother catches her!" Fern cried out. A man a block behind her bobbed his head up in surprise.

"But where?" I asked. "We don't know where she is."

"You'd better get to her house so you can be there when she arrives," Ted said. "That will confuse her mother. Maureen confuses easily anyway."

"I'll come too," Fern said. "I have a good excuse because I promised to read the girl's hand."

"I won't come," Ted said. "Two of you are enough to overwhelm Maureen. Three of us would seem ridiculous. But" — he looked me hard in the eye — "you call me if you need any kind of help for any reason. That's what our new car phones are for. I'll be in the car until I get home."

Ted got the car phones after a friend of his had a heart attack on a back road and was able to call for help in time. And I hope having those phones is like carrying your umbrella so it won't rain. Now we won't have heart attacks on back roads. Or other catastrophes.

The Baylors live in Biltmore Forest, where a lot of doctors live. And lawyers, too, evidently. There's a country club with a golf course, and a lot of the houses are big and fancy. The nice thing about Biltmore Forest is that, since the houses are on large lots, there are plenty of trees. And it's a pretty safe place. It's cheek by jowl with Asheville, but it has its own police, who patrol.

Fern and I headed that way, through Asheville's downtown, past the hospitals and such, and turned onto a woodsy road with banks of rhododendrons on both sides — from city to wilderness in one quick turn. She quizzed me about what John Baylor had said, or mostly hadn't said. She had only one comment: "I don't trust him."

After two or three minutes we began to pass houses, back from the road and mostly behind banks of rhododendrons or other semi-wild growth. We could just glimpse some houses down long driveways, but some were large enough and close enough to be seen in full glory. I liked one with white columns in front, à la Scarlett O'Hara's Tara. Another was stone with one wing of plaster and half-timbered wood like a British country house.

"Maybe I should move my real-estate business here," Fern said. "At least the houses don't slide down hills the way they do in California."

We passed the town hall, the police station, and finally came to the Baylors' large brick house on two levels. Tall central core and two wings. The garden was full of evergreens and rosebushes. Roses to match the frame on Maureen's picture.

We drove up a circular drive which let us park

right in front of the door. We got out and tapped the big brass door knocker.

Maureen appeared. Somehow I was never quite prepared for John Baylor's wife to be so frail and yet pretty at the same time, even now when she was obviously over forty. Cords stood out on her neck, and blue veins stood out on the backs of her hands. I'd always felt kindly toward Maureen because folks said she could be even vaguer than I am. It's always good for the morale to know someone who's worse than you are.

Maureen not only forgot names, she forgot nouns of all sorts. At a dinner party she'd say, "Please pass me the . . ." and then blush. The word wouldn't come. So I'd told her about flow-arounds, just describing the word some other way, which breaks the logjam. As in "Please pass me those little, green, round things that grow in pods." People figure you say it that way as a joke, which is fine. And, in fact, Maureen has been doing it ever since. So she ought to be grateful to me, right? But I think she's forgotten I taught her the flow-around trick.

She gave us her lovely floaty smile, which said she was glad to see us. But I knew she wasn't. She was pretending.

Actually, she's smarter than your first impression of her. She once worked in John's office, briefly. He kicked her upstairs by marrying her. And perhaps such a very precise man would need a wife dreamy enough to agree that he must be right all the time.

"I was over at Cousin Gertrude's this morning," Maureen said abstractedly. "That poor woman has migraine headaches like I do. She has to lie in a dark room with a — with one of those things woven of cotton and dipped in water — on her head." Maureen seemed shrunken, with her eyes half shut and her face drawn. "I'm glad to see you, but I'm afraid I have a migraine headache myself. Could I get you to come back another day?" She enunciated the words slowly as if speaking hurt. Logic said she was putting on a show, and yet I had a feeling she really did have a headache.

"We came to see Lucy," Fern said boldly. "I promised to read her hand."

Maureen's rosebud mouth still smiled. "I'm sorry to say Lucy's not here." It occurred to me that Maureen's eyes and mouth often disagreed.

She was opening her mouth to make some further excuse when a voice said, "Here I am. I just got here, Mom." Lucy had come up in back of us. Incredibly perfect timing! Mom probably hadn't had a chance to warn her off.

I turned around to say, "Hi." Lucy was all braces and knobby knees and glasses and earnestness. She looked much younger than seventeen, and yet she was the same age as Kim. She moved well, though. Smoothly, like a kid who knew where she wanted to go in life and wouldn't be stopped.

"Perhaps this isn't a good time for you to visit," Maureen said to us.

75

But Lucy cried out, "Oh, Mama, Cousin Fern promised to read my hand, and she's going to have to leave and go back to California, and then I'll have to wait a year! We won't bother you. You go on."

Lucy pulled Fern into the large living room with the high ceiling and large furniture in scale with the room. All mahogany and polished to the nines. I followed. Maureen came right along, frowning as if she wasn't quite sure what to do. She seemed unwilling to let us out of her sight. She stared at me disapprovingly, as if I should be polite and take a hint and leave. I was not about to be polite. First things first.

Fern told us to sit on the brocade couch. "You sit in the middle, Lucy, because Cousin Peaches is interested in learning to read hands, and she'll want to see what's in yours."

Maureen edged nervously into a high-backed, striped satin wing chair, near enough to hear. If she was putting on an act about the migraine, she kept it up. Pain was written in the careful way she sat down and the tense lines on her face. If she hurt as badly as she looked, she must have had a tremendous desire to hear what Fern and I said, no matter what. Otherwise, she would certainly have excused herself and gone off to lie in a dark room with a damp cloth on her head.

Fern took Lucy's right hand and gently bent the fingers back. They didn't bend far. Fern had told me a flexible hand equals a flexible mind

76

and vice versa. So Lucy wasn't easy to bend. Fern touched the fingers, knobby like all the rest of Lucy. "Your fingers tell me you don't like change. You think things out carefully and make up your mind slowly. And you change your mind slowly and carefully in the same way. That's true of most folks who have fingers with obvious knots at the joints. Which is unusual in someone as young as you are." Fern kneaded Lucy's hand to feel the texture. She compared the left hand to the right. "There's so much more to read in a hand than just the lines on the palm," she told Lucy. "For example, your hand is flat and firm. You work hard to get what you want. Things don't come to you by luck."

"Is that bad?" Lucy asked earnestly. "Am I unlucky?"

"Not at all," Fern said. "It's just your style. Look at Peaches's hands. They're a little that way, too. You make your own luck with sweat. And you're not likely to run off half-cocked and fall into trouble. You think ahead."

Fern turned to me. "You see how that all adds up, Peaches?" she said. "Bony finger joints mean making up the mind slowly, based on the facts. That's especially true in a long, thin hand like this." She held up Lucy's hand like exhibit A as Lucy watched, eyes magnified by her glasses. "The inflexible hand enlarges on that. Also the large, determined thumb." Fern kneaded Lucy's hand again. "The flat palm without much padding adds the bit about get-

77

ting things by hard work, not luck. This is the hand of a skeptic who thinks for herself. Sure, she's a kid. But nobody takes candy from this baby just because she's naive. This is basically the shape of hand we call philosophic, the same shape as Eleanor Roosevelt's. This is the hand of the thinker."

Lucy grinned and showed her braces. "Philosophic!" she breathed. "Wow."

All that from a hand. I made up my mind to watch and see if it worked.

As I looked sideways at Lucy, I could see a glass-front set of shelves beyond her, all holding the most exquisite coffee cups. Maureen collected them. She had good taste. This room was beautiful, from Audubon prints on the wall to Chinese urn lamps to a large green Chinese rug, obviously an antique. If Lucy had to work for what she got, that must mean later. Not now. She lived in the lap of luxury.

Maureen stood up, both frowning with annoyance and wincing with pain, as if to announce the end of our visit. Lucy and Fern ignored her. I pretended to watch the hand reading so closely that I didn't see Maureen.

"But you said I had that line in my hand — the one a lot of us have." Lucy was avoiding the old name: the Mark of Murder. I saw her mother wince extra hard, as if she couldn't stand it if Fern said anything bad.

"Yes," Fern said, "and it's unusual to find that line in a long, thin hand like yours. Obviously you are an original thinker. You have an interesting hand."

"What should I beware of?" Lucy asked. Maureen cleared her throat, as if she was about to make an announcement, clasping one hand tightly with the other.

Fern laughed. "Everybody wants to know that. You should beware of worrying too much. See all those little lines all over your hand? They're worry lines. Listen to moody music or go for walks in the woods when your worrying gets out of hand. And sometimes a very logical hand like yours means you don't listen to your intuition quickly enough."

Maureen opened her mouth then shut it. She sat back down. Maybe she'd become interested. Maybe a headache plus Lucy was more than she could handle all at once.

Fern told Lucy some stuff about her heart and head lines and such, but I was on overload. If I was going to remember what she'd said so far, I had to go over it in my mind. I looked across at Maureen's hands to compare them. One hand lay on each thigh — twitching slightly. Maureen's hands were almost the opposite of her daughter's. Maureen's were long and thin but so smooth you might imagine she was without bones. And like the rest of her, her hands were pale.

Maybe I should have been sorry for Maureen with her headache, but I was too busy wishing she'd go away so we could talk freely to Lucy.

No such luck, but she still didn't throw us out. So when Fern finished, I asked Lucy if I could photograph her hands. She said she thought that would be fun and asked for a set of the photographs with some of the things Fern had said written on the back. Maureen looked wary but still didn't object, so I asked the next question while I worked.

"You used to be good friends with Kim, didn't you?" I asked Lucy. I spread her hands out flat on a small mahogany coffee table.

"Yes," she said, shifting on the couch uneasily. "When we were small, we played together a lot. She was my best friend." I moved the camera around to get it in the best position.

Maureen stood up again. Now she was entirely frowning, not wincing.

"We used to live close to each other, but when I was eight, we moved here," Lucy said, staring at her hands. "I missed her a lot. Kim still used to come play with me in the summer because her mother worked near here." She looked up at me and smiled. "We had fun." The smile drained away. "But then her mother got another job. I didn't see her as much. But we still got together as often as we could."

I clicked the camera. "Have you seen Kim in the last few weeks?" I asked Lucy quickly.

Maureen rasped, "Lucy, don't gossip."

Lucy paused as if trying to decide what to say, then said, "No." She'd curled her hands tight. I took a picture of that.

Maureen told me, "It's time for you to go."

Lucy caught her hands together, like a parody of her mother. "Kim was all steamed up about this wild, sexy boy. She didn't have time for me." Was that spite in Lucy's voice?

But wait. "Everybody else said she was running away from him," I said.

Lucy just shrugged.

Talking to Lucy in front of Mama was not going to work anyway. "You may know that Kim has left town and didn't tell anyone where she's gone," I said. "Her mother is very worried that something has happened to her."

I caught a frightened widening of Lucy's eyes as Maureen stepped in front of her. "You need to go now," Maureen ordered me and Fern. "Please leave this — this building where we live."

I made my pitch to Lucy's ears. "If you have any thoughts about why Kim might have left or where she might have gone, please call me," I said. "I'm trying to help her mother be sure that Kim is all right." Lucy leaned around her mother to nod at me, and I handed her a card with my car-phone number and my home number. "I'm at one of these two places most of the time," I said.

Maureen glared as if she wanted to take those cards with my numbers and burn them with the fire from her eyes. And I admit I was being pushy. There was something in Maureen that brought out the mule in me.

Lucy read the numbers aloud twice. I had the distinct impression she was memorizing them in case of need. I hoped that was a good sign. She obviously knew more than she was going to tell in front of her mother.

Chapter

7

Monday, 1 o'clock

We weren't even back at Fern's motel when the car phone rang. I picked it up and pulled into the parking lot of the long, low downtown post office. I'm too old-fashioned to zip along and talk at the same time unless I have to. Old One Track Mind here could have a wreck.

"This is Lucy. I need your help," said a shaking voice.

"What can I do?" My ears pricked up. Those who need help are more likely to tell all.

"Could you pick me up at the Bitlmore Forest town hall? In half an hour? I may have heard from Kim." Her voice trembled with excitement. "She wants me to meet her. And who else would know about our old play place? I'll be in front. Don't tell anybody!" She said that as if it were a matter of life and death.

I gasped. "Wait! In front of the town hall?" But she'd hung up.

Next to me in the car, Fern was leaning toward me, wanting to know more. I guess I looked electrified. But Lucy had said not to tell anybody. I was dying to tell Fern or to call Ted on the car phone and tell him. But I knew I should talk to Lucy and find out what was up — why this was hush-hush. So I told Fern somebody had called me about a confidential matter. Fair is fair.

Naturally Fern objected. She complained that I didn't trust her. She glowered, even when I explained that this secret wasn't mine to tell. I invited Fern to dinner with Ted and me. I bribed her with the hope that I'd have something more to tell her then.

She was still bursting with curiosity — and plainly mad that I wouldn't spill the beans — when I dropped her off at the Best Western. But she agreed to come to dinner.

Once she was inside the motel doors, I pulled into a space in the parking lot and found some peanut-butter crackers in the glove compartment. I called Ted and told him what was up. He made me promise to call him back as soon as I knew more. Then I set out for the Biltmore Forest town hall, munching crackers instead of lunch.

The town hall looks like a small country club except the sign says what it is. Behind it are the fire station and the police department, which look like outbuildings of the country club. Lucy was waiting for me right by the road. She wore a black T-shirt, black pants, and black sandals. Her glasses were the only twinkle in the whole outfit. She climbed into the car with less exuberance than I would have expected.

"So how did you hear from Kim? Did she sound okay? Where has she been?"

She turned to me with a puzzled frown. "I'm not positive it was Kim," she said, "but it could have been. I hope. This person using a phony voice telephoned me and said she has a message to me from Kim. Thank goodness my mother was in bed with her headache and didn't answer." She flushed. "Sometimes my mother listens."

I felt let down. And I noted that Lucy didn't trust her mother.

I noticed somebody near the fire station, washing down a fire truck with a hose.

"What kind of person called?" I asked.

"Some girl, I think. She was kind of whispering, like somebody might hear. But it didn't make sense. Why didn't she just tell me whatever it was over the phone? Why did I have to meet her in the woods? She hung up before I could ask all that."

"That does sound odd," I said, "so maybe we shouldn't go alone. And here we are at the police station. We could get help." I started the motor, ready to turn in toward the police.

Lucy gasped. "No!" And her eyes were huge

with horror behind her glasses. "If it's Kim, she's afraid. She doesn't want anyone to know where she is, or she'd have said it was her. She told me not to tell about the call."

"But if it was Kim, why wouldn't she have said who it was?" I asked. "To, you, her friend."

"But I know it must be a message from Kim." Lucy's voice grew shrill, a little desperate. "This person talked about our special place where we used to play as kids. She said she did that so I'd know she really knew Kim. It's a place near a brook and an old fallen tree, and she mentioned how we pretended the space near each branch of the tree was a room." Lucy put her hand over mine on the steering wheel. "Please! That's where we have to go. That's where she said to meet her!"

I let the car idle while she finished her pitch. "And she knew about the other tree we used to climb, with a basket on a rope and a pencil and paper so we could write each other notes and send them up and down. And I was so busy remembering all that and checking if the person had it right that I didn't ask what I needed to ask until suddenly she hung up, almost as if somebody came in the room. Nobody but Kim would know all that. So maybe it was Kim. But I don't know."

You want it to be Kim, I thought. Wishful hearing.

I still wondered if we shouldn't enlist the police. But if they scared this girl off, we might never know what she had to tell, or even who she was. The fireman back beyond the town hall looked so sure of himself, squirting water from a hose. I wished I were sure.

"And what do you need me to do exactly?" My curiosity was getting the better of me.

"Could you give me a ride to that place where I'm going to meet this girl, and park nearby and wait?" Lucy's voice was hopeful but still quavery. "I told the person I'd meet her there, near our old house, in an hour. I figured that would give me time to work out somebody to back me up. And the place is right near the road. It's hidden because it's down in a kind of hollow and full of trees, but you can hear the cars from there. It's not far."

"But will you be safe?"

"I have a thing of Mace with me," she said. "My cousin Ellie from Chicago gave it to me. It's for if you're mugged or something. I don't know why she thought I'd need it here, but maybe I will. You never know." She sounded so determined, and so desperate to find out about her friend, that her voice carried me along.

And, boy, I thought, *Lucy may look younger than Kim, but she sure thinks out the details.*

"It's especially important not to call anybody who will blab about this," Lucy said. "This girl said what she had to tell me was very confidential and I mustn't tell a soul. But I know I can trust you, Cousin Peaches. I know you've helped people before."

87

So how dangerous could a girl be who wanted to give Lucy information about Kim? I asked myself. We drove along the winding road with pines on each side, past a golf course with a big KEEP OUT sign by a green.

"So tell me about this boy Kim was mixed up with," I said. I might as well find out what I could as we drove along.

"He's older," Lucy said with contempt, "and he drinks too much. And I know Kim has better sense than to go off anywhere with a man like that." There was doubt in her voice. "His name is Abner Hale," she said on a surer note, "and maybe Kim thinks she can reform him. If she does, she's a fool." Lucy spit that out.

I started to blurt out that her own father had said Kim was running away from Abner Hale, but then stopped myself. Before I could say anything, Lucy pointed.

"There," she said, "that lamppost with the curved neck means we're close. You can park in the end of the drive. It's so long that the people in the house won't even know you're there."

"Unless," I said, "they decide to drive down their own driveway. What's the address of this place? I might need to know." I'd wait and ask more about Abner on the way home.

"Fifty-five Stuyvesant Road," she told me, and I wrote that down on the pad I keep near the automatic gearshift. The drive curved so much that a little way into it I could see neither the road we'd just come down nor the house beyond me. Which meant nobody could see me, I hoped. On my left the woods sloped up, floored with ivy, proving that this wasn't a wild area but somebody's tame woods. On the right the woods sloped down, carpeted with brown leaves never raked away from last fall — possibly never raked at all. Untamed woods. I could see only a little way into the maze of green.

"If I don't come back in fifteen minutes, maybe you can come into the woods and see what's wrong," Lucy said as I parked by the edge of the drive. She got out — as silently as possible, I noticed. No slamming car doors. I watched her walk up the drive a short way and turn into the woods near the brown trunk of a large tree. She walked slowly, looking this way and that, stopping every so often as if to listen extra carefully. My heart began to beat faster. Were we foolish to be here? Soon the trees hid her. The secret place wasn't too far in, she said.

I called Ted on his car phone, told him what was happening, and gave him the address. "Look," I said, "I certainly don't expect anything to go wrong, but if anything should, I might not have time to call again."

"Chat for a minute," he suggested. I realized his left-brain logic was telling him we ought to be as careful about this as my right-brain intuition was telling me.

"There is still absolutely no reason to think that Kim is anything but out on her own and glad to be left alone," I told Ted, mostly to convince myself. "Mary Mary-Sue must be a smothering mother. So maybe Kim just needed a breathing spell. Maybe she's here in person to meet her old friend Lucy and tell her what's up. She wants to send her mother something to prove she's fine. And Lucy can give an eye-witness account." I hoped it was something like that. The woods stayed thunderingly quiet. I heard a car pass by on the road. My car windows were rolled down to catch even a snapping twig. All I heard except the passing car was a slight breeze in the trees, very welcome.

Then a shrill scream hit me in the solar plexus. I dropped the phone and jumped out of the car, but I had hardly gone more than a few steps when Lucy came hurtling toward me out of the woods, out of breath, glasses askew. She grabbed my arm and began to pull. She screeched. "She's bleeding. There's a knife!"

We ran down the hill through the rustling dead leaves, jumping over fallen logs, grabbed by outstretched branches from the taller trees, unable to see far ahead of us. Finally Lucy stopped short and held me back. A few feet beyond us was the body of a girl. The first thing that registered was the black-handled kitchen knife stuck in the chest — a knife with brass rivets in it. I have one like it. I looked into the staring eyes. They did not look back.

The girl was on her back with one leg twisted under her and dead leaves all around. She wore a white T-shirt, now blood red across her chest around the knife, and faded jeans. My mind was working in all directions at once. Wondering how she fell backward. Noticing that those staring eyes were violet. And that the hair was the dark, vibrant brown-black of Kim's. The face seemed the right shape. Death had made it more wooden. Because plainly those empty eyes meant she was dead. I didn't want to believe it was Kim, who enjoyed life with a flair. I heard Lucy crying.

And the dead girl lay there in the brown leaves with her hands thrown open on both sides of her body, almost in supplication, as if she were begging for mercy. Too late now.

Chapter

8

Monday, 2:30

Between sobs Lucy gasped, "We have to call the police." She was a practical girl, even at a time like this. "I'll go up to the house." She blew her nose resoundingly on a tissue, swallowed, and stopped crying. "I know the people. I can run faster than you." Before I could tell her to use the car phone, she was running up the hill.

I have seen bodies before, but this one upset and unhinged me, I guess because she was so young. The tears in my eyes made it hard for me to look around as I wanted. But then I realized I had my self-focusing camera. Cameras never cry.

I pulled it out of my trusty shoulder bag, stood back, and photographed this poor dead girl in the dead leaves. She lay near a small spring with rotting black leaves in it and a trickle that meandered off through the gully as a small sluggish stream. I photographed the knife in her chest close-up. So ugly! Even through a mist of tears. I clicked a picture from farther back.

Suddenly I thought of Fern. I knew what she would have told me to do. I took a picture of each hand from a low angle so that the lines would show in spite of the slightly curved fingers. Fern said lines changed. She'd want to know how they'd changed since the print we'd seen. That might even be a clue to what had happened. As I began to photograph the hands, I heard a siren. What? So fast? And then I realized. Of course. Ted had called the police the minute I dropped the phone and ran after Lucy. The police might not be pleased with my amateur photograph. I took several shots of the scene around the body as quickly as I could, then stuffed the camera down into the depths of my pocketbook.

I heard a car screech to a stop, and the siren stopped. I called out, "Down here!" Footsteps crunched toward me through the dead leaves. A very young policeman appeared. Or have I just reached the age when everybody looks very young?

He asked if I'd touched anything, and I said only the ground with my feet, and as little of that as I could manage. I told him the dead girl must be Kim Gordon, the daughter of Ward and Mary Mary-Sue Gordon. I told him part of what I knew as we stood in the leaves and more as other police arrived, and he took me up to sit in the police car and give him a statement. That seemed to take forever because he wanted all the details of how I happened to be there. I saw another policeman talking to Lucy, and then John Baylor arrived, rushed over, told me I should have consulted him before I said a word, and took off with Lucy. My policeman thanked me and said I could go. I looked at my watch. Four o'clock.

Something was still bothering me about the body lying there in the leaves — something I'd seen that wasn't quite right, if a murder scene ever could be called right. And yet I couldn't for the life of me lay my finger on what it was. It'll come to me, I thought hopefully. God willing.

Chapter

9

Monday Afternoon
and Tuesday Morning

Kim. Just seventeen. Maybe in love. I was in love with a stinker once, years ago. Even after I managed to pull myself back, to realize he was quicksand, the guy fascinated me. He was in such pain and so sharp. But in love with his own pain. Not trying to pull out of it, but trying to pull other people in. It hurt me to pull back because it hurt him. Thank God, I knew I had to do it or fall into quicksand. Was this Abner What's-His-Name quicksand? Did he have something to do with how Kim died?

Was Kim running away from the boy, as John Baylor had said? Or was it possible she had run off with him, as Lucy had implied? Which should I believe?

All that kept running through my mind, even as the police asked me about what I'd seen at the scene of the crime. The police were so businesslike, asking again and again about every detail. They needed to be. But that depressed me somehow.

By the time they let me start home, I felt bombed out. I thought of calling Mary Mary-Sue, but the police had asked me to let them notify her. That would be terrible enough. I'd send her my love later. I stopped at a wide place by the side of the road, near the golf course with the NO TRESPASSING sign, and tried to call Ted at home. No answer. That was odd, and I began to wonder why Ted hadn't rushed to the scene of the crime. That's what I would have expected him to do after he'd heard the mayhem on my car phone and called the police.

I arrived home to find Fern there but no Ted. She opened the front door and welcomed me into my own pleasant wood-paneled living room, as if she were the hostess in her fancy yellow pants suit. Oh, yes, I'd invited her to supper. But where was Ted? And she was early. "I just got here," she said breathlessly. I noticed a small plaid suitcase and a tote bag by her side. "Ted left the key in the mailbox. Also," she said more insistently, "he said something terrible was wrong?" She said it like a question. I felt disoriented.

"He reached me at my motel," she said, "from the airport. He just had time to call the police and check that you were okay." She took my hand as if I might need comfort. "He said he tried to leave a message."

"What was it?" I asked. "Tell me quick." Good Lord, what could have happened to Ted?

"His father had a heart attack." Fern placed her hand dramatically over her heart. "Ted's mother called from Nashville and begged him to get there just as fast as possible so he could see his father alive. Ted took the first flight he could." She paused to let the drama of that sink in, then rushed on. "And what was wrong where you were? He said the police had things in hand but someone was dead and you'd tell me the rest."

So Ted heard Lucy yelling. And then he called the police and then his mother got through to him. He must have called the police back, since he knew something dreadful had happened. And heard I was safe and rushed off to his parents. And somewhere in there he'd managed to call Fern.

I was relieved Ted was okay, but poor Papa. I liked him, though Ted's family were funny, prickly people. They adored Ted, but they'd had another daughter-in-law, who was trouble. Married to an older son, who'd died in an automobile crash before I'd met Ted. Their cautious attitude toward her rubbed off on me. Besides, Ted's parents were a great age. Papa was ninety-four; Mamma was ninety. Old enough to have a right to be crotchety. We were lucky they were self-sufficient at that age.

My mind was wandering. I pulled myself together. Fern was fond of Kim. I thought of them laughing at reunions. Fern was going to be upset.

"Ted said he'll call as soon as he can," Fern told me. "He said not to call him — he'll call you tonight. He asked me to be here when you got home because it always made you feel better to have somebody to talk to when things went wrong." Fern scanned my face, waiting for me to explain.

"Come sit down," I said to Fern. She was going to be shocked. She sat in the leather chair that used to be Ted's before we married. I sat in the big plaid, overstuffed chair and made myself tell her the terrible truth.

"Kim has been murdered."

She gasped. "Mary Mary-Sue was right to be scared!"

Then I told Fern how Lucy and I found the body in the woods. I waited till she'd had a good cry to tell her how I photographed the hands. That might get Fern out of the dumps. She always felt better when there was something she could *do*.

"I can develop the pictures," she cried, leaning forward. "Toto Small said I could use his darkroom if I ever wanted to. I won't tell him why. I'll call him up right now." She waved at the phone on the small mahogany table near the front door. She jumped up. "All we can do for poor Kim is help to find her killer. And, Peaches, I may find important clues from those hand pictures." She smiled proudly. "I'll blow them up."

In my mind I saw an explosion. I *was* upset.

Fern hurried over and reached for the telephone, then stopped and said, "Oh, yes. You have a telephone message from Marsha at Malaprop's Bookstore." I was amazed that Fern would think about that at such a time, when her mind was on murder, the Mark of Murder, and her poor young friend Kim. "This Marsha called Ted before the shit hit the fan." California language. "Ted said Marsha said to call back anytime tonight. This is her home number." Fern pointed with one red-nailed finger to a slip of paper fastened on the clipboard that sits near the phone.

I tried to switch gears. I'd made up my mind that murder and mayhem weren't going to get in the way of promoting my book, *How to Survive Without a Memory*. No matter what. Right? Boy, was I into no-matter-what up to my eyebrows! But I wasn't going to change my mind. I'd already been around to every bookshop in town: Accent on Books when I went to have lunch at the Fine Friends restaurant nearby, Books-a-Million as I went to Circuit City next door, Waldenbooks and B. Dalton when I went to the malls, the Bookshop on Wall Street and Malaprop's when I was downtown. I told the managers I could read or sign books or give a talk or whatever. Now Malaprop's was calling back. What a moment to call!

When Fern got off the phone, pleased because she could use the darkroom the next morning, I called Marsha.

"Is there any way we could get hold of some of your books tomorrow?" she asked. Actually, there was. My writer friend Sharyn had advised me to get about fifty to have on hand so that if books ever failed to be delivered to a bookshop in time for a signing, I'd be prepared. Those books had arrived just the day before. I explained, and Marsha said, "Oh, that's wonderful! We want you to come and talk or read and answer questions tomorrow." Tomorrow! I gasped, but she explained quickly. "We had scheduled Oliver Sacks, the neurologist, who's written a popular book about how the brain works in unexpected ways, and we've advertised it, and we expect a large crowd, and our author has taken sick. There's no way we can get in touch with everybody. And at least your *How to Survive Without a Memory* is sort of about how the brain works. About how we can get around what happens when the brain doesn't work exactly as we'd like it to. So we thought if people came and found you were speaking, they might at least enjoy that and not be so disappointed."

I took a deep breath. Beginning authors should rise to opportunities. "It's possible I could come," I said, "but there are a couple of things I have to check before I say a final 'yes.' I'll get back to you shortly. What time would you like me if I can do it?"

"Seven," she said, and I figured that unless Ted's father died, Ted's mother would prefer not to have me there. Once before, when Ted's father was really ill, she told Ted that the only consolation was having some time alone with her boy. Still, I'd have to check with Ted. Certainly Kim's funeral couldn't be that soon. And yet, perhaps out of respect, I shouldn't rush out and promote books. Perhaps I was being callous.

Fern was waiting when I hung up, all eyes and ears. "How wonderful," she said when I explained. "Of course you have to go. Kim would want you to. And a gathering like that is a good place to find clues."

"What?" That didn't make sense.

"Of course," she said. "The people who come will all be people who are interested in how the mind works. And that's what detection is all about — right? I just have a hunch we'll find out something we really need to know." She stood straight and threw her shoulders back. "This is an opportunity, Peaches. For us both." She'd turned her grief into determination and was firmly ensconced as my Dr. Watson. Maybe a more enthusiastic Watson than I wanted. Thank you, Ted.

Ted called at eleven. He sounded fine, and his father was a little better. "Vital signs stabilized," they'd told Ted, so the doctor was guardedly hopeful. I explained about finding Kim and managed not to cry on the phone. I mentioned the possible talk at Malaprop's and how I felt I should go and also felt I shouldn't.

Ted said, "Go for it. You can't bring Kim back to life. And you know Mom. She's not pining for you to be here. So good luck."

"You see?" Fern said when I told her. "Your talk is important. Do it."

I called Marsha back, said "yes," and told her I'd drop the books off the next day.

Which meant I had to be ready. I showed Fern to the guest room. Yes, the suitcase did mean she was spending the night. I took the film of Kim's room out of my pocketbook while I thought of it, and asked Fern if she would develop that with the hand pictures.

Actually, I'm a great admirer of Oliver Sacks. He writes such fascinating books about the ways in which people with neurological problems develop unusual talents to get around them. His shoes would be hard to fill. Tired as I was, I got into bed with a copy of my book and tried to decide what to read or talk about.

People would arrive at Malaprop's expecting to hear about the brain. I could tell them how I made friends with mine. I mean, *life* is detection. You find out how your brain works best and go with that.

I leaned back on my pillows and yawned. My brain may waste time in the day forgetting things, but I can *save* time by asking it to work while I'm asleep. That's a fair exchange. While I'm asleep, my mind arranges all the details without struggling to remember each one. Don't ask me how. So I skimmed through *How to Survive Without a Memory* and pointed out to my brain that I needed to make people laugh and have a good time but give them some useful stuff, too. I asked my brain please to do its thing. I fell asleep with the light on, came to again, and turned it off.

But the path of true sleep-think is not smooth. I woke up sweating in the night. I'd dreamed I saw a knife in my chest and then suddenly there were two of me, lying there dead. I turned on the light and wrote that dream on the pad I keep by my bed. I looked around my familiar room with the stained-glass cardinal on the window and the green flowered curtains. My safe place. Somehow, I finally drifted off to sleep.

In the morning I overslept. Good grief, the clock said 9:30. But I lay in bed and worried about my dream. Was it a warning?

Warning or not, I had to compose my Tuesday evening talk. I jumped out of bed and went to the room we use as an office. No sign of Fern; she was evidently still asleep. Even this late. I sat down at my computer, and my fingers on the keyboard began to put down one or two sayings you can use when you forget something or lose something, such as "I haven't lost my mind, it's backed up on a floppy disk somewhere," and then . . .

The phone rang. It was Fern. Not asleep at all! I glanced at the clock. 10:35. "I'm here at

Toto's," she said breathlessly. Boy, she had snuck out without even waking me. "I have developed the pictures," she said and paused, as if that meant something revolutionary. "I have studied the corpse's hands." She paused again. I pictured her fighting back tears. "Now, lines do change, but not that much."

Fern's voice grew warm. She almost sang. "And this is amazing, Peaches, but there's no Mark of Murder." Crescendo: "That dead girl can't be Kim!"

Chapter

10

Tuesday, August 29

I stayed put, waiting for Fern, and ate some cornflakes and drank some coffee at my favorite thinking place: the kitchen table by the window. Outside, a lovely clump of big red and white dahlias — from bulbs my niece Mary gave me when she moved to Texas — bloomed beyond the birdbath. My feelings bloomed, too. The dead girl was not Kim! I was so glad. But then who was the poor stabbed girl? I saw her in my mind and shivered. Could I be sure that Fern was right — that the dead girl wasn't Kim? I could hardly wait to see the pictures.

Fern had said it would take her about three-quarters of an hour to get to my house from Toto's. I tried to call Mary Mary-Sue, but her line was solidly busy. I called Pop. The sitter said he was asleep. Wow — at quarter of eleven in the morning. Still exhausted from the re-union.

So I went back to my notes for my talk. Thank you, sleep-think, for the raw material. But my mind found it hard to concentrate. Who was the dead girl?

Fern arrived about 11:30, throbbing with importance but also a little tense about the face. She had on an off-the-shoulder, Gypsy-looking purple blouse, a full purple skirt, and hoop earrings. Mourning clothes? She swept into the kitchen, welcomed by the smell of coffee, and put the pictures of the dead girl's hands on the white-topped kitchen table. "I had to force these a little so you can really see the lines," she said. She also laid down Mary Mary-Sue's copy-machine print of Kim's right hand. "I like sugar and cream in my coffee," she added imperiously. She put the rest of the pictures in another pile. They would be of Kim's room. I'd get to those later.

I brought us each a blue mug, and we sat down at the table to study the hands together. The photographed hands were pitifully limp-looking and lightly curled. Half-curled hands among the half-curled dead leaves. I shivered again. The copy machine hand was more like a map. "You see," Fern announced, "the shapes of the dead girl's hands and the shape of Kim's handprint are almost exactly the same. They're rather small hands, with the smooth fingers that mean impulsiveness. Also they have large thumbs. The owners of these hands were determined, like you and me."

Thank God, we were alive.

"But," Fern added, "the line patterns in the two right hands are not the same. Not at all. The dead girl's hand has not just two, but three lines across. A most unusual mark. I've seen it only once before, on the handprint of a yogi, and once on the print of the artist Salvador Dali. Needless to say, it's not the same as Kim's."

I looked and was amazed. Fern was right. Three horizontal lines were clearly marked in the right hand photograph. There was the top line that Fern called the heart line. I had that one. The bottom horizontal line — which she called the head line — that one made a sharp angle with the line around the thumb she called the life line. I had those lines. But between the heart line and the head line on the dead girl's hand was another horizontal line. I did not have one of those. I had never seen one of those.

Fern nodded triumphantly. "It can't be Kim."

I looked at Kim's hand map. There the usual two horizontal lines, like those in my hand, were combined into one. The Mark of Murder. And the lines were unsure, wavering.

I went back to the photographs of the dead girl's hands. "Her left hand," I said, "doesn't have that triple marking. Just the usual two lines. Who can she have been?"

"And why haven't we heard of her before?" Fern asked.

"Kim must have known the dead girl," I said, suddenly excited. "Maybe someone told Kim she had a ringer, and Kim went to find her. Or the girl came and found Kim. How else did the girl know about Kim's childhood playing place? And who would have followed the girl to that place and killed her? And why? Or did they mean to kill Kim?" I sipped my coffee and pondered. "You knew Kim better than I did, Fern. Don't you know anything to help us understand?"

But Fern's mind was evidently on something else. "I have already called Mary Mary-Sue," Fern said, setting down her empty coffee cup and glancing at the pot.

That was just like Fern, to get straight through to Mary Mary-Sue when I couldn't. Why did that annoy me?

"I feel for her so," Fern said, pointing to her heart again. "She was so grateful to discover that Kim might not be dead."

"She must have had an awful shock when she thought it was Kim," I said.

Fern got up and fixed herself another cup of coffee, then sat back down. "Yes, Mary Mary-Sue had identified the body, but she hadn't thought to look at the hands. She had a good cry right on the phone, just from relief." Fern smiled and shook her head as if she couldn't believe what Mary Mary-Sue had said next. "But she's so practical. She said thank God she took the call in her own room by herself where she could talk."

"But why?"

Fern shrugged. "To do things her way! Mary Mary-Sue said she'll notify the police. In fact, she'll take Kim's handprint down to the morgue and compare them. She'll tell the police she began to have a feeling that the body she'd seen couldn't be her daughter because that girl did look a little different. But Mary Mary-Sue had thought that was because the girl was dead or because Mary Mary-Sue couldn't see well with tears in her eyes." Fern shrugged, as if everything had been taken care of. "Mary Mary-Sue said we didn't need to come forward. In fact, the police might be annoyed that you took pictures if they knew."

"Now, wait a minute." I leaned toward Fern and looked her straight in the eyes. "If Mary Mary-Sue wants us to hide what we did, she has a personal reason. She looks out for number one."

Fern shrugged again and looked away. "Well, she did say she didn't want this death mixed up with something unorthodox like hand reading." She frowned. "I don't think she wanted me to get into the act."

I laughed. "That's like her. And for now we can lay low. This has been taken out of our hands. Excuse the pun. Let's go drop my books off at Malaprop's and go out to lunch. I need time to sort out my thoughts." I looked out the kitchen window at the fluffy white clouds against the blue sky. Scattered, like my thoughts.

And right then, my dream came back to me like a hit over the head. "I had a nightmare last night," I told Fern. "I dreamed I was two people and that both had been murdered." I described the two of me with a knife in each chest. The dahlias out the window became a pool of blood. I warmed my hands on the heat from my coffee cup.

"A precognitive dream!" Fern cried. "A prediction of the fact that just today you would discover that two girls who looked alike are involved in this!"

"I hope to gosh it's not a dream that predicts," I said tartly, "since the two girls were both dead and they were both me."

I jumped when the phone on the back of the table rang. It was Ted. His voice cheered me up. He sounded fine. Oh, how I missed him. I was pleased when he said his father was a little better. He was glad to know the dead girl was not Kim. And after we talked about the serious stuff, he told me Papa wished me good luck with my talk. And Papa sent me his mother's favorite face-saving-when-she-forgot line. Now, that was better to think about than me dead twice. I grabbed the pad and paper by the phone and took notes.

Ted said his father had reminded him that

when somebody caught his grandma standing in the middle of the room, looking puzzled, and asked her what she was doing, she was likely to say she was "studying on the hereafter."

"You mean heaven and hell?" I asked Ted, amazed. Fern stared at me with both eyebrows raised.

"That's just what they would ask," he said, "about heaven and hell. And she would say, 'No, I'm trying to figure out what in heaven's name I'm here after.'"

I laughed and sent thanks and get-well-quick wishes to Papa. I filled Fern in. "Maybe," I said, "Papa will fit into my talk. I want to mention how once people know you write about remembering and forgetting, they kindly contribute their own tricks and jokes."

"Yes," Fern said. "You must concentrate on Malaprop's." She stacked the hand photos with the others and stared into her empty coffee cup. She got up, went over to the pot on the counter, poured herself another cup, and added so much cream and sugar I wondered how she stayed so thin. She sat down and took a long sip. "Good coffee. Now, what else are you going to say?" She spoke as if she was planning to help whip me into shape.

"I was going to talk about some of the usual things, like remembering names," I said, "but also about how mechanical devices can improve the chances for your brain."

"To people interested in neurology?" She eyed me as if I might be a mosquito. Tact is not Fern's long suit.

"Like my computer," I said. "God's greatest gift to the absentminded, with a spell-check and a schedule I update every day."

"Any young person knows more than you do about computers," Fern said, "and older people don't care."

"Simpler devices work, too," I said firmly. "My friend Helen Andrews has a basket in which she keeps everything she might need to take with her at all times — her pocketbook, library books to be returned, pens, pencils, her grocery list, and so forth. She never gets in her car without the basket over her arm. She never comes back to the house without her basket, and she always puts it in the same place."

"I bet she looks silly, like Little Red Riding Hood." Fern was not in a good humor. She was obviously feeling let down after rushing off to develop the pictures of the dead girl and then reading those dead hands. Even when Fern was a kid, she occasionally used to get in a nasty humor. Now was the wrong moment. I talked back.

"Listen," I said, "why shouldn't we be as helpful to the inside of our heads as we are to the outside? You don't hesitate to help the outside of yourself put its best foot forward, so to speak. You paint your face, get permanents. As I remember, you dye your hair. And some folks I

112

know even wear girdles and get nose jobs. My friend Joyce had a face-lift."

Hey, maybe the dead girl deliberately had her face remolded in order to look like Kim. No. That was crazy.

"So why shouldn't we give our brain its chance to put its best foot forward with whatever helps?" I asked hotly. "Look silly, indeed! We'd be silly not to do that!"

Fern shrugged. "Okay. Touché. And dyeing my hair wasn't enough. I called Richard last night, and he told me he is marrying somebody else. They're going to be married by a Buddhist monk on Friday." Richard? Oh, yes, Fern's boyfriend. How very California to be married by a Buddhist monk!

She burst into tears. Poor Fern. I grabbed her hand and squeezed it hard. "But that means," she sobbed, "that I can stay even longer — until we solve this. And I don't care if I never go back to California."

Solving crimes as therapy, I thought. Well, why not? It had certainly kept Fern percolating while she talked about the dead girl's hands. I was truly sorry for Fern, but I was sure she'd bounce back. Fern was like that.

As for finding Kim, or discovering her double, we were still at square one.

Okay, I'd rest my brain. I suggested to Fern that we have lunch downtown at the Cafe on the Square. Heartbreak plainly didn't hurt her appetite. After lunch we left off the box of my books at Malaprop's. Marsha said she'd arrange a display and see me at seven. Fern and I went back to my house. I called to check on Pop, but he was taking a nap. Again? I put the final draft of my talk on slips of paper which just fit in my book. I was ready.

We had a quick supper and set forth. Fern was smiling again, even if it was a bravado smile. She wore bright green and earrings shaped like suns. She made me wear green, too, saying it was the color of beginnings and this was my first talk. We arrived at the bookstore looking like spring had sprung.

Marsha took me down to the meeting area of the cafe below the bookshop and up to the end of the long, narrow room. I sat down on a front-row chair near the small podium and looked over my notes. The folding chairs for the audience began to fill up. Interesting looking people: a young woman in a gray suit carrying a briefcase; a friendly-faced man with a wispy beard, wearing jeans, a Guatemalan-looking shirt, and one silver earring shaped like a feather.

Meanwhile, Marsha came up to the podium and gave folks a pep talk about me as a substitute speaker. I was grateful. Hey, this was exciting!

I started by making the audience laugh about the hereafter. Hey, what a good crowd. They were even interested in the part about my friend the history professor trying to teach me the medieval systems of memory with shocking images, puns, and such. The story about Helen's Red Riding Hood basket both amused and struck them as a good idea. Most people asked interesting questions, like were my systems all for people who are right-brained? I said I never tested the brains of folks who contributed ideas, but each trick was guaranteed to work. I'd tried them all.

Fern raised her hand. Actually, she flapped it, very expectantly. I nodded, and she said she had an interest in physical signs of mental attributes. Did I know of any signs that show a good memory or a bad one?

"No," I said, "except a string around the finger."

But Fern managed to get a rise from a pompous-looking type who raised his hand and told about the single line across the palm that doctors used to help diagnose Down's syndrome. "I assume," he said, "that someone suffering from mongolism would have a bad memory."

Fern said she had heard that line could have other meanings, and would love to talk to anyone who knew about it. Boy, she was going to milk anything she possibly could out of this occasion!

Marsha announced there was wine and cheese and that I would be glad to sign books. And those lovely people bought books. Not entirely tactfully. One man said it was for his wife who couldn't find her way around the block.

One young man said he was a poet, and poets had more right than other folks to be absent-minded. But some folks were so glad to meet a fellow forgetter that we became instant friends. That was great. I could almost stop thinking about the dead girl. I could almost stop wondering where Kim had disappeared to.

Finally the crowd thinned out. I looked up to see Fern in the back of the room in deep conversation with the man with the silver feather earring. They were standing in front of a large bulletin board with hundreds of business cards and messages all over it. Fern beckoned me to join them.

"This is Mike," Fern said as if she were introducing the crown prince. "He's half Cherokee, and he works in a bookstore in Hendersonville." By his left ear a card on the bulletin board said, in large print, KNOW YOURSELF THROUGH MASSAGE. I guess I was tired. I thought of someone massaging his ear. I felt like laughing.

I gave Mike my best bookstore smile. By his right ear a card said LEARN HOW TO SELL.

"I was explaining to Fern that two lines across the hand combined into a single line is not confined to Down's syndrome," he said. He had the I-know-the-answer voice of a radio announcer. Good. That would help me to remember his name was Mike.

Fern was absolutely bursting with self-satisfaction and smiling up at this Mike as if he might be God. If she missed that boyfriend of hers, you couldn't tell. Something was up. I started to say that, in fact, the one line instead of two ran in my family, but Mike kept talking.

"I'm a woodworker," he said. "I go to fairs in Cherokee. I go to ceremonies. And I was telling Fern here that I've heard that when we Cherokee are looking for the right child to train to be a shaman — what you might call a medicine man — we look for an anomaly, something that makes the child different. And one sign of that is sometimes the single horizontal line across the hand. Combined with natural intelligence, of course, and other factors. I don't know what else."

Fern gave me a significant look. This is interesting, I thought, but what does it prove that makes Fern act as if she discovered America?

"I was telling Fern that I met a pretty girl in the shop a few weeks ago. Her name was Eileen," Mike said, "and she asked about my feather earring. We got to talking about my being part Cherokee, and she asked if we had a book that might tell about this very line we are talking about."

"And did you?" Maybe this would be fruitful.

"I told her no. But the Cherokee give a meaning to that line. And someone I knew could tell her more. That was Anna Littledeer, but I see her only at fairs. I told Eileen that Anna would be at a fair in Cherokee a few days later and she could find her there. I don't have Anna's home address."

"Did the girl you met in the shop have the shaman line in her hand?" I asked.

"No. She said her sister had the line and was afraid it meant some weakness of character, some bad flaw."

Fern reached in her pocket and pulled out a slightly dog-eared snapshot. "Is this Eileen?"

He stared at Fern in amazement. "Why, yes, it is!"

"No," she said dramatically. "It isn't! This is the girl with the combined line in her hand. Kim Gordon. She sure looks like the girl you saw, doesn't she? That girl you met seems to have been murdered, and Kim has disappeared." Were the girls sisters?

Now it was Mike's turn to rock back with surprise. "Good Lord," he said, "what a shocking story!"

"Watch for it on the evening news," Fern told him before he could ask more. "Would it be possible," she asked, "to get the address of this Anna Littledeer you sent Eileen to see? The one who knew the Cherokee belief about the combined line."

"I'll try," he said. "I know someone who knows where to find her. I'll get in touch."

"You always learn things in a bookshop!" Fern said as we got in the car to start home. "And that line, the mark of difference, will lead us to Kim. You'll see."

Chapter

11

Tuesday, August 29, Evening

"Fern, I've got to hand it to you," I said as Fern drove us back to my house. "I never thought you would discover anything related to Kim at my book signing. I am positively floored. And imagine! The dead girl may be Kim's sister. And until yesterday we hadn't even known she existed. This is strange! And how amazing that the line that runs in our family can be typical of a shaman's hand. That will certainly please Pop."

Fern zoomed past a huge, multicolored totem pole, which seemed to move in our headlights. It belonged to the Boy Scouts and graced their headquarters. I reminded myself not to let Fern drive the next time we went somewhere, even if I was very tired from talking. I am married to a fast driver, but Fern is a maniac. "Could you go a little slower?" I asked as she swerved out onto Merrimon Avenue. "This isn't the California freeway."

Fern laughed gayly as if humoring *my* craziness and slowed down to semi-maniac. "It's nice of Mike to say he'll try to get us the address of this Cherokee who can tell us more about the line in Kim's hand." When Fern said that, I had the oddest feeling she had some secret about the line. But that would be silly. I looked at her profile in the half light. She wore an enigmatic kind of smile as she zoomed past signs for pizza and frozen yogurt. We were near the college, and students like to eat.

There was more to this situation than had come to light yet. "You know Kim better than I do," I said.

"Yes," she said, "Kim calls me in California."

"Often?" I prayed the present tense was still correct.

"Sure," she said. "We were both adopted, you know. My mother was really my aunt. My birth mother was killed in a tractor accident."

I had forgotten that. Of course. That was a bond.

"Kim needed someone to talk to about being adopted, about how she felt about that. So she talked to me." Fern sounded almost smug, pleased with herself as she whizzed along.

Just then a battered pickup turned into Merrimon in front of Fern. Her brakes screeched, but we managed not to hit the truck. I gasped. Two boys and a coon hound in the back of the truck opened their mouths and stared with fear. An old man in a black felt hat looked out the driver's-side window as if Fern should be ashamed of herself. I regret to say that all the rest of the way home she complained about male drivers. Not another word about Kim. Never mind — at least Fern slowed down.

By the time we came to my nice, comfortable square-cut-log house, we were both yawning. We stopped inside the front door. "I'll tell you more about Kim and me tomorrow," Fern said, stretching. "I'm exhausted."

I was exhausted, too, and I sensed I would do better to let her tell me in her own good time in the morning. Fern was a natural force just like Pop. She had to run her own course. And would you believe we actually forgot to watch the eleven o'clock news? The latest on the investigation into the death of Kim's look-alike, maybe her sister, was certainly on the news.

Listen, I said to my brain — or was it my mind? — as my head hit the pillow. *You did a good job of sorting out my Malaprop's talk. Thanks for that. And if sleep-think can do that, maybe it can do more than that. So please, while I'm asleep, will you help me figure out what on earth is going on with Fern? Something is odd about the way she's acting. And while you're at it, brain, I'd like to know how that relates to Kim and why she's vanished. But I think that may take longer.*

I kind of laughed at myself for trying to be a detective in my sleep. But, hey, whatever works, works.

Chapter

12

Wednesday, August 30, Morning

I woke up and thought: *coincidences*. Too many. And with the last one — the bit about how Mike showed up at my signing and told us about poor Eileen and the medicine-man line in Kim's hand — even Fern, with all her nerve, had had an odd look on her face. I'd been distracted at the time — or, rather, amazed — but Fern's face came back to me in the night, and I woke up knowing how she'd felt: embarrassed.

And yet I didn't feel as if this Cherokee earring man she'd met at the book signing, this Mike, was lying. Somehow I was sure that wasn't it. Was Fern mixed up in something sneaky? But what? And why?

I jumped up and threw on my favorite denim skirt and a T-shirt. I ran to the kitchen to see if she was up for coffee yet. I would confront her head-on.

The kitchen was silent except for the ticking of the clock and the cat meowing. Empty except for the cat rubbing my ankles, the sunshine through the window, and the smell of coffee. In the middle of the kitchen table was a large note. I'LL BE BACK AT ELEVEN. FERN.

But I wanted to confront her then. I said "Stinker!" so loudly my cat, Silk, cringed. I patted him to reinstate his self-esteem. He had been my father's till Pop announced he was too old for cats. So Silk was used to outbursts.

At least Fern had left me some coffee. I almost suspected arsenic in it. But that wouldn't be Fern's way. Too obvious. Besides, it smelled delicious. I poured myself a mug and sat down at the kitchen table, fuming.

I grabbed the pad and pencil that live by the phone and began to make a list of things that fit together too neatly. First, Fern alerting us all to the Mark of Murder. Then Mary Mary-Sue just happening to have Kim's handprint with that mark. All that right after Kim, who had the mark on her hand, had vanished. And then I photographed the dead girl's hands, and the Mark of Murder wasn't on her right hand so she couldn't be Kim. But I was the one who took the picture. Nobody could have predicted that. And what good could any of this do anybody? But something was up, damn it. I could feel it in my bones.

Silk came over and jumped in my lap. Did he see steam escaping from the top of my head? Did he want to help? I wished he could.

And why had someone killed the girl who looked like Kim? Hey, the police might have tracked down the girl's identity by now. At least they would have learned something. This was not the right time for local television news. I went to the front door, opened it, and reached for the *Citizen-Times*, which lay near the front steps. The sun shone, but the air was morning cool and smelled of summer. A nice day to pull weeds in the garden and relax. I shut the door and went back to the weeds in my mind.

I hurried back through the living room, spread the paper out on the kitchen table, and there on the front page was a picture of Kim waving. A smiling, candid shot. My stomach wrenched with sadness. The caption said it was Kim.

DEAD-RINGER MYSTERY MAY INVOLVE TWINS, the headline said, and the story told how the body found in Biltmore Forest was first mistaken for Kim, but was now totally unidentified. The story asked that anyone who could identify the murder victim, who looked like Kim, call the police. Nothing there I didn't know.

No picture of the body that looked like a twin. Too gruesome for the paper to run, evidently. If the dead girl was a twin, could her hand be different? Or would it have to be exactly the same?

Could Kim have known she had a twin when apparently nobody else did? Why keep it secret?

Suddenly it came to mind that, a little over a month ago, Kim had cut her lovely long hair. When I had seen her, I'd just thought, *Too bad.* But could it be she cut it on purpose to match the girl I later found dead? That thought gave me goose bumps.

The newspaper story went on to mention that family and friends hadn't seen or heard from Kim for over ten days and were worried that she might have met with foul play. The story told how Kim was the adopted daughter of Mary Mary-Sue and Ward Gordon and said those with any information about Kim's whereabouts should call the police.

If the police had talked to John Baylor, they had not told that to the press.

I realized that it was only the previous day when we had realized the dead girl couldn't be Kim. It seemed much longer ago.

The telephone rang. It was Pop. "I am ashamed of you, Peaches," he said. "You have no respect at all for your old, sick father."

Oh, boy. I hadn't gone by to tell him firsthand about finding the body. I had lowered his prestige as a purveyor of gruesome news. "I was feeling badly yesterday," he said. "But in the evening, when I was feeling more myself and learned the news, I called you to find out about this body business, and you weren't even there. All I got was your damn machine. I suppose you thought I'd fool with that. I would have expected you to come and tell me about this murder in person, Peaches, to lessen the shock. At my age shock could simply carry me off. And I'd think you would care about that."

I apologized and looked at the clock. 8:30. Fern was not due back until eleven. I said I'd come right over. And then I made my first big mistake. I told him about the Malaprop's signing.

"You mean to say," he said, "that anybody in town who wanted one could get a signed copy of your book before you gave one to me?" He sounded as if violins were playing sadly in the background. "Don't you remember you promised me the first one off the press?" I did not. But it worried me. Could I have done that? Pop is very good at making you wonder about things like that.

"Pop," I said, "you're going to hate my book because I admit I'm not perfect. And you've heard most of it anyway." But I felt badly. I had lowered his prestige even more because he was not the first to have the book.

"Perhaps," I said to cheer him up, "you can help solve who killed the mystery girl and where Kim has disappeared to." That was my second big mistake. Never, *ever* say the first thing that comes into your head when you're feeling guilty. Especially to my father.

But, boy, did I electrify Pop. I hung up the phone and hurried over to his place to find him sitting at his favorite table near the big window, looking out into the garden. He was beaming. "I'm ready to help," he sang.

Allie, his favorite current sitter, was by his side, helping him clip newspapers. His latest hobby was clipping crime stories. Actually, Allie did all the work since Pop is almost blind. She had crimped gray hair and wore blouses with Peter Pan collars. She looked as if she should be in a church choir, but she certainly could spot gory stories.

"I know the killer!" Pop cried out as soon as I sat down beside him. "It was Ward!"

And knowing that Pop usually manages to stay plugged into the gossip network, I listened carefully.

"He wants the money," he said, "from Kim's trust. He thought he killed her, but he got the wrong girl. He wants to leave Mary Mary-Sue and live in the manner to which he wishes to become accustomed. Can you imagine having that woman run your life?" He made a face.

So the gossip mill knew about Kim's trust. "But why would the money come to Ward, and not to Mary Mary-Sue or someone else, if Kim died?" I asked.

"All that," he said, "is for you to find out. I can't do everything for you. Now, tell me what you know."

Pop had, of course, heard that Lucy and I had found the body. The gossip mill was on to that. He knew about the kitchen knife, so I could tell him a little more about that knife and about the woods where the girl was lying, and make him feel he was getting an eyewitness account. I managed to draw it all out until he felt satisfied. The gossip network evidently had not heard about the hand photos. And I deprived the network of that juicy fact by not telling Pop.

"At least," Pop said, "you have to go out to find bodies. They don't arrive at your door. How many have you found now?"

"Too many," I said with a sigh. "It seems like after the first one, you get in the habit. Because people expect you to snoop, and that's dangerous."

"But it could be worse," Pop said. "Allie found this story about a police dog that brought home two human legs, one leg one day and one the next. They'd been sawed from a body." He turned to Allie. "Show Peaches the clipping." Then back to me: "The police had to put a tracking collar on the dog, like they use to track wildlife, in order to try to find the body, and even that didn't work." He turned back and smiled at Allie as if she were the most marvelous woman in the world. She smiled back primly. Not Pop's usual flashy taste in sitters.

I shivered. Why this gruesome new hobby? Was it Pop's way of coming to terms with death? Or maybe he simply needed to reassure himself that terrible things happen to other people, not just to us. I wished Allie weren't so helpful. She strove to please, even with that story about cut-off legs.

"I am certainly glad you don't have a dog," Pop said to me.

I changed the subject. "Fern is staying with me while Ted's away."

"She'll help solve this murder and disappearance case by reading hands!" he cried. "Oh, this is going to be interesting! It will drive John Baylor crazy. He hates things like that." Pop reached over and patted my hand. "If you have to leave to go help Ted's parents, Fern and I can take over the case. Allie will help."

Fern. Ha! I looked at my watch. Ten o'clock. I explained that I had to get home because Fern would be back, possibly with some new facts we'd need for the case. She wasn't due until eleven, but I had some snooping I wanted to do before she came.

I drove home through the sunshine, past the overlook to the far mountains, down Webb Cove Road — a closed-in corridor of green in August — and past some kids canoeing on Beaverdam Lake. I drove into my driveway. Fern's red rental car wasn't there yet.

Still sitting in the living room was the paper shopping bag Fern had brought with her when she moved in. I figured that meant I was perfectly free to look through it. I carried the bag over to the coffee table in front of the couch and began to pull out the contents. There was a light sweater for our cool mountain evenings. An extra pocketbook: bright green. I brazenly opened that. Nothing inside but a crumpled tissue, three dimes, and a comb. At the very bottom of the paper bag was a book. I pulled it out and laid it on the table: *Cheiro's Language of the Hand*, big, black, and flat. The *C* was a crescent moon surrounding the rest of the title. The *i* was dotted with a star. "Revised and enlarged edition, 1897," it said inside. I leafed through. Boy, this Cheiro had famous clients. I found Mark Twain's handprint, and Sir Arthur Sullivan's. He was half of Gilbert and Sullivan, right? And W. E. Gladstone's. Ted had read some book about him. They named a kind of suitcase after him. He was a famous prime minister of England under Queen Victoria.

Maybe Fern figured we might demand proof about the Mark of Murder. Why else had she brought the book? Well, I wouldn't mind knowing that she hadn't made up everything she said. She'd called the Mark of Murder an old sign. *Language of the Hand* was about a hundred years old, especially considering this was not the first edition. New in comparison to cave walls, where Fern had said handprints were found, but older than I am by a long shot. No index. I leafed through and looked at the pictures. Hand shapes mattered, Fern had said. A picture of the "conic"-type hand had tapered fingers like Janet the Planet's. Cheiro called it artistic. The "philosophic"-type hand, with knots at the finger joints, was shaped like Lucy's and John

131

Baylor's. There was a square-type hand with a square palm and squared-off fingertips, which Cheiro called the useful hand, and several other types. I skipped through to the chapter on the line of head. Cheiro didn't mince words. He had one page devoted to insanity shown by the line of head. And a page and a half on murder.

I began to read about the murderer's head line. "The line of head divides the hand into two hemispheres, that of mind and that of matter." He said if the head line was high in the hand, giving the world of matter greater scope, "the subject is more brutal and animal in his desires." I looked at my hand, and the line of head was slightly more than halfway up my palm. Was that high?

"This has been amply proved by the hands of those who have lived a life of crime, particularly if they have been murderous in their propensities (Plate XXIV)." I looked for the picture, hoping for a reprieve. This was like reading a medical book and getting the diseases as you read along.

But as I turned toward Plate XXIV, I found another whole chapter on "Propensities for Murder."

That caught me. "As regards the hand, it divides murder into three distinct classes," Cheiro wrote. "First, the murderer made so by instinct to kill, as exhibited in the brute creation through passion, fury, or revenge." That sounded bad enough, but Cheiro said that class was ordinary with no sign in the hand but un-governable temper and brute passion. Those people, he said, merely got carried away, and after they killed, they felt broken by remorse.

"Second, the murderer made so by the greed for gain; the nature that will stop at nothing to gratify the covetous tendency." These people would not appear abnormal, he said. "The most striking peculiarity will be the line of head, which will be heavily marked but with a decided growth upward. It completely leaves its place on the right hand; as the propensities become stronger, it enters the line of heart, takes posses-sion of it, as it were, and completely masks all the generous or kind thoughts of the subject." But it wasn't just the head line Cheiro said you were to go by — there had to be other clues. "The hand is unusually hard, the thumb not ab-normally thick but long, very stiff, and con-tracted inward. The entire formation gives covetous propensities and an utter want of con-science in the pursuit of gain." I shivered. One of us could conceivably be like that. And appear normal in most ways! I was referred again to Plate XXIV.

I found it in the back of the book. "The hand of Dr. Myer, convicted of murder, 8th June 1894," the caption said. It was an ugly hand, the lines deep and wavering. And straight across the palm was a combined head and heart line, more or less like what Fern was calling the Mark of Murder. I felt a chill.

But Fern was exaggerating. She was including any combination of the head and heart lines into one. Cheiro did not. In this murderer's hand the heart line — the top horizontal line — began on the heel of the hand in the normal place and curved up between the index and second fingers, just like mine. But the head line, which began in the normal way near the beginning of the life line, rose and joined the heart line. It was a distinct pattern. And when Fern said members of our family had that Mark of Murder, she was oversimplifying by a long shot. Fern was twisting the truth, damn her.

And for what reason? Why was she putting us all through this? And how was it related to a real murder?

I turned back to Cheiro's description of the third type of murderer. Maybe I was doing Fern an injustice. Maybe there were other markings such as Fern described.

In the hand of this subtlest and deadliest murderer, Cheiro had written, "there will be nothing abnormal in connection with the hand itself. It is only by examination of the characteristics that the treacherous side of the nature will be discovered. The leading features, however, will be a very thin, hard hand, long, the fingers generally curved slightly inward: the thumb long — giving both the ability to plan and the strength of will necessary for execution."

And here came the head-line stuff:

"The line of head may or may not be out of its

134

proper position. It will, however, be set higher than usual across the hand, but will be very long and very thin, denoting the treacherous instincts." So this most terrible type of murderer, in Cheiro's estimate, didn't even necessarily have Fern's Mark of Murder at all! Fern was a fraud.

Unfortunately, I kept on reading.

"Murder with such persons is reduced to a fine art, in the execution of which they will study every detail — so skillfully that the verdict is usually 'Death from natural causes.'"

Wow! Folks must have read Cheiro partly to scare themselves to death.

Whom did I know with a long, thin, hard hand? Fortunately or unfortunately, I couldn't think of a soul.

I heard a car stop in the driveway. I envisioned long, thin, hard hands on the steering wheel. I looked out the front living-room window, but before I could get near enough to it to see around to the driveway, a key turned in the lock of the front door. Fern opened it and stepped inside.

She was dressed in a simple white skirt and blouse. No earrings. As if she wanted to play Babe in the Woods. Babe in the Woods, my foot!

"Where have you been?" I asked angrily.

She looked me over, walked over, and looked down at the book on the coffee table. She sat down in the leather chair at a right angle to the table. I sat back down next to the incriminating book.

"I have been driving around, trying to think how to tell you the truth in a way that will make you believe me," she said in a humble tone which wasn't like Fern at all.

I looked at the backs of Fern's hands, laid flat on her thighs. The conic type, tapered fingers. Artistic, Cheiro had said. Smooth fingers. Impulsive, Fern had said about Janet the Planet.

"I know you didn't tell the truth before," I said.

She squirmed, but she kept her shoulders back. "I almost told the truth," she said wistfully.

"You used me to try to get what you wanted," I said. "Whatever it was. And what we got was murder. You took a little bit of fact about a mark Cheiro said helped show a murderer and blew it up into a farce. What in God's name are you up to? And how can I know when to believe you, ever again?"

Fern took a deep breath and held herself still. She let her breath out slowly and then, with an air of working hard to speak distinctly, said, "I did exaggerate about the Mark of Murder."

"And there was a great deal you neglected to tell me, right?"

"Yes," she said, "but I had a reason." She bowed her head slightly but spoke with careful clarity. "I didn't mean for things to go wrong."

"Naturally," I said.

She raised her eyes, and they were full of pain and apology. Not like any Fern I had ever seen before. "But now that things are going so wrong, and I don't know exactly what to do, you've got to help me. You've got to believe me, Peaches, or you and I will be in danger — even worse danger than we're in now."

Chapter

13

Wednesday, August 30, Noon

"I meant for this to turn out well," Fern said again. "And now some killer is on the loose, and anything could happen, even to us." She pressed back in the brown leather chair as if the arms could protect her and fingered her empty earlobes as if they could inspire the right words. This was the only time I'd ever seen her without dramatic earrings. The lack stood out like nudity. Out the window behind her, I noticed my favorite pine tree begin to toss in the wind. We were probably going to have a storm. Yes, the barometer must be low; I felt pressed down. A storm would at least break the unusual heat.

Fern fidgeted in her chair. She said, "Kim and I planned the Mark of Murder thing . . ."

"Kim!" I blurted out.

She shrugged. "Yes, we made the plan a while

back, before she disappeared." Fern paused as if she wasn't sure how to go on. In the distance I heard a growl of thunder. I felt like growling myself.

"Like I said, we were both adopted," Fern said, raising her head as if in challenge. "But you knew all that. And Kim didn't have anybody to talk to about how being adopted feels." Fern gave me a pleading, large-eyed glance as if to beg for understanding. Part of her act? "Kim wanted to talk about finding her parents. She needed to figure out a way to learn what her mother was like and what her father was like and why they gave her up for adoption. And nobody would help. So she called and talked to me." That last was said with a ripple of pride.

"Called long distance to California," I said. "How could a kid afford that?" Another thunder growl, coming nearer.

"Yes, it was important to her. I told her to call collect. In fact, last year she heard the rumor that she was one of us by blood. That her real mother or real father was a member of our family. She was upset because John Baylor wouldn't tell her yes or no. So she was sure it was true. And why did it have to be a big secret? And she kept looking at each one of us asking herself: is that the one? And after that she got depressed."

"And exactly what was your secret plan?" I tried not to sound sarcastic, not to let my voice ask if they meant to plan murder. Because I wanted to believe Fern was capable of a perfectly innocent plan that could cause disaster, which is at least better than on purpose. Maybe she really had meant to help. I'd had experience with that kind of thing, with Pop. Loud thunder crash. Fern winced, as if she expected to be the target. Was she feeling guilty? Or just dramatic as always?

To what extent is character genetic, like blue eyes or brown hair? Some members of our family had that one mark across their hands, and some were born to be dramatic, not to mention outrageous. And a certain number were just naturally strong-willed. And when the strong-willed and the outrageous and the dramatic were in one and same person, what then? Another crash. Fern hugged herself.

I looked at Fern's thumbs, flat against her hands as she clutched each arm. Her thumbs were as big as mine. I wondered how a hand reader would spot outrageousness. And, good grief, was I outrageous?

But all this speculation was getting me nowhere. The first patter of rain hit the window. "All right," I said evenly, "tell me exactly what happened."

"I'd read Kim's hand before. Kids love to get their hands read." She smiled as if I should appreciate that. "And I knew Kim had that mark in her hand which is a little bit like the old-fashioned Mark of Murder." There was a flash of lightning. Thunder followed. She flinched again.

"But just a little bit like the mark," I said, my outrage gathering steam.

"Yes," she said, "the real sign of murder was supposed to be the heart and head lines joined but in a more exact pattern and in a hard hand with a long, curved-in thumb. But, nevertheless, the Mark of Murder was very much like the one line across the hand instead of two. That single line is unusual and therefore kind of a genetic marker."

A graduation picture of my daughter Eve hung on the wall, not too far from Fern. There was a sameness about their eyes. I had to admit it. Kinship did mark us. "By genetic marker, you mean . . . ?"

"If you found two people with that unusual line and a number of other things the same, like maybe a crooked little finger and a double-jointed thumb, you could figure that there was a good chance those two people were closely related."

"You could figure, or you knew?" Over Fern's shoulder, my eye fell on my favorite lamp. Made from a wooden log, it has a carved face beginning to emerge, as if the carver hadn't finished. I needed to turn the lamp on. The storm had sucked away the light in the room around us.

"Well, it makes sense they'd be related." Fern smiled sweetly, like any fool could see that. "And besides, it made Kim so happy to have a plan. The last few months she's been depressed. She needed a plan. And beginning about a month ago, Kim even suspected she had a sister out there somewhere." Thunder and lightning came almost together; that meant the lightning was close. "I hate storms!" she said. And she hated my asking questions.

I wanted to see every twitch of Fern's expression. I got up and clicked on the lamp by the window. Outside, the pine tree just beyond the terrace still waved, and a loose paper blew across the lawn beyond. Fern's red car in the driveway was a bright spot in the gloom.

I sat back down across from Fern. "Faces would be alike in twins, so why would you need the hand lines to find your twin?" I demanded. In fact, I figured, the hand lines had shown that Kim and her look-alike were not identical twins because their hands were not alike. This was getting confusing.

The phone rang. I hoped whoever called would make some sense. And of course, he did because it was Ted. He said his father was better. The telephone line was full of static, but I could hear. He said he was coming home and then perhaps going back for a while when his father was out of the hospital. I was for that. Immediately I felt better. Even the next crack of lightning didn't bother me. But I didn't want to discuss Fern's fraud with Ted, not in front of her. I wanted to wait until I could speak my mind. I told Ted I was fine and mighty glad he was coming home.

I felt more kindly toward Fern. She'd be

leaving my guest room. She was one of those people you could love more if she wasn't staying in your house.

"You have discovered a lot," I said, "but why did Kim believe she had a sister?" This got stranger and stranger. "How could she figure there was one out there?"

"Several times people told her they'd seen her in a place where she'd never been. And she wanted to believe it. She wanted to find a sister." Big flash. Fern winced. Big bang. We both jumped. I was afraid the lightning had hit my tree, but no, there it waved.

"So what happened?" I asked.

Fern gripped her hands into fists. "Okay, I made a mistake. I felt like I ought to do something. But I couldn't think what to do, with me way off in California. And Kim was so depressed. This was about two months ago." She glanced to see how I took that, then went on.

"And Peaches, I just naturally have to try things. I believe in that old saying: 'It's better to try to do something and fail than to try to do nothing and succeed.' I'm that kind of person. Would you believe my hands are almost exactly like Amelia Earhart's?"

I didn't think it would help to point out that even though Amelia Earhart was a pioneer in aviation, she did vanish in the middle of the Pacific Ocean.

"So you talked to Kim," I encouraged.

"I think Kim was holding back. I don't think

she was telling me everything about what depressed her. But that's hindsight." Another flash. The light flickered, and I had the strangest feeling the lamp face winked as the thunder crashed. Fern said, "How can we hear ourselves talk?" as if the storm was bothering her on purpose. Then she sighed. "I didn't know how to help Kim, but I couldn't just give up."

"Not in our family!" I said. "We'll go to hell for the things we've done, not for the things we've left undone."

Fern glanced up, startled. She obviously hadn't been planning to go to hell at all.

"And then I had an idea." Fern's hopeful, pleading eyes were locked on me again. "I suggested that since I knew one or two other members of the family had the same single line across the palm that she did, we'd talk it up at the family reunion. We'd call it the Mark of Murder, which it almost was, and find some excuse to read everybody's hands. And maybe we'd find a good bet for a close relative, or maybe if we kept everybody talking, we'd hear about somebody somewhere else who had the line. Well, it was a chance. And the idea made Kim feel so much better. Like it might somehow help her find out who she was."

"And you could count on Pop," I said dryly, "to jump in with both feet and make much of something called a Mark of Murder!"

Fern had the grace to look embarrassed. "Yes, I did think of that."

"So what can I believe?" I asked. "What's true? Do you know where Kim is?"

"No," she said, "I haven't heard from her in two weeks. But I figured I'd go on with our plan." Slight thunder rumble. "I figured that maybe in some way it would even help us to find Kim. If I found a mother or a father or a sister, that would sure make Kim want to come back. I guess the hand-reading thing was a dumb idea. And the girl who looks like Kim, who could be her twin, doesn't even have the same hand lines. Perhaps she's a fraternal twin, not an identical twin. It's all very strange."

"Perhaps she's not even closely related," I said. Not likely. But then people said that, at least from a distance, I looked like Cousin Gertrude (Gertrue-blued, Gloria's sister), except that Gertrude always looked bored. And she was a third cousin once removed.

The storm was abating. Even the rat-a-tat-tat of the rain had lessened. Storms can blow by like that in the mountains.

"Perhaps your plan worked," I said, "but not the way you wanted it to." I hoped real murder wasn't the way Fern wanted her plan to work! "When we know who the dead girl is, we may know more about Kim's family."

Fern got up and looked out the window. "I think the worst is past," she said. Unfortunately, she seemed to mean the storm and not our problem.

"I need to ask you something else," I said.

"Please sit down. Now, about the Cherokee thing . . ."

Long pause as Fern sat. She crossed her legs, swung the top one, and tried to look nonchalant. But her hands were clenched. Ha! Fern had said to look at hands, and now I was! "Of course, I knew the Cherokee thing all along," Fern said casually. "About that one line instead of two across the palm, and how it's thought to be one possible sign that a child can be trained to be a shaman. I forget who told me. Maybe Cousin Jane over in Sandy Mush, who's interested in Indian stuff. I told Kim about that shaman stuff because I thought it would cheer her up to be special. But I guess that line worried her more than I knew. Because of Cheiro's name for it."

Fern looked down, saw her hands, and unclenched them. She gave me a sheepish look, turned her hands over, and stared at the palms. "If I could read the future correctly," she said, "I would have kept my big trap shut, right from the first."

"And so the look-alike who said she was Kim's sister, who somehow found out about Kim and the across-the-palm-line, wanted to find out more. But why?" I asked. Was Fern still putting me on in some way I couldn't figure out?

Outside the sun was shining again. The pine tree shone. But I didn't feel enlightened.

"I guess that girl was curious about her look-

146

alike, too," Fern said, "so curiosity can be lethal." Her voice rolled with drama: Fern, the human thunderstorm. "I think we need to watch our backs."

Chapter

14

Wednesday, August 30, 1:30 P.M.

I sat back in my chair and sighed with pleasure. Alone at last. Just me and my beautiful Swiss-cheese sandwich with lettuce and pickles and a tall, cold glass of skim milk. And, boy, was I hungry. I needed fuel after my morning with the Mark of Murder, not to mention Fern and thunder.

I sat there at the kitchen table, looked out on the rain-washed garden, and took a delicious bite. I looked out at the birdbath with a blue jay splashing and red dahlias behind it. Red for celebration. Fern was gone. I had told her I needed some time to be alone and sort out my thoughts, and God bless her, she believed me. And of course Ted was coming home that night. Hoorah! Two minds are better than one. He'd help me sort out all the craziness. I took another sip of cold milk and wiggled my toes with pleasure. Too soon.

Somebody was knocking on the front door. I put down my milk. Who now? I hurried to the door and peeked out the little window by the side. There stood a tall, gangly man with one lock of his longish brown hair hanging down over his face. Fortyish.

He brushed his hair back and knocked again. All the lines in his face ran downhill, lines of sorrow. His knock was angry, getting louder. He wore a denim shirt and jeans. And even at a glance he looked disorganized, as if someone had just woke him in the middle of the night. But this was early afternoon.

My gut hunch was that he needed help. I opened the door to midday warmth and his anxiety.

"I'm looking for Peaches Dann," he said in a broader Southern accent than we have in our mountains. He had a thoughtful question-asking voice, but anger and anguish made his words resound. "Somebody killed my daughter!" Two birds on a tree in the front yard flew away, startled.

He paused and looked at me as if he couldn't quite understand what he'd just said. Then he said, "A woman named Peaches Dann was the one who found my daughter. I have to talk to her. Is that you?" He stepped forward as if he were ready to do something desperate, if he could just think what.

So this must be the father of the dead girl. My sympathy leaped out to him, but my sympathy was guarded.

"Yes, I'm Peaches Dann," I said quickly. "If there's any way I can help, I will." I grabbed my shoulder bag which hung by the door in case I needed a pencil and paper plus a box of tissues from the table near the door. "Let's sit out in the yard here," I said. Maybe he just needed help. But he seemed so scarily balanced on a sharp edge. Better we should be outdoors where anyone who drove by on the road could see him if he went berserk. They might call for assistance.

"Come sit on the terrace," I said and quickly led him to the chairs around the glass-topped table where Ted and I like to sit on a pretty day. I grabbed a handful of tissues and wiped the last rain moisture from two cast-iron chairs. He followed me as if he were half in a trance. He almost tripped over a rough place on the stone terrace but caught himself. As he sat down on the edge of one of the iron chairs, I took the chair catercorner to him.

"I need to find the son of a bitch who did this terrible thing," the man said, clenching his fists on the tabletop, "to a girl everybody loved. Not just me. Everybody."

I nodded. He didn't seem to need questions. He needed to talk.

"I didn't even know she was dead, not until I saw the picture in the paper." He stared as if he didn't see me and shook his head. "I saw the picture of the girl who looked like my daughter! The story said the police thought that a girl named Kim had been murdered, stabbed, and then they found it wasn't her. And nobody knew who the dead girl was. And I felt like it was me who was stabbed. Because the picture was exactly like my daughter, my Eileen." He stopped and I felt he was replaying the newspaper scene in his head.

"They looked like twins," I said.

"I thought my daughter was at her friend's house!" he cried. "And I called and she hadn't been there. And I called the police and they told me to come identify —" He choked, and tears filled his eyes. Finally he pulled himself together and went on more calmly. "And it was her. Eileen. Dead. They said you were the one who found her." He swallowed, and his large Adam's apple bobbed up and down. "And what were you doing off in the woods as if you went to meet my daughter?" His eyes were angry but questioning. His voice trembled. Across the road in the woods, a bird was singing sadly like a counterpoint to his words.

This is a man who will listen, I thought. Crazy or not. I picked my words carefully, kept my voice steady. "Someone telephoned a young friend of mine and asked her to come to that place in the woods. She asked me to come with her and give her a ride."

"Who called her?" he demanded. "Who?"

151

"I don't know," I said. "She didn't know."

He moved impatiently in his chair, as if I should know more, but he continued to listen. "The person who called said she wanted to tell my young friend, Lucy, something important about the girl who vanished, Kim, the one who looks like your daughter. Kim was Lucy's friend from the time they were kids."

"A policeman said you told them that," he snapped, "but you must know more than that. I have to know what happened, or I'll lose my mind!" He ran a large, bony hand over the top of his head as if to be sure his mind was still there. "And you found my daughter dead in the woods."

He blew his nose on a large, white handkerchief, like an elephant trumpeting. I could see he was one of those tragic people who are more tragic because they are almost comic at the same time. Not stupid, I decided, but unpredictable.

"You daughter was a lovely girl," I said. "I'm so sorry about this." Those words were inadequate. In my mind I saw her. Even in death she was beautiful. "But, please, tell me who you are and how you found me," I said.

He stuck out his hand. "I'm George Stackhouse," he said almost formally. "I called your cousin Ward Gordon, the one the paper said was the father of the other girl. He said maybe you could help me, maybe you could tell me more."

So should I thank Ward? A car drove by on the road, an open convertible with laughing teens inside, oblivious to us. Joyously alive. I winced for Eileen's father.

"Tell me what you saw," he begged. He wiped one large, bony hand over his face as if wiping the anguish off. "Tell me everything, even the parts you believe I'm not strong enough to hear. I don't believe the police are telling me everything. Why do people think I can't stand the truth?" he cried. "I can stand it. I have to. My God, my life is full of truths I have to stand. I can't give up."

I waited until a bright-red pickup truck, with the windows down and rock music blaring from the radio, passed out of earshot. Our street is usually quiet. The loudest noise is the rustle of wind in the trees across the road or a dog barking or the children five houses down. Not today. But once the blaring music faded, I explained how Lucy wanted me to go with her to a meeting place, wanted me for backup in case there was some kind of trick, since we didn't know how or why Kim disappeared.

"Lucy who?" he demanded, and I explained she was not only Kim's friend but also a distant cousin and the daughter of the lawyer who arranged for Kim's adoption.

"A lawyer arranged this Kim's adoption? Baylor?" Eileen's father went rigid, as if he'd touched a live wire. I nodded.

"Baylor! That's the man who arranged for us

to adopt Eileen!" George Stackhouse glared with suspicion. "We were so pleased to get that lovely baby girl. We were so trusting! But something was fishy even then, wasn't it? If there were two girls just alike. And there's some connection between the two we weren't told, isn't there? Which maybe led to this."

He said "this" with such sorrow that I knew he meant Eileen's murder.

"Yes," I said, "I think there must be a connection. But I don't know even as much as you do. How did you meet John Baylor?"

"My wife's father once had connections here in the mountains. Though we lived in Texas until a year ago. Baylor called and said he'd been a friend of my father-in-law's a number of years back, and he'd bumped into him on a trip to Texas and heard we were looking for a child to adopt. And he had a child he wanted to place, far from her relatives in the mountains, he said. A child from what he called a good family. She was a beautiful baby. My wife fell in love with her picture."

He paused, then groaned. "Oh! If we'd just stayed in Texas. But it never occurred to me that Baylor wanted to place Eileen away from her relatives because there was danger. I was dumb. And how would anybody recognize my girl? She sure has changed since she was a baby. And we lived in Hendersonville, an hour away from here. And why in the name of the Lord would they kill her?"

154

Someone recognized her because she looked like her twin, I thought. "And why did you come here?" I asked him.

"The National Weather Records Center moved me here," he said. "That's in Asheville. I'm basically a weatherman. And I never thought — and I never stirred things up. I never told Eileen she had any connection to these mountains. And I never looked for her relatives. Why would I want to find them?"

"Did she try to find them?" I asked.

He froze and considered, then spoke fast like I'd opened a hole in a dike. "Not that I know of. Eileen would have known that searching for her birth parents would have hurt her mother. I mean Alice. Because that would show that Eileen felt we weren't adequate parents, we weren't enough. But lately she's had some secret. I could feel it. Eileen was a smart kid, too. She could have fooled us. We thought we were so lucky."

"What kind of a secret?" I asked.

He jumped up. "How would I know? I had a feeling. That's all. But something was wrong from the beginning, wasn't it? I'm sure of that. I'm going to see John Baylor, and I'm going to find out what! I have an appointment in an hour." He glanced at his watch.

In my heart I wished him luck getting anything out of pompous John.

"I'd go now, damn it, but Baylor won't be there. He said he'd be out till three." Eileen's father began to pace around the table.

"Well, he sure hid the very existence of Eileen from *us*," I said as Stackhouse passed in front of me, then plunked back down in his chair.

"But *you* get on with it. Tell me what *you* found." He fastened his eyes on me and didn't even seem to see the yellow butterfly that flitted back and forth between us before it took off for the flower bed. I felt annoyed at the butterfly, as if it should know better than to flit around at a moment like this. Because telling this man wasn't easy, telling how Lucy screamed and I ran after her into the woods and I found what I thought was Kim with a kitchen knife in her chest. My voice kept trying to break, but I managed to keep it flowing.

He cried, but only briefly. "Go on," he said.

I told him how Mary Mary-Sue had her daughter's handprints. And how, because the lines were not the same, we knew the dead girl wasn't her adopted daughter, Kim.

Eileen's father stared at his own square-cut hands, now holding on to the edge of the table. There was a gold watch on his left wrist. He'd said he had an appointment in an hour. I pulled a pencil and small yellow pad out of my pocketbook.

He frowned. "And, you know, it's strange that in the last month Eileen got interested in hand reading. And I just had this feeling that that was connected to some secret."

Aha! But I didn't break the flow of his words with a question.

He was now so calm I was afraid he was in shock. He held one hand up and contemplated the palm. "She said I had a square-type hand, which meant I was a practical person who wanted everything in its place." I noticed his fingers were almost squared off like two-by-fours, but with bony joints, and the main part of his hand below the fingers was roughly square.

Tears came into his eyes again. "And God knows my daughter is not where she ought to be. My poor girl."

"Was your daughter ever interested in the markings on the hands of Cherokee Indians?" I blurted out.

He sat up straight and stared at me. "Now, how could you know that Eileen was interested in that?"

I told him about the so-called Mark of Murder line and how Kim had it on her hand and how a line like that apparently had special meaning for the Cherokee. And Eileen evidently tried to buy a book that would tell about that line in Carolyn's bookshop in Hendersonville, and told the bookseller — Mike — that her sister had that line in her hand. I told Eileen's father how I showed Mike the picture of Kim, and he said, yes, that looked like the girl who came to the bookshop. I tried to say this in a low-key way.

But Eileen's father began to tremble. "And Eileen didn't tell us?" He pushed the hair back from his eyes as if to see better. "Oh, we knew there was something, but we never suspected she met a sister. I can't believe it!" He eyed me suspiciously, as if I were making up lies.

"I have no proof Mike got it right about the sister," I told him.

"We did wrong," he groaned. "We didn't make Eileen tell us all her secrets. We gave each other space. My wife, Alice, grew up in a family where kids didn't have any say. Or any privacy. They had to do exactly what they were told or else. Alice didn't want us to be like that. Maybe we should have been." Tears were in his eyes again.

I leaned back in my chair and figured the hardest part was over. I'd told him the worst.

He shook his head unhappily and groaned again. "So much is happening to me. Lord, give me strength. About Alice's sister, too." He let go his rigid grip on the table and dropped his hands in his lap.

Now, wait a minute. What about Alice's sister? This was getting complicated. I was lost.

He turned and stared right through me. "It's too much," he said. "Alice is home in bed, sedated. She's in a state of shock."

Good heavens, there was more! I *am* a good listener, so people tell me things. I sensed I should encourage him very gently. "Shock," I repeated softly, then left a judicious pause. The bird was singing again off in the woods.

"Just six weeks ago my wife learned her sister was murdered — and now this had to happen."

"Murdered?" I asked. What now?

"It was unreal. You see, her sister vanished twenty-one years ago. And ever since it's worried her."

I should think so! "And Eileen's twin vanished, too. Is there a connection?" Hey, maybe we were on to something.

"No," he said firmly. "My wife, Alice, knew why her sister left. Their mother demanded that they all be perfect. So Susan and her mother had towering fights because Susan wasn't perfect. Susan couldn't hack that. So the kid just vanished. She went to California — we knew that much."

Like Fern, I thought. "And then?"

Stackhouse got up and paced up and down on the grass. "You won't believe this!" I waited. "A month ago we got a letter, forwarded from Texas, from a prisoner in California. His name was Andrew Frank."

Odd, I thought. Frank is usually a first name.

"He said he was married to Susan and had been convicted of murdering her. We had never heard of him before."

"What a shock."

Eileen's father nodded soberly. "This prisoner said he only had the nerve to write us now because someone else had now confessed to Susan's murder. He sent us a description of that murder. She was shot in the head as she lay asleep in bed, one night when he claimed he was out driving around because they'd had a fight.

159

He said he felt terrible about that. Naturally. He said he was sure we would rather know what happened than to wonder forever."

"And he waited years to let you know! Is he out of prison now?" Hey, maybe he was mixed up in Eileen's murder somehow.

"He said that, even with a confession, there was still red tape to getting out of prison. But when and if he was cleared, he would like to meet Susan's family. And tell them that she'd been happy. But he wanted to be legally cleared before he contacted us any further."

"And did you meet him?" I asked.

"No. Alice wrote an enthusiastic welcoming letter, which worried me. Maybe he was trying to con us. But this guy, Andrew Frank, wrote us back a short formal note. He said please not to get in touch until he was cleared. He was too damn proud, if you ask me. That's how it seemed at first. Well, then I wanted to find out more. To demand information. To help him if he needed help. And Eileen wanted to help him, too. She was a great kid, damn it! But Alice was adamant — we should honor her brother-in-law Andrew's request. I couldn't move her, no matter how I tried. Because, like I said, Alice believes in giving other people space. Maybe too much space.

"But I got John Baylor — that damn John Baylor — to check for me. To see if this Andrew Frank was still in prison out there, and he was. And John found out that the man who confessed to the murder — a hippie type who said he had been high on drugs at the time — was now dying of AIDS. And John said he might not be reliable. And Alice made me wait, as Andrew wanted us to. Alice can be stubborn. And she was so cut up about her sister, Susan." He groaned. "And now this! How can one family have so much grief?"

"And Eileen wanted to help this Andrew?"

"Eileen wants — wanted — to be a lawyer. And she was so interested in what would have to be done to get the conviction overturned. But she'll never know now." Tears seeped from his eyes. The inappropriate butterfly danced back and lighted on the table, wings waving gracefully.

"What was your daughter like?" I asked, because now, I felt, he was ready to talk. He'd blown off his steam and was ready to speak more clearly.

"She was smart," he said, perking up slightly. "She was a volunteer at Pisgah Legal Services last summer vacation. That's the group that helps people who can't afford expensive lawyers." He stopped short. "You know, Eileen did get a threat about that. From some crazy man who thought everybody who was helping his wife was on his wife's side in their divorce battle. He was a drunk who blamed everybody else. Harold Hornsby from Brevard. So I wonder — but how could he be mixed up in this?"

I wrote down "Harold Hornsby from Brevard" on my yellow pad.

All of a sudden Eileen's father hit his forehead with the flat of his hand. "I forgot to tell the police that! This is too much. My wife has collapsed." He sounded defensive. "Of course she's upset. This makes three."

Now I was really confused. "Three?" Was there no end to this?

"Her first husband was shot in a nightclub brawl. He was a Cuban jazz musician. A very talented man. And then she heard her sister was killed. And now this!"

"So you felt your daughter was keeping secrets?" I asked, to get back to Eileen.

He jumped up and looked down on me. "She was a wonderful person, and if she kept a secret, it was just to help out somebody else. I can tell you that." The startled yellow butterfly zoomed away.

Eileen's father sat down again and did another switch. "Why are you asking me questions about this? Why is my daughter your business? You aren't the police!"

And why was he suddenly so belligerent? I was annoyed as well as flabbergasted. "I'm not the police, but as it happens, I've worked out the solutions to several murders."

"Murders?" He seemed amazed. He demanded details, and I gave them. He actually looked impressed.

"Therefore," I said, "my family gives me

credit for being able to find things out. And Mary Mary-Sue has asked me to try to find Kim. And Lucy asked for my help. And that's how I happened to find your daughter in the woods."

"Eileen," he said soulfully, as if he'd forgotten her for a minute and remembered her death again fresh. He sagged and swallowed.

"The voice," he said, "the voice this Lucy heard on the phone — what was it like?"

I said that Lucy didn't recognize it, but that she thought it was possibly Kim's.

He nodded, as if that made sense. "Yes. Eileen must have been helping somebody. Maybe this Kim, who was her look-alike. Maybe they were twin sisters, like the paper said." He shook his head in a confused way. "And there was something Eileen felt she had to keep secret about it." His face wrinkled in a puzzled frown. Then he jerked straight up again, as if something had stung him.

"Maybe that was why she ordered some strange things through the mail. We found them on her desk after she was dead." He clenched his hands into fists. "Oh, God, why did this have to happen?" Tears choked his voice, but he fought them back. "Eileen got a whole packet of stuff from something called the False Memory Syndrome Foundation. Have you heard of that?"

"I suppose I should have," I said, "because I write about memory. And the name sounds vaguely familiar."

"I brought this stuff with me to give to the police," he said, "and forgot to take it in with me. My mind is not working right. Then I was mad at the way they treated me, like I could be a suspect. I left without remembering to go get them the false-memory stuff. And it may have nothing to do with what happened to Eileen, anyway."

"Could I see it?" I asked. Because you absolutely never know what will turn out to be important. In the midst of all the terrible drama in Eileen's family, the fact that she sent off for information about false memory could be a clue. Detection is finding out what really happened, right? And also finding out what appeared to happen and never actually did. Could false memory fit in with that?

Chapter

15

Wednesday, August 30, 2:30 P.M.

Eileen's father picked up a briefcase lying on the flagstones near his feet and pulled out a stack of printed material. "This is just some articles and newsletters from the False Memory Syndrome Foundation. They seem to be about brainwashing, but it's what Eileen sent off for, just before . . ." He choked and pushed the printed pages across the table toward me.

I looked down at the top paper, titled "Making Monsters." What on earth? This was not some comic-strip thriller. It was a paper by a Dr. Richard Ofshe of the Department of Sociology at the University of California at Berkeley. Eggheady stuff. What did a seventeen-year-old girl want that for? And what did monsters have to do with memory, even false memory? I was tempted to sit down and read the stuff quickly, but there was too much. And at any moment Eileen's father was going to jump up and go see John Baylor.

"If Eileen ordered this material just before she was killed, of course you have to take it to the police," I said. "But before you do, how about giving me a copy?" I wanted a chance to study it. "I might be able to be useful. After all, I knew Kim and the police didn't." He looked desperate enough to clutch at any help he could get. Good. "We can go right over to Mailboxes Etc. and use the copy machine. It's not five minutes away." I explained where. He hesitated. "And you'll want to keep a copy for yourself," I added firmly. That got to him.

"All right." He picked up the papers, reached in his pocket, and took out his car key.

I reached in my shoulder bag and took out my key. "We'll go in convoy," I suggested. "Unless you'll give me a ride," I added on second thought. "Then I'll walk back. The exercise will be good for me." Actually I wanted to give him a chance to say anything else that was on his mind as we drove.

"I have to get to that lawyer soon," he said and glanced at his watch. "There's time if we hurry. And you did know Eileen's sister — if she was her sister. You might spot some connection I'd miss. So, thank you."

It always amazes me how taking action, even a small action, calms people down.

"Wait just one second," I said and ran into the

166

house and grabbed a two-handled canvas bag which lives near the front door. Great for carrying papers. I hurried out to his car, opened the door on the passenger side, and jumped in.

He was silent as we drove out onto Lakeshore Drive, so I asked a question. "How did your daughter act the last few weeks? Did she do anything strange?"

"No," he said, shaking his head. "Not really. Except she was moody, which wasn't like Eileen. She was a smart girl, good in school. She was going to be at Mars Hill College in the fall. She wanted a car, and we said 'no.' I wish to God we'd said 'yes'! But she didn't complain." He paused and frowned. "Except, like I said, I had this hunch she might be hiding something. I'm not usually irrational, so I dismissed my feeling. Why didn't I pay attention? Maybe I could have saved her." We were going down a steep hill to the shopping center. He clutched the steering wheel as if he might crush it.

I started to say, *You couldn't have known,* but I knew instinctively he wouldn't accept that.

We stopped abruptly in a line of cars in front of Mailboxes, which is one in a row of small shops: Accent on Books, a craft shop, and some others. He grabbed up the pile of papers, and we hurried in together.

There were two copy machines, so we split the work. Boy, there were a lot of pages to copy, some of them newsletters which had to be turned inside out to get all the pages. We worked silently except for the rolling noise of the machines.

Meanwhile, people came in and out, mailing packages of various sorts. Nobody I knew — until, just as I was smoothing out a page to put in the copier, I glanced up to look straight into the face of Cousin Elvira. As always, she looked wildly curious and thrown together. She wore a pink man's shirt, buttoned wrong, tan Bermuda shorts, and orange sandals. "I have to mail this sweater I knit to my daughter," she said. I hoped it had two sleeves in the right places.

"You know, her husband is stationed at Fort Bragg, and the baby is due next month," she said. Then, without hesitating or missing a beat, she added, "What an interesting title, 'Psychiatric Misadventures.' "

I'd put the copier top down, but not before her eagle eye could see what I had put in the machine. "I'm so glad you are helping Mary Mary-Sue look for Kim," she said in a knowing tone. "We are all racking our brains as to where that poor girl can be, especially after this latest tragedy. And I suppose you think that Kim has lost her mind."

The temptation, of course, was to explain to Cousin Elvira why she was wrong. To tell her "Psychiatric Misadventures" had nothing to do with Kim's state of mind, at least not that I knew of. I resisted. "This is something I am copying for a friend," I said, praying Eileen's father would lay low. The only safe course with

Cousin Elvira was to say as little as possible. And I thought — at least I hoped — she'd long ago figured that out about me, that I couldn't be pumped worth a dern.

She seemed about to turn to Eileen's father. She'll ask anybody anything. I moved between them. "Elvira," I said, "I am trying to pursue a line of inquiry that you would approve of. But for now I need to keep it to myself."

Her eyes became larger and brighter. She looked at a page on the pile to copy. " 'The Lies of the Mind,' " she whispered with relish. "How absolutely fascinating. Of course, I won't tell a soul." She probably meant that. At least for the moment. I was glad the woman at the counter was discussing a strange-shaped package with a young man in sneakers and nobody seemed to notice us. Eileen's father had quietly covered what he was doing with the manila folder it was in to begin with. Smart man.

"When I find something out," I said to Elvira, quietly but firmly, "you'll be the first to know if you'll help me out by leaving me alone right now." I stared her down, which with Cousin Elvira is not easy. She has gimlet eyes.

"Oh, I can keep a secret," she said, patting me on the shoulder as if I should know that. She hurried out as if she couldn't wait to get to a phone. She'd report what she'd seen, add some wild guesses, and weave a tale. I hoped to goodness that wouldn't make trouble.

Eileen's father finished his copying as fast and

as quietly as possible. I did the same. We sorted out copies, one of each page for him and one for me, and I put mine in the canvas bag I'd brought just for that purpose. He paid, and we went back to his tan Ford.

As soon as we started off, I told him about Elvira, our family super-gossip.

To my surprise, he didn't seem upset. "It's just possible," he said, "that if she spreads the word that some kind of false memory could be related to our tragedy, someone who knows something about that will come forward." I admired his optimism.

He offered to give me a ride all the way to my house, but I knew he was late. He did insist on giving me a ride to the top of the steep hill. I insisted on walking the rest of the way. I needed the air. I needed to look at the green leaves and hear the birds. That might help my mind work.

He stopped the car, reached out, and clasped my hand tightly. "I'm going to trust you," he said. "Please let me know anything you find out."

And I said: "Please do the same for me. It may be too late for Eileen, but maybe we can find her sister."

Tears came to his eyes. "I think Eileen would want us to do that." He blew his nose. "She was a great kid." Then he began to shake and clenched his fists by his sides. "It's not fair!" he cried. "Life's not fair."

I knew it wouldn't do a bit of good to tell him he was right.

Chapter

16

Wednesday, August 30, 3:15 P.M.

I was a little short of breath by the time I went up some of the hills on the way to my nice log house with green solitude around it. When the trees are in full leaf, houses half vanish. I like my isolation. Most days, at least. I opened the front door to a ringing phone. I grabbed it up from the hall table. The voice that hit my ear was Pop's.

"Peaches," he boomed, "you come over here now! Cousin Mary Mary-Sue is standing right here and she's driving me crazy! I need your help, and I can't talk now, but come as fast as you can." He hung up.

That was like Pop: to summon without explanation. The bag of false-memory papers was still in my left hand where I'd switched it when I opened the front door, so I took it out to the car with me before I noticed. Oh well, why not? I hurried up Town Mountain to find out what on earth Mary Mary-Sue was doing at Pop's house.

I parked in the circular drive which loops in front of the house. Banked impatiens along the drive bloomed fire-engine red. Red for alarm. I was alarmed, all right. What was Pop up to now? I hurried up the front steps, grabbing the iron railing to pull me up faster. I rang the bell by the oak door. Pop keeps the door locked, but it opened so fast I almost fell in. Two people were waiting for me, right inside — Pop in his wheelchair and Mary Mary-Sue in plain navy blue, as if she were one step from mourning black.

"I'm glad you're here," they said in chorus, each glaring at the other as if they wanted to shoot. Mary Mary-Sue, being so tall, could look down on Pop. But Pop, with his Franklin D. Roosevelt in-command chin lift and flashing blue eyes, was not to be outdone. Without moving back one inch, they began to talk at once so I couldn't understand a word.

Mary Mary-Sue stopped first and crossed her arms, evidently seeing that I couldn't hear her. Pop went right on: ". . . and so I said five thousand dollars was ridiculous. And Mary Mary-Sue said, 'Get Peaches. She'll tell you what a stingy old bastard you are.' " His voice rose in outrage. He pointed one skinny finger at Mary Mary-Sue.

"But you summoned me over here," said Mary Mary-Sue, "on a day when I have more than I can do anyway. When I'm worried sick. You lured me over by promising to put up a handsome reward — you used those words — for anyone who had information to help us find Kim."

I studied Pop. Now he was half sheepish, half pleased with himself, eyes sparkling. He'd figured out how to be in the middle of things. "Old bastard" was right.

"So, of course I came," said Mary Mary-Sue. "I have to find my daughter." She shivered. "I know she's in danger. Someone meant to kill her and got the wrong girl." She glanced at me. "They meant to kill Kim. I'm sure of that." She turned to Pop, hands on her hips. "And all you want to offer is a reward of one thousand dollars. Five thousand is more like it. Five thousand could smoke out the ones who think they're protecting Kim. The fools."

"Like who?" I asked quickly.

She flushed. "If I knew who, we might not have to offer the reward. If I got my hands on them, they'd tell! But someone must be helping that girl hide! And, believe me, I've called all her friends. And not a one admits a thing."

"I know you've called John Baylor," I said.

Mary Mary-Sue nodded and at the same time went so red in the face I wished I hadn't said that. "Talk about bastards," she choked.

"Come sit down," I said. "Let's figure out

what we should all do next." If I couldn't get them calmed down, they were both going to burst into flames. Spontaneous combustion.

I took the handles of Pop's wheelchair and wheeled him firmly over to his place at the table where he likes to sit. Mary Mary-Sue followed and plunked herself down in a chair by his side. I sat on his other side.

"George Stackhouse, the father of Eileen Stackhouse, the girl who was killed, who looked like Kim, came to see me," I said. That shut them up. They didn't want to miss a word. Pop raised his head and looked me straight in the eye, as if to say, *I'm waiting. Tell all!*

Mary Mary-Sue sat perfectly still.

"I liked Eileen's father," I said. "He said he called and talked to Ward, and Ward told him that I found Eileen's body."

Mary Mary-Sue shrugged. "I hope you didn't mind. Ward figured the man might tell you something useful." Translation: Ward didn't want to fool with him, himself. Mary Mary-Sue squirmed in her chair. "That man was angry at the world. He even asked Ward where we were early Monday afternoon." She snorted like an indignant horse. "I gather that's when the police think someone stabbed his girl. He had a nerve." She twitched as if someone had poked her with a live wire, then took a deep breath. "It's lucky Ward and I were at home together when that girl was killed."

I pulled a pencil and pad out of my shoulder

bag and wrote down her alibi, such as it was. Suspect everybody.

"What did you find out, Peaches?" Mary Mary-Sue demanded.

"We expect to be kept informed," said Pop imperiously. Now he was "we" with Mary Mary-Sue.

"I discovered," I said, "that Eileen was interested in becoming a lawyer. She wanted to help her adopted mother's brother-in-law, who apparently had been falsely accused of murder years ago. Somebody has come forward to confess to the crime, but helping the brother-in-law get out of prison is complicated, I guess. And Eileen was interested in something called false-memory syndrome, which has to do with people remembering things that never happened. But I don't know how any of that fits in."

Pop leaned back and narrowed his eyes. "Who was it," he asked dreamily, "who said, 'My life has been full of terrible disasters, most of which never happened'?"

"It sounds like Mark Twain," I said testily. This was no time for Pop to go off on a tangent. "But murder *has* happened. Eileen Stackhouse was stabbed. And Kim has disappeared. And John Baylor is the lawyer who saw to the adoption of both kids."

Mary Mary-Sue stood up. "I am going to see that man right now and demand to know who these kids really are. Who their parents are — or were. And this time he's going to tell me!" She turned to Pop. "And how about a five-thousand-dollar reward?"

"Pop and I will figure that out," I said. "Pop needs to talk to *his* lawyer to word the reward notice. And remember, if you want me to help discover where Kim is, let me know everything you find out."

Mary Mary-Sue nodded and strode out the door like a general with a battle plan in hand.

"So the dead girl was interested in false memory?" Pop mused, ignoring the reward. "Why don't you know about that, Peaches? Memory is your department, so false memory must be too."

Mine? Pop can remember things that never happened with no help at all.

"Listen," I told Pop, "it's important to find Kim quickly, before the killer does. So it was great of you to offer to help. But Mary Mary-Sue doesn't come cheap. She knows you're rich, Pop, whether you admit it or not. If you want to be in the middle of this, it's going to cost you five thousand dollars."

He groaned, and I could see a terrible inner struggle going on.

"Of course," I said, "you could word a statement so that the reward is payable only if it leads to the finding of Kim and the arrest of the killer. You could word it so that, if two people give information, they split the reward. So it isn't five thousand to each."

A look of utter horror crossed Pop's face as he

considered *double* five thousand. Finally he shuddered and said, "Okay. I'm a fool, but I'll do it. Call Homer."

Homer *Sawyer* was Pop's *lawyer* (self-contained mnemonic device), a man Pop trusted, with longtime mountain roots. He wore dark suits, white shirts, and a pallbearer expression to make sure you took him seriously. But he claimed his father was a mountain character in Thomas Wolfe's *Look Homeward, Angel.* And now and then he'd break out with an old-fashioned salty expression to restrain Pop from foolishness, such as, "If I were you, I wouldn't get into a pissing match with a skunk."

So Pop respected Homer. I called him, and Pop seemed satisfied that Homer would be by later. Pop yawned and said, in the meantime, he'd take a nap. That meant I could go home. He also said he'd call Cousin Georgianna, who's the librarian in Marshall, and ask her to bring us a book on false memory and murder. I figured one book was not likely to be about both, but Pop would probably forget to call Georgianna anyway, unless she happened to call him in the next five minutes. I took off quickly before Pop thought of something else for me to do.

I arrived at my humble abode at the same moment that John Baylor arrived in his black Cadillac. I drove into the driveway, jumped out, and went over to meet him. He got out of his car and shook my hand. He had on a dark suit, a white shirt, and an expression like a pallbearer. I think it's catching among lawyers. But he was supposed to be at his office, conferring with Eileen's father, wasn't he? Or had enough time passed so that was over? And he was supposed to be on hand at his office to be the subject of Mary Mary-Sue's wild truthfinding attack. But here he was at my house instead.

"Well," I said, "this must be some kind of occasion. Since when do lawyers make house calls?"

Chapter

17

Wednesday, August 30, 5:30 P.M.

I led John Baylor inside, not paying much attention to my surroundings, anxious to know what he had to say. We sat down on either side of the fireplace. "All right," I said, "shoot."

He pulled himself into the most dignified possible position, cleared his throat, and adjusted his suit jacket. "I suppose," he said, "that you were surprised to learn that I was the lawyer who arranged the adoption of Eileen Stackhouse as well as Kim. I have just talked to Eileen's father at my office. He's making all sorts of wild accusations about how I'm hiding something. I informed the police of my role in this matter as soon as I discovered that a girl who resembled Kim was found dead. As soon as I knew it was not Kim, I knew it must be Eileen."

"So?" I said.

"I was dreadfully upset about her death," he said. "And I realized you would be upset that I hadn't told you she existed." He gave me a properly sorrowful nod. "You have to understand," he added defensively, "that even beyond the legalities in this matter, I was sworn to confidentiality by a client who trusted me. I keep my word. You can count on that. Even when it's difficult." He smiled at me as though, if I were older or wiser, I'd have approved.

"So?" I said again.

Brevity flustered John. Not that he showed fluster much, but he blinked faster. "I was asked to place the twins," he said. "They were twins, but fraternal rather than identical, I'm told. They were so alike they seemed identical when they were not side by side." He cleared his throat again. "Anyway, I was asked to place each one in such a way that neither family would be aware that they had adopted one from a set of twins."

"And you got away with that," I said, "for a while. And what about money? Was that for both?"

"I was asked to administer a trust fund for each twin. I told you about the one for Kim. I suppose the relative who requested my services assumed that, as the twins grew older, they would look less alike and no one would spot their relationship. But lately they seem to have looked more, not less, alike."

"Because Kim cut her hair." I sighed. Oh, the small coincidences that can change a life!

"You placed Kim with kin," I said. "At least there's been a rumor to that effect. And her hand is marked with a line that's very uncommon in the population at large. That line is quite common in our family." I watched to see how he'd react to that.

He became inscrutable. "I do not care to talk about relationships," he said coldly. "I have told the police who the parents are in strictest confidence. And we agree that it would not be productive to release the names of the birth mother or father at this time. In fact, under North Carolina law, I am not allowed to reveal this." He was so far up on his high horse that I wanted to smack him. I refrained.

"And you placed Eileen far away in Texas," I said. "Why did you do that?"

"I followed the wishes of the relative who put the twins up for adoption," he said. "That's all I care to say."

"The Asheville police chief," I said, "is related to your lovely wife, Maureen, I happen to know. I don't suppose he is helping you cover something up?"

I said that to make him mad. If John ever loosens up, it's when he's mad. Boy, did my ploy work!

"I'm only doing my duty," he said loudly and stood up. "I am doing my best to live up to what I promised a poor distraught man who asked me to find a good home for each of the girls. And what right have you got to meddle?" He screwed himself up to an even higher fury. "And what right have you got to make snide marks about Maureen or Maureen's kin? My wife does more good for sick, unhappy people and old people than anyone else you know! Just today she took some hot chicken soup to Cousin Anna. She's spending the day helping her out. Cousin Anna broke her arm yesterday."

I must not get distracted by Cousin Anna's arm. "And what did you really come here for?" I asked.

"I came by because I wanted to tell you in person about the twins."

I found that hard to believe. He could have called me. Did he hope to discover what I had found out? But he seemed to know everything I'd found out, and more. So why was he here?

He finally made himself plain. "Now, I'm sure the police have enough leads to find Kim. You and I should stay out of this from now on."

Chapter

18

Wednesday, Early Evening

I followed John out of the front door onto the stone terrace which wraps around one corner of the house, past the glass-topped table where I'd sat with Eileen's father. The cool of evening sent a slight breeze quivering. I watched John drive off in his black Cadillac, around the curve and out of sight.

Now I'd have a chance to look at those papers. Good Lord, where were they? Stop that, I told myself. Think. Where was I last? Of course. In the car, coming back from Town Mountain. I found them on the floor of the car on the passenger's side and brought them in the house.

Just inside the front door, by the small table where we put letters to be mailed, I stopped. My heart beat faster. Something about the room was not right. I hadn't noticed with John there, but now it hit me. I looked all around. At the fireplace, far over on my left, empty of ashes for the summer. At the two overstuffed chairs on each side — we'd just sat there, John and I. The green striped couch at right angles to the fireplace was exactly as usual. My eye couldn't immediately spot anything wrong, but the hair on the back of my neck stood up.

I asked myself why. What was up? Silk the cat wasn't sitting in his favorite place on a couch cushion. But I knew he might be sitting on the kitchen table, waving his tail as he watched the birds outside in the birdbath. Silk wasn't supposed to sit on the table, but when I wasn't looking, he wasn't perfect.

Perfect. Everything was too perfect, that's what it was. The pile of magazines on the end of the table in front of the couch was neatly squared, Ted's *Editor & Publisher* on top. The newspaper I'd been reading the night before was neatly put together in a pile on the table by the rocker, not slightly helter-skelter as I had probably left it. But how could I be sure? Maybe I'd put everything just so. Unlikely but possible. Or had John straightened papers as he passed? Was he nervous-neat? Or suppose someone else was still in the house? I shivered. Someone hiding?

I began to tiptoe, which was silly because I hadn't been quiet before. John and I had talked quite normally. But it made me feel better. I tiptoed into the kitchen. No cat. Odd. I was sure I'd left him inside. My sandwich, curling slightly at the edges, and my glass of milk, now tepid, still sat on the kitchen table, undisturbed even by the cat. I took a bite of the sandwich and realized how hungry I was. If it was a little stale, so what? The phone book and some bills were just so in a stack on the kitchen table. I was sure I had left them scattered. I began to feel annoyed. Someone was imposing his style on my house. Or did I imagine it?

Did Fern still have a key? I was sure I'd taken my key back. Who else had a key? My cleaning woman, but she came on Fridays. Ted. He'd be back shortly. Hoorah! But not yet. I hurried around from the kitchen to my office, still munching the sandwich. The office was so full of papers that I couldn't be sure how each pile had been, but again I had a feeling of more order than I would have expected. It made me feel a little crazy. I envy folks who can be absolutely sure how they put things.

I went over to the computer and turned it on, I'm not certain why. Just a hunch that if everything else had been touched, maybe the computer had been, too. All seemed normal. I pulled up the database and jumped. A message came up: "This file was not closed properly. Filemaker is now performing repairs."

I got the message occasionally when the power blipped while I was using the database list of names, addresses, and phone numbers. But I was quite sure that the last time I looked up a name, the power had not gone off, even for a second. I'd shut the computer down properly when I was through. Hadn't I?

What was true? The sandwich in my mouth tasted extra-dry. I shut down the computer and then carefully cased the bedroom. Nothing obvious was wrong. The red stained-glass cardinal on the window was cheerful as ever. The double-wedding-ring patchwork quilt on the bed was smoothly in place. I opened the sliding closet door with some caution but found no secret burglar hidden behind my clothes or Ted's. I looked through the bureau drawers. Again I had the eerie feeling that someone had been through my things. My scarves were folded too well.

I went in the bathroom off the bedroom and swept my eyes around. My Indian-print bathrobe and Ted's white terry-cloth robe hung behind the door on two hooks as usual. I finished the last bite of my sandwich and picked up the glass by the basin to run a glass of water. The glass was already wet inside. My stomach turned over. I didn't remember drinking water from that glass that morning. And if I had, would it still be wet? I put it back down. My mouth was puckery dry, but I didn't draw water to drink.

I went upstairs and looked over the guest room with the white ruffled curtains and the white chenille spread. I looked in the closet. Nobody was hiding there among the empty hangers.

I half wished I'd been over the whole house and taken notes before I left, so I'd know if things had changed. But you can't go through life taking that many notes or there'd be no time for anything else.

At least I was now sure that nobody was hiding in the house. So okay, I had things to do. I went in the kitchen and got out the largest knife to have near at hand, just in case. I spread the false-memory-syndrome papers out on the table, which was the largest bare spreading-out place I had.

I picked out a paper to read and sat down. *FMS Foundation Newsletter* said the first page. So, who was behind these newsletters Eileen had sent for? I read a little further. They were published by a group of parents of grown children who believed they had discovered in therapy that they were abused as children. In fact, they had accused — and in some cases sued — their parents. Apparently this was going on all over the place, with the parents swearing innocence. So some accused parents and some scientists had formed the False Memory Syndrome Foundation, dedicated to proving that even vivid memories could be false. But what did that have to do with Eileen?

On the wall a framed picture of my daughter, Eve, as a child of about six caught my eye. She held a kitten and smiled with vibrant happiness. I shivered. How terrible to have memories of childhood horror.

I looked back at the papers. Somebody, probably Eileen, had circled a boldface paragraph on the front of one newsletter: "The American Medical Association considers recovered memories of childhood sexual abuse to be of uncertain authenticity which should be subject to external verification."

I just naturally love external verification.

I read a little further about how people "recover" memory with the help of hypnosis, medication, guided visualization, and such like. They begin to "remember" things that are said to have happened twenty or thirty years before. Shocking things they've never even suspected. Yes, I'd read something or other about that in a newspaper or maybe a magazine, about some show-biz type who said it had happened to her.

But how could anyone be sure? And why wouldn't someone check against medical records and such?

I read stories of families split, half believing the accusers and half the accused. And stories of psychiatrists and psychologists sued by patients who said these therapists had used their powers of suggestion, hypnosis, and so on to encourage memories of things that had never even happened.

How amazing that people were fighting and suing each other over this: over the nature of *memory!*

Memory made misery. I read the story of a young woman who accused her family and then, after all the sorrow and turmoil, came to the conclusion that her "memories" weren't real.

How terrible if you falsely accuse a person close to you of abusing you as a child. And yet how terrible if such a memory turns out to be true.

Why would Eileen, a girl of seventeen, want to find out about all this? Why would she have looked into it at a time that turned out to be just before someone murdered her?

I was glad I'd have someone to explore this with — that Ted would be home before long. I looked back at Eve's picture, grateful I'd had a happy child.

I realized I was still thirsty. I went to the refrigerator and got out a pitcher of iced tea — a new kind of herb tea I was trying, lemon-spice. I poured a glass. I had to meet Ted at the airport at 9:30, but I had time to spare. I was so thirsty I took several long swigs of tea. Tangy. Spicy, in an interesting way.

I went back to the table and leafed through the false-memory papers. Some of the "recovered memories" went back to birth, yet some of the scientists said we don't remember things that happen before we are two and a half or three years old. Was that what interested Eileen? Did she want to know whether she or Kim could accurately remember back before they were adopted at two and a half? Did something frighten her about that time?

Yes, it sure would help to discuss all this with

Ted. I glanced at my watch. It was 7:30, and it took me nearly an hour to get to the airport. Plenty of time to get ready. I took another swig of tea to refresh myself.

The phone on the kitchen table rang. Fern said, "Pop tells me you met the dead girl's father!"

I told her briefly what I'd learned about Eileen, how she seemed to have been a great kid and how I liked her father. I felt tempted to cry, but that wouldn't help. I started to tell her the false-memory part but shut my mouth before the words got out. I'd never get off the phone if that came out. I'd tell her later. I did tell Fern about feeling that somebody had been through the house and how glad I was that Ted would be home soon.

Fern got all worked up about what she called "the break-in." I'd managed to convince myself to be calm about it, to allow for the fact that it might all be in my imagination. Fern didn't help.

"Of course," she said, "you know you are in danger. If I were you and Ted, I'd spend the night in a motel. In case somebody has put a time bomb in the house or something. Get the locks changed first thing in the morning because someone could enter at any moment, and there you are — a sitting duck. I bet you don't even have the curtains drawn. Someone could shoot you through the window." She was right. I took a sip of tea to steady my nerves. "I'm only telling you this for your own good," she said.

190

She was also telling me because, like Pop, she couldn't bear not to be in the middle of the action, even vicariously by phone. A family trait? Heredity? Something that cropped up here and there in our family like the Mark of Murder? Would the need for excitement show in Fern's hands? She said her hands were like Amelia Earhart's. Would Fern die for excitement?

I looked out at the gloom beyond the sheen of window glass. Ted and I had never bothered with kitchen curtains. Anyone who passed through the backyard could see me plain as day. I drank some more tea. I'm a nervous sipper.

"People with big thumbs and firm hands like yours can be overconfident," Fern said. "Why don't you take the phone off the table and sit on the floor where you'll be out of sight? You're sitting at the kitchen table like you usually do, right?"

Well, why not move? I took the phone in one hand and settled on the floor. I reached up and got the iced tea. Nobody shot at my hand. I drank another swallow and felt the least bit queasy. I'd made it too strong, but I was still thirsty, so I drank it anyway.

I readjusted the phone. "I'm going to meet Ted shortly," I said to Fern. "There'll be two of us, so if there's just one killer, he'll be outnumbered. And besides, what good would it do him to kill me? I don't know anything yet, not anything that adds up. God knows I haven't found Kim." Looking around under the table, I saw two pens, a spool of white thread, and a ball of dust. Okay, I'm not efficient.

"I have been looking into all the ways Kim could have left town," Fern was saying, "like I said I would a while back, remember? There's no sign of Kim leaving by plane unless she used an assumed name. And she's not registered in any likely Asheville hotel or motel." Fern *had* been busy.

"Thank you," I said. "I'd like to talk longer about that later, but right now I need to go pull myself together to meet Ted."

"I'll call you," she said, "if I think of any hint of what could have become of Kim. Now, you be careful."

I took a last swig of the tea and headed into my room to take a shower and put on a pretty dress for Ted. After all, he'd been gone a while. I felt slightly dizzy. That wouldn't do.

I looked at the clock by the bed. I didn't have to leave for three-quarters of an hour. Good. I went over to the closet and pulled out a blue-and-white-striped dress with a swishy skirt. I hung it on a hook in the bathroom and laid out my underthings on the closed toilet seat. I reached for a towel to hang by the shower and noticed something strange. My moving hand left a trail behind it, a trail of luminous hands like a movie in slow motion. I blinked to clear my eyes.

I stepped out of my clothes and flipped the sandal off my foot. The sandal made a trail, too

— a curve of shining sandals. Kind of nice. But why?

I'm just shook up, I told myself. *A cold shower will help me pull myself together.* I got in the shower stall and turned on the water. Every single spray of water was luminescent with light. *I'm part of the light,* I told myself. I felt a rush of joy. The light beat around me. The spray touched my skin in a thousand places. It wasn't spray; it was butterflies. They were all around me, butterflies beating against me in the light. I was a butterfly bush in a shower of flashing silver rain. And that was so ridiculous that I began to laugh. I couldn't stop laughing. The water around me was full of rainbows. Rainbows on my arms, my hands, my watch. I should have taken off my watch. Watch. I tried to pull myself together. Time. Ted. I had to meet Ted.

I got out of the shower. The water with the rainbows ran on. Splendid.

I began to sing. My voice was lovely and fluid in my ears, yet there were no words. *Fly,* I said. Airport. Something was wrong with me. I couldn't keep my mind on the airport.

I needed to call the airport, to let Ted know I couldn't come, because how could I get to the airport like this? Naked as a jaybird and wet all over. I sat down on the floor in my bedroom and laughed some more.

Some little faraway part of me repeated, *Something is wrong.*

My eye fell on the telephone. What a funny

black thing with buttons. Buttons like on a flute. I saw thousands of buttons of all shapes and sizes like stars around me. I crawled toward the telephone. There was some reason I should be near it. Apparently it knew that. It rang.

"Peaches," said a voice. It was a voice I didn't quite trust. There was a phony waver in it. It was Fern's voice.

"Fern," I said, "you lied about the Mark of Murder."

"Listen," Fern said, "Cousin Elvira just called me. She says you think that Kim has lost her mind. Did she make that up? It sure would be bad news."

I began to laugh. "News, shmooze," I said. "Booze cruise." I liked the *ooo* sound. I sang it to myself. *Ooo-oo-oo-ooo.*

"Peaches," she said, "have you been drinking?"

"Iced tea," I said. "And I can't get to the airport without clothes on."

"I'll be right over," Fern said. "Don't do anything. Stay where you are."

By the time I heard Fern coming, I had found the forest. I looked at the green rug under my hand. It was a forest, a wonderful tiny forest. If I could just see down beyond the tops of the trees, there'd be deer and possums and maybe even Indians. I was enthralled. I lay my cheek close to the rug and tried to see into it. I began to see a deer when I heard the bangs. Hunters?

No. I heard the door banging. I crawled toward the door. Down the hall. The hall was black. There was thunder. I was going to be hit by lightning. But the kitchen was brighter. I managed to open the door.

Fern said, "I've lost the key you lent me." Then she stared at me. "Open your mouth," she demanded.

I tried, but my teeth stuck together.

"A symptom of acid," she said. "But you wouldn't take LSD. You're not the type. Where is the tea you drank?"

I pointed at my mouth and began to laugh again.

She went to the phone, and I heard her say Ted's name. I lost the rest.

She got my clothes and began to help me put them on. Hey, I was a baby again. I looked at her right eye. I saw me in her right eye. And suddenly her eye was as big as a swimming pool. I knew I might fall in. And she had lied to me about the Mark of Murder. And I saw a lying line beside her mouth. The kind of line that grows from telling lies.

"You must come with me, Peaches," she said.

No! I tried to scream. *No! No!* Nothing came out.

Fern's whole face was suddenly as big as a house. The lying line was like a road. *No!* I screamed inside. *No! No! No!*

She was back to the phone again. The phone was my enemy. Black. It began to grow till it was as big as an elephant. The phone could run me over. It could trample me to death.

Fern was back by my side. She was trying to tell me I was okay. I was okay. She leaned close to me. Her hair was made of snakes. "I can tell by your eyes," she was saying, "and by the way you can't open your mouth. This is a bad trip. Try to relax. You're going to be okay."

Trip. I was supposed to go to the airport. The snakes of her hair hissed at me like air going out of an inner tube. Out! Out! Out!

"LSD," she said. "Somebody slipped you acid." Fern was from California. They took LSD in California. "Safe place," Fern said, and the lying line near her mouth got larger and larger. "Taking you to a safe place."

And then, no matter how I fought, the men came and carried me off. They should have been red because I knew they were from hell. They were Fern's men. She'd called them to take me away before Ted could come. And Ted would never know where I went.

Chapter

19

Thursday, August 31, Morning

When I woke up, Ted was in the chair by my bed. I was in a pale room, standard-issue hospital-plain, with a chair and a rolling tray-table at the foot of the bed. The room did not even waver. Ted didn't turn into a monster or change size, thank goodness. He smiled his most comforting smile. I reached for his hand and said, "Hello. Welcome home."

He said, "Thank God, you sound all right." And then, "You are, aren't you?"

And I was. A little weak, but in my right mind. When I moved my hand, I saw just one hand. There was no IV dripping liquid into my arm. That was a good sign. Ted said Fern had called him and had brought me here. He said his father was doing fine. Good. I sighed and dozed off again for what I thought was just a moment. When I woke up a second time, Ted had turned into Fern.

She sat there reading some book about yoga, as normal as Fern could be, in a dress covered with chickens and wearing copper chicken earrings. To proclaim her country origins, no doubt. The room around her stayed solid. Her nose and eyes behaved as features are supposed to behave. I said, "You look better this morning."

"And you're behaving better," she announced. "They're pretty sure all you had was a dose of LSD. Scary when you're not expecting it. But they think you're probably fine now. I bet they'll let you out today. Who do you think spiked the tea?"

She might call it "all you had." I called it a nightmare. And I had no idea who had searched my house — who had created that nightmare on purpose. Had John Baylor been in my house before I saw him and put something in my iced tea? But he'd been with Eileen's father. So who? And I didn't even drink much. Suppose . . . I shuddered.

"Where is Ted?" I asked.

"He went off to eat breakfast," she said. "No point in two of us sitting here."

I looked at a small travel clock which someone had kindly put on the bedside table. It said 9:45. "I brought the clock," Fern said, "because it's good for us all to know how fast time is passing." She shook her head sadly. "Meanwhile, that poor girl is out there somewhere by herself, scared to death. She must have heard the news of how you found her sister stabbed. She's grieving for the person who was closest to her in the whole world.

"And by the way," Fern continued, "a policeman was here because of someone having broken into your house or slipped in or whatever and maybe put something in the iced tea. I talked to him, and so did Ted. Of course the police are mainly worried that this could somehow be related to Eileen's death and even to Kim disappearing — since you found Eileen and all that." Fern shut her book, which had lain open on her lap. "Your karma is attracting trouble."

Why my karma and not Fern's? I shivered. Poor Kim. I squooshed myself up higher in the bed. My head seemed surprisingly clear. "I hope Kim was closer to Mary Mary-Sue and Ward than to her sister. She'd just met her sister." At least that's what we thought. My head didn't even ache. I was definitely going to live. "At least Kim will have someone comforting to come back to." I heard myself sounding falsely positive. I stopped.

"Closeness to people has nothing to do with whether you just met them," Fern announced. "People can be close to the damnedest people. That boy nobody likes is sitting outside, asking to talk to you. That Abner Hale."

John Baylor sure didn't like him. He said

199

Abner looked like you were an oyster and he was looking for his oyster knife. Was pompous John right this time?

"Abner swears he is going to marry Kim," Fern said. "Can you beat that?"

I couldn't. Not in a New York minute. But he was certainly somebody I ought to talk to.

"He showed up right after Ted left for breakfast," Fern said. "Somewhat hysterical. He looks like hell. The boy, not Ted. The boy swears he was off camping in the back woods because Kim told him to. Says he just heard about the girl who was killed and how she looked like Kim. He just recently heard that nobody knows where Kim is. Or so he claims." She raised a skeptical eyebrow.

"Why did he come to see *me?*"

"He says he came straight here after he called Mary Mary-Sue's house and talked to Ward, and Ward said they had no idea where Kim was and that you found the other girl's body." Fern pulled a red comb out of her copper-colored pocketbook and gave it to me. "Ward told him you were in the hospital."

Good old Ward. He must hope I'd pump this boy and that he and Mary Mary-Sue wouldn't have to bother with him. Of course I was curious about this Abner, who either scared Kim or was going to marry her or whatever. The one John Baylor said had burned down a barn. I was so curious, I felt better and better. "Could you get him?" I asked.

She smiled with glee. Fern does like to watch

confrontations. I combed my hair and pulled the sheet up to my chin. She came back shortly with the boy, then stood quietly in a corner.

He wouldn't have fit in a corner. He arrived pulsing with energy, black eyes glowing. He couldn't stay still. He shifted from foot to foot, ran his fingers through his hair, wriggled his shoulders as if to keep them from getting a kink. I will say that he seemed less arrogant than I remembered. Certainly less cool and collected. He wore cutoffs, a wrinkled shirt, sandals without socks, and a frantic expression.

"You've got to know where Kim is!" he blurted out.

"With your help," I said, "maybe I can figure it out."

That floored him. He did a double take. I decided he wasn't used to thinking of himself as someone who could help.

"Well, damn it," he started, as if he were going to complain about my inadequacy. Then he stopped himself. He reached for the pack of cigarettes that bulged in his shirt pocket, then stopped his hand with a jerk.

"When was the last time you saw her?" I asked.

He stood more quietly, and I could feel him counting up the days in his mind. Or was he thinking up a lie? "Maybe a month ago," he said. "She made me quit drinking." He looked at his feet and shrugged. "I thought I'd go off and camp and get my head clear. I like to camp and live in the woods. We made a bet that I could stay entirely clean and sober for a month in the woods, away from folks who . . ." He stopped. In my head I finished the sentence for him: *away from the folks who would encourage him to go back to drinking and maybe drugs.*

He was good-looking. Unpredictable looking. Terribly alive. I could imagine why Kim might think he was worth the trouble. He had well-muscled arms, a tight body, and those piercing eyes. He was sexy, and he was the kind of man a woman would want to reform and help. Except that never seems to work. But in this case, he was saying it had. Was he lying? Or did he really care enough about Kim so that he might work as hard as was needed to impress her? She was a beautiful girl. Confused, maybe, but beautiful.

"Have you talked to the police?" I asked.

He backed away from the bed. "I stay away from police," he said warily. Then he smiled brilliantly. His teeth were very white. "What do they know?"

And what did Kim know about why he was afraid of the police?

My intuition said, *Watch out.* Some other part of me wouldn't have minded taking him on myself, trying to reform him. *Yes, watch out.* I felt sorry for him and for Kim. He was working so hard to please her. Or, if that was a lie, he had a spectacular talent for twisting the truth.

"How did you find out that Kim was missing?" I asked.

"Oh, first I heard it from my friend Al, who hunts," Abner said. "He came by my camp in the woods. I didn't worry about Kim going off. I figured she needed to leave her crazy family. Like I did. But then, when somebody killed that other girl . . ." He floundered.

"Eileen," I said. The shock of death had engraved that name in my mind. "Eileen, who they say is Kim's twin sister."

"All of a sudden, I was scared," he said, coming over, sitting down on the edge of my bed, and leaning toward me. He smelled of fresh sweat and tobacco. "Kim's not careful. I'll help you find her," he said with that brilliant smile again. "Got a match?" Signs all over said NO SMOKING, but what a smile.

Was I going to be his oyster? I looked at his hands to take stock. They were palms up in his lap.

At least his hands weren't long and thin and hard with one line across — Cheiro's Marks of Murder. In fact, his hands were broad, highly padded, and almost bright red. Didn't Fern say highly padded meant good luck? But extremes were bad. His hands were extremely red. And full of the little lines all over that she called worry lines.

"I need Kim," he said, clenching those hands into fists. "I never had anybody before like her. Hell, I've been falling apart for five years. I'm tired of falling apart. But I can't stop without her." A picture flashed in my mind of Abner going down for the third time and grabbing out. Don't try to save a drowning person unless you know how. They taught me that at camp. Throw a life preserver. Hold out a long stick or paddle. But don't get close, or he'll pull you under with him. I'd been under enough for one week or I wouldn't be in this dern hospital bed.

"I have to find Kim." Abner couldn't sit still. The bed bounced. "You don't understand. Somebody is trying to kill her, and I've got to stop them!"

I came to attention. "Who?" I asked. "Who has a reason to? And whom would she trust to help her hide?"

Fern was still standing in her corner behind Abner, not saying a word. She pointed toward the door into the hall. Great, I thought. The nurse is going to interrupt us. And Abner will be out of here fast. But the nurse did not appear.

Instead, along came Pop. Allie, the sitter who found true crime stories for him, was pushing the wheelchair. "I had to come and be sure you were all right," Pop proclaimed. His eyebrows hit the ceiling when he saw Abner on my bed. Abner started.

Oh, wonderful! Just when I needed to find out more from Abner. I reached out to grab his arm, but the boy twisted away from me and swiveled around Pop so fast that he vanished in a second.

"Abner, wait," I called out. "We can help each other." But he was gone.

"Good riddance," Pop said with a sniff. "I

never did like that boy. He has bedroom eyes, and his mouth looks like he might bite. And even you find him sexy, don't you, Peaches? And God knows you're old enough to know better — I hope."

Pop's eyebrows stayed up. "I do worry, Peaches, about the way you don't take care of yourself. About the people you consort with. If your mother could see you, she'd be shocked. Your mother is gone to her just reward," he said sadly, "but of course she's still with you. Still a part of who you are. I've come to talk to you about that."

"That was Kim's boyfriend," I said, annoyed. "He might have told me more about Kim if we hadn't been interrupted."

I should have kept my mouth shut. Pop reared up in his wheelchair like a snake about to strike. "Do you have any idea," he demanded, "what a supreme effort I've had to make to come and visit you in the hospital? Me, a poor half-blind old man in a wheelchair? You ask too much, Peaches. I should have peace in my old age."

We both knew perfectly well that he spent his whole life trying to avoid peace.

"You can get in more trouble, Peaches, and cause me more trouble than anyone else I know," he said sadly, like a saint about to be burned at the stake.

That was too much. "If I cause trouble," I said, "it's all due to heredity. I get it from you."

At that he smiled. "At least you understand

the power of family ties," he said sweetly, "and how they can be a matter of life and death. That's what I came to talk to you about."

Chapter

20

Later That Morning

"I'm glad to see you looking better," Pop remarked, which made no real sense because he hadn't seen me when I was worse. He seemed to have forgotten he'd arrived to talk about life and death. I decided to let him take his course, which is what Pop does anyway.

Allie pushed the wheelchair so that Pop sat near the edge of the bed. She stood behind him, prim in her round-collared shirt, evidently not wanting to take the only chair while Fern stood. Fern came over, kissed Pop on the forehead, and sat down in the chair.

"So what's the status of the case?" Pop asked, dignified as Perry Mason. Eager as a dog on the scent. Of course curiosity was what had really brought him here.

"Somebody wanted to slow you up," he said

without waiting for my answer. "The doctor tells me it was LSD. Something kids take to try to get a thrill. I assume you didn't take it yourself on purpose." He rolled his eyes toward me and raised those craggy, white eyebrows as if that were possible. "If you'd taken a large enough dose, it could have made you crazy for good." He pointed one finger at me. "You need to take better care of yourself, Peaches. And take better care of your key."

I was glad the nurse wasn't taking my blood pressure. Pop sure was raising it.

"Somebody came in my house while I was gone," I said, "probably while I was at your house. I think they searched the place and drugged the iced tea in the fridge."

"Thank God you didn't drink any more of that tea than you did," Fern said, preening. "It's a good thing I came when I did."

Pop leaned back in his wheelchair and sighed. "You need better locks at your house." He raised his voice like this was a television commercial. "But at least no one has attacked your reputation!"

Aha! Now I was going to find out what was really worrying him. He looked at me wide-eyed. "Cousin Elvira tells me they're saying it could have been me."

As I've said, Elvira would repeat anything — the worse, the better. The more impossible, the louder. "What? How could you have been the killer?" Pop in his wheelchair?

"That's ridiculous," Fern said staunchly, but she leaned forward in her chair to hear more.

Pop smiled benignly. "They're not saying I'm the killer, Peaches. They're saying I could be the father of the twins! Could have set up the trust funds for them. That I know all about that part and won't tell!" He actually looked rather pleased with himself. "They're saying that Kim is your sister, and that's what's ridiculous." Was this where his talk about heredity fit in?

"Who's saying all that?" I demanded. I needed to talk to them quick.

He frowned. "It could be Elvira," he said slowly, "but I'm sure somebody told me that. I can't think who."

And maybe he dreamed it.

"And is it true?" I asked. Naturally I hoped it wasn't. But with Pop, absolutely anything was possible. Could Kim and Eileen be my sisters? It would be even worse to have a sister dead than a distant cousin.

"Of course not!" he bellowed angrily. "Your mother would never have put up with that!" I expected nurses to come running, but they didn't.

"Pop," I said, "you just naturally inspire rumors."

"The worst part," he said, "is that three different people have called me up to tell me that they don't believe the rumors — that I would be too stingy to set up trust funds like that. So I hope you're going to clear this up quickly, be-

209

cause it's very messy the way it is! And it's important not to let people get away with rumors," he said self-righteously. "And here you are, just lying in the hospital, doing nothing. Do you know what they're saying about you?"

At that moment the nurse did come in to take my pulse. *I will be calm,* I told myself.

"They're saying that you believe Kim is crazy, but that's not all. They're saying you should realize that Mary Mary-Sue was the one who secretly encouraged Kim to get money from John Baylor and go out on her own. That Mary Mary-Sue wanted her to get out of town and away from that Abner what's-his-name that we just got rid of. And John Baylor is so dumb he didn't know he was being used. But something backfired. And the other girl was killed. What do you think of that?"

The nurse lingered, which is exactly what I would have done. Her ears almost flapped, she so obviously wanted to hear more. I could see Fern quivering to ask questions, but she and I both held out until the nurse left.

As soon as she was gone, I burst out: "Who told you that?"

"Why, Cousin Elvira, of course. Who else in the family keeps track of everything people say?"

"And," Fern asked with a delighted smile, "Elvira said that Mary Mary-Sue is putting one over on John Baylor?"

I blew up. "I am going to resign from this

family. Why spread poison like that? We ought to work together. We stink!"

But Pop just relaxed in his wheelchair and shrugged. "You won't resign," he said confidently. "Even tadpoles help their relatives. Even sea squirts, which have no brains at all, claim kin." He smiled, totally pleased with himself. "Peaches, you get upset too easily," he said. "And I didn't come here to upset you. I came here to help you out. Heredity is going to help you! You'll be delighted, wait and see."

"I'll believe that when you prove it," I growled.

Pop looked hurt. His eyes became hound eyes. The corner of his mouth went down. "You know how you told me you were sure heredity had something to do with the solution to this murder?" he asked. "Well, Allie here has been reading me some very interesting articles. I get tired of hearing about murders. After one in Greenville where they tortured the man for three days, I'd had enough. So Allie found some stuff about relatives."

"I do the best I can," Allie said, bending her head in a self-deprecating way.

I remembered the story she had found for Pop about the dog bringing home human legs. She couldn't have gone anywhere but uphill from that.

"So Allie's been reading me an article about how even sea squirts with no brains know their kin. Even paper wasps look after their own. I think this will be useful to you, so I brought it over."

"I can't quite see how it'll help me, since I'm not related to any wasps," I said, still feeling peevish, and was tempted to add, *except for you and Cousin Elvira.*

"Read to her about the cannibals," Pop ordered Allie.

The sitter reached in her large, worn pocketbook and brought out an issue of *Scientific American* with flowers on the front. Obviously brought just to read to me. She smiled at Pop as if she was overjoyed to please him. "It says here," she said, "that creatures that recognize their kin have a better chance of surviving and proliferating than those that don't." She held the magazine toward me and pointed to two charts. I did a double take. They were family trees for salamanders. One had more branches and subdivisions and little pictures of salamanders — decidedly more than the other. "Now, when there's a food shortage, these little things resort to cannibalism," she said sweetly.

"And so do humans," said Pop with relish. "Like all those people who ate each other when they were stranded in that snowbound pass on the way to California."

I couldn't see what Pop was trying to prove. Even Cousin Elvira, the super-gossip, doesn't actually eat people, except in a figurative sense.

"So it says here," said Allie, "that in the third generation only half the salamanders that can't recognize their kin survive to have babies. The rest have been eaten by their relatives. But three out of four salamanders in the family that recognize kin and, therefore, avoid eating them, survive. They have devoured other families instead. It says here that, by the fifth generation, the family that is genetically disposed to recognize kin predominates."

Pop beamed. "Like us. Why, Peaches, you don't know how lucky you are to be my daughter."

I did not answer on the grounds that it might incriminate me.

"Why, take Cousin Elvira," he said. "Her father moved to Florida where she couldn't watch him, and then married his practical nurse when he was ninety-five. So the nurse got all his money when he died. I haven't done that, have I?"

I did not point out that he was not yet ninety-five.

"Or take Ward," Pop said. "His father and mother split. Boy, that was ugly. Ward's father never saw his kids again. Just had a sexy new wife and moved to Texas and had new kids that rode horses, and to hell with the old. Gives Ward an ugly streak." Pop began to laugh. "If Ward were a salamander, he'd eat his father."

"And will that help me find Kim?" I asked. I try to be patient with Pop's diversions.

"Of course not," Pop said. He turned to Allie. "Tell Peaches about delphiniums."

213

"It says here the mountain delphiniums can tell relatives from nonrelatives by their pollen," Allie explained. "And they try to breed with flowers that are not too closely related or too genetically different." Allie said that with some distaste, as if she didn't approve of flowers breeding.

"Those flowers are smart," said Pop. "Toto Small married a first cousin, and their children all have big feet and cross-eyes."

"But not because he didn't recognize his kin!" Fern cried. "We recognize our kin by their faces and by the markings on their hands, if we know how. We aren't so dumb."

Pop ignored her.

I was suddenly terribly tired. I guess my adventure with the LSD — my terror at not knowing what on earth was going on — had taken a lot out of me. "And how does all this help solve who killed Eileen and where Kim has gone to?" I demanded sharply.

"Why, it goes to prove that Kim and Eileen were trying to protect each other," Pop explained in a careful tone he might have used for an idiot. "They found each other, didn't they? And you can't be more closely related than twins. And certainly they were smarter than a bunch of tadpoles. So while you try to find out what happened, you can keep that in mind. They tried to protect each other, and that somehow provoked someone to murder Eileen."

Pop's logic was a little wavery here and there, but I had a strange feeling he might be right.

214

Chapter

21

8:00 A.M., Friday, September 1

I was mighty glad to get home, especially since Ted had had somebody change the locks on the doors and put in dead bolts. We were sitting in our favorite spot at the kitchen table, finishing breakfast. Out the kitchen window everything was hazy near at hand and foggy farther off, beyond the birdbath. The fog seemed appropriate. I was glad Ted taught just a few classes, not a full load, and none were scheduled for Friday mornings.

Of course Ted and I had talked about who would want me to be out of commission. The person who killed Eileen? But who was that? Not knowing was no fun.

As best I could, I'd filled Ted in on things that had happened while he was gone, even my reading at Malaprop's and how Fern had admitted a Mark of Murder scam.

We looked through my photos of Kim's room and found nothing immediately significant there, except Ted was surprised, as I'd been, to see the envelope marked RATTLESNAKE EGGS. Very odd. Everything was confusing.

"And nobody tells the same tale about Kim," I complained. "When we went to see John Baylor, he told us he believed Kim wanted to get away because she was afraid of Abner Hale. Mary Mary-Sue seemed red-hot angry that John Baylor encouraged Kim to leave. But now Pop's gossip circle is saying that Mary Mary-Sue was the one who egged Kim on to get money out of John Baylor to go off on her own. That Mary Mary-Sue wanted her out of town, away from Abner Hale. And that John was so dumb he played along and didn't know he was being used. Once in a while that gossip circle is on to something." I sighed. "Whatever happened, I am quite sure that Mary Mary-Sue is puzzled and worried sick now."

"Apparently," Ted said. He meant "take nothing for granted."

At least my thoughts were behaving themselves. The doctor said I might conceivably have a recurrence of hallucinations but certainly not as bad as before. I felt okay so far. The police and John Baylor had both given me a lecture on staying out of this murder investigation, but I had a right to look for Kim. She was — apparently — my blood kin. And somebody was evidently trying to do us both in. And as for Ted — well, he'd half-heartedly told me I should stay out of it. But that old nose-for-news, former-reporter curiosity made it easy for him to agree when I said I intended to find Kim, and that was that.

So now, to help sort out what we knew, he was taking notes on a yellow legal pad. I usually feel everything is under control when Ted takes notes, but today even that hardly helped.

"Mary Mary-Sue is smart enough to fool everybody," Ted said, underlining her name. "That may be what inspired the rumor that she's doing just that."

"Also," I said, "she has fights with Cousin Elvira when Elvira tells tales about the senator. Mary Mary-Sue loves her boss. So Elvira likes to think the worst about Mary Mary-Sue." I drank a large swallow of my coffee, bitter and stimulating. I needed that.

Ted shook his head as if to say he couldn't guess about lies.

"And Mary Mary-Sue," I said, "certainly didn't expect Eileen to be killed. I hope. Maybe the whole gossip thing was just hot air, foul hot air." That thought made me mad. "The telephone system farting," I said and was pleased with that way of putting it.

"But it still bothers you that there might be some truth in the farts," he said. Ted knows me well.

I nodded.

Right then the phone on the table rang. I was so wound up that I jumped. Ted picked it up, put it to his ear, and said, "Good morning." He winked at me. "Yes, Mary Mary-Sue, she's much better." He made a wry face at me as if to say, "Well, one way better." "In fact, here she is," he said and handed the phone to me.

Mary Mary-Sue, who did or didn't tell the truth, was full of kind words. Pleased, of course, that Pop now seemed ready to put up a big reward. "Be easy on yourself," she said, "that's what I'm trying to do. I'm going to stay home today and look through Kim's things once more in hopes of finding some clue." She wanted to know if I had any idea yet who might have done it. I gathered her "it" meant somebody giving me LSD.

I didn't say much except "no." I wanted to wait and confront Mary Mary-Sue about the possibility that she had lied about Kim — confront her in person where I could see her face. "I may drop by in a while," I said.

"We'd better go talk to her right now," I told Ted as soon as I hung up, "and sort this out." When Ted frowned, I added: "I'm impatient to get moving, I know I am, but why not? I'm all right. Honest."

We finally agreed that he'd drive. That way, any possible recurrence of hallucinations wouldn't be a problem. "But I'll stay out in the car," he said. "She opens up more to you."

I was glad Ted would drive. This was a spooky

morning, with fog that retreated, almost like an hallucination itself. As we drove down our road, the far trees seemed to be dissolving, but the near trees were green as we moved along. Unsubstantial as — as memory. Phlox near us along the road was vivid purple. There were bright yellow daisy-like flowers, too, but in the distance colors faded out to gray-white.

The yellow pad in the car between us was close and, therefore, vivid. "Let's go over what we know before we get there," I said, "complete with who was where and when." Ted is good at that kind of detail. I picked up the pad and began to read the neat chart he'd made of all my ramblings.

He had dates down the side and names at the top. "Let's start with Kim," he said as he made a sharp turn. "Fern told you Kim had been depressed, right? Abner told you that Kim persuaded him about a month ago to go off into the woods and dry out, right?"

"Yes," I said, "and, John Baylor gave Kim money to leave town about two weeks ago. And she left a note and vanished." A car passed us, zoomed ahead, and vanished, all but the red taillights which glowed through the milky air. "Where would a young girl go by herself? Maybe she went off into the woods with Abner!" I said, but I didn't believe it. Abner seemed too worried.

"Before Kim disappeared," Ted said, "she and Fern cooked up the idea for the Mark of

Murder scam, in order to compare hands and see which members of the family have the same genetic markings that Kim has. Fern said she figured those folks might be close relatives." Ted half grinned as he said, "A very strange method."

We both were silent, thinking about that. The mountains around us faded out except for a shadow here and there. But the tall grasses near the road, which I hardly noticed on a regular day, were wet, which made their tassels shimmer rusty red and stand out.

After a while I spoke again. "Fern said she went along with the Mark of Murder thing to cheer Kim up. Because it made Kim feel they were doing something to figure out who she was. By then Kim may already have known about her sister, but if she did, why didn't she tell Fern? And why does John Baylor have to be so dern secretive about the whole thing?"

A bird flew out of the fog on one side of the road and back into the fog on the other, as if it existed only in the blink of an eye.

We turned into another road, which seemed to go straight into no-man's-land, with lots of trees on each side. On one near hill the trees stood in a row like paper-doll cutouts, backed by white fog. Down by the road I could see every detail of a sign for a Baptist church.

"John could be the worst of all," Ted said. "Even back when you and I visited John, he didn't add up. He said he gave Kim money to get away because she felt in danger from some-one. He said he assumed she felt threatened by Abner. *Assumed,* not *knew.* But it seems strange for a high-powered lawyer like John to give out money from a trust without being sure of all the facts."

"Also," I said, "when I went back to get my notes and heard John on the phone telling Maureen not to let us talk to Lucy, that was odd."

"Some things we do know," said Ted. "At the family reunion Fern put the Mark of Murder scam into operation and then told you she did it so that, if she did find Kim's mother or father or sister or brother or such, Kim would hear about it and come back. That does seem far-fetched."

"And because Kim's hand contained the mark and was interesting in other ways, Fern asked me to come look at Kim's handprints at Mary Mary-Sue's house. Although Fern had ac-tually seen Kim's hands before and hadn't told Mary Mary-Sue. Fern told me she had read Kim's hands last year. But Fern said hands change. Maybe she wanted to see how Kim's hands had changed over the years. And Mary Mary-Sue seemed so afraid that Kim was in danger. If Mary Mary-Sue was lying, she's a world-class actress."

The sides of the road were suddenly steep around us. Rocky and sprinkled with candle-like yellowish mullein plants and small pine trees. The tops of the bluffs dissolved into fog high above us. I felt small.

"So I don't know whether a single one of these relatives of mine is telling the truth," I groaned. "Which seems unfair and makes me mad. And I would quit looking into this except I can't. Because Lucy led me to the body of poor Eileen, who turned out to be Kim's twin. And even that could have been rigged by someone, though I can't think why anyone would particularly want me to find the body. But somebody *did* want to fry my mind with LSD."

I shut up as we turned onto a twisty smaller road. Trees arched over us, half hiding the fog above. A child sat in a swing in the yard of a small, friendly house.

I thought about John Baylor's daughter, Lucy. Not a child anymore, but still so young. "If the person who called Lucy wasn't Eileen, then maybe whoever it was wanted Lucy to find the body. What a cruel thing to have happen to a young girl. And why?"

"We need to know who would profit from Eileen's death," Ted said, using his practical let's-get-back-to-brass-tacks voice. "John Baylor must have had to tell the police who set up the trusts and who would benefit if the twins died. But when I talked to the police about the LSD, they wouldn't tell me a thing about the rest of the investigation."

I sighed. That was frustrating, but there was plenty we did know. "Okay," I said, "alibis."

Ted glanced at the chart. "Abner told you he was off in the woods by himself on Monday morning when Eileen must have been killed. Fern was with you and then said she was in her hotel room. No proof, but she was there when I called a little later. Mary Mary-Sue said she was with Ward. They would probably lie for each other. John Baylor was with a client. Maureen was supposedly at home with a headache. Lucy was with you."

An old basset hound ambled in front of us, and Ted's brakes screeched. The hound ambled on. The screech hit my nerves worse than it did his.

"Before I heard her scream, Lucy was alone in those woods where I found Eileen's body. Alone for several minutes," I said, "but there was no other scream. No sound of struggle." I wished I could forget the body. "And how could Lucy have killed Eileen without my hearing something?"

"Who else do you suspect?"

"Like you say — whoever benefits when the twins die," I said. "Whoever called Lucy if it wasn't Eileen. I don't see how Mike, who told us about Eileen and the Cherokee hand line, could be a suspect. But it's odd the way he came forward at my book signing, almost as if Fern had arranged for him to do it. I guess we ought to find out where Eileen's adoptive parents were at the time she was killed. Her father sure didn't look guilty — he looked mad."

We came around a curve, out of the fog, and there was Mary Mary-Sue and Ward's house, just up ahead, looking as white as purity and as old-fashioned traditional as apple pie. A sporty red car I didn't recognize stood in the curved driveway. I looked at my watch: 9:15. "Early guests?" I asked.

Ted parked at the beginning of the curve, back from the house. "I'll wait here," he said.

Chapter

22

Immediately Afterward

I hurried up the steps across the wide porch and rang the bell. From down the dark hallway Ward ambled to the front door. He wore jeans and a faded plaid shirt, and he held his head carefully, as if he had a hangover. His eyes were wary, and a vein jumped in his forehead. He did not ask me to come in. I was family. Not asking was not polite. He knew I was helping to look for Kim, so he should have been overjoyed to see me.

"Good morning, Ward," I said, super-politely. "How are you? I came by to talk to Mary Mary-Sue." I was sure she must be down the hall in the kitchen. Wonderful smells wafted from there. Country-fried potatoes, my nose said. Sausage. Coffee. Ahh. Ward would never have gone to all the trouble to cook those good things.

"I'll tell her you're here," Ward said, leaving the screen latched.

Then, just as I was beginning to seethe, Mary Mary-Sue came striding down the hall, unlatched the door, pulled me inside, and gave me a hug. "How lucky you've come now," she said, smiling down at me. "I would have summoned you to this powwow except I was afraid you were still shaky on your feet. I'm glad you're better." She had on her senator's-assistant costume: crisp blouse and straight skirt, and on top of that a ruffled apron with a smiling cartoon pig on it. A woman of contradictions. If she was lying, she did it gracefully.

"You know Ward's sister, Sandra Redmon," she said as she led me down the hall. She paused and swallowed, as if she didn't want to go, but she did with a rush. "Sandra's been telling us how Kim told her she'd been having nightmares. A few weeks before she vanished." Mary Mary-Sue all but choked. Her voice went hard and angry. The angles in her face stood out. "I'll get her to tell you about it."

"And Ward's sister is telling you now? For the first time?" I blurted out. I thought: *How could she keep quiet? After Kim vanished? Then, after the murder of Kim's twin? Why on earth didn't Sandra tell Kim's mother and father anything that could possibly help them figure out what happened?*

Mary Mary-Sue answered my unspoken questions. "Kim made Sandra promise not to tell anyone." Mary Mary-Sue's voice wavered, as though she wanted to cry. Kim hadn't told her adoptive mother about her nightmares, so why would she tell her adoptive aunt?

I could see Sandra, a dark-haired woman in a red suit framed by the doorway at the end of the hall. She was sitting at the table in the big country kitchen. A strongly defined woman. Middle-aged. She had jet-black hair cut in wedges. A wedge of bang swept across her forehead. The rest of her hair hung in a black Dutch-boy wedge, cut straight. Her red mouth was straight and strong, her eyebrows the same. She had on the kind of suit you'd expect on a lady lawyer in her office, not in this wood-paneled room with bunches of dried herbs hanging from a beam and black iron muffin and corn-bread pans hanging on one wall. Except that the lady lawyer would wear gray. I wondered if this woman's red suit matched the red car or swore at it.

I hadn't seen Sandra in years. She was energetic, moved fast, so I used to remember her name as quick*sand Sand*ra. She and her husband, I'd heard, had moved back to the old family farm in the mountains. Apparently her husband, Arthur, had caught the farming bug and even started a marketing co-op.

"Hello," Sandra said, eyeing me as though taking inventory. Behind her loomed Mary Mary-Sue's big, old-fashioned gas stove, even more imposing than Sandra.

"You know," Mary Mary-Sue said, using her

legislative formality, "Peaches is trying to help us find Kim." The image of Eileen lit up in my mind. All I'd found was Kim's twin — and found her too late. I sat down heavily at the big, round kitchen table.

"I should think the police and sheriff's folks and the state investigators would have all sorts of sophisticated ways to search, using computers and such," Sandra said. She had sharp, white teeth and talked quickly. "But I suppose we can use any kind of help we can get."

I noted she said "we." But I thought of myself as helping Mary Mary-Sue, who had sat down beside the red-suited Sandra and was sipping coffee. Helping Mary Mary-Sue, not Ward and his side of the family. Was I like a paper wasp, preferring blood ties? Do wasps have blood? This woman did not smell right. She had on some kind of perfume that smelled expensive and citified. An odd combination with the aroma of the country-fried potatoes and the sausage. And perhaps I couldn't even trust Mary Mary-Sue, who smelled of cooking that good breakfast.

Ward's sister spoke as though she'd memorized her lines. "I do psychological counseling at the high school." She looked too formal for that. "But Kim didn't come to me as a counselor," she said. "Kim came to me privately as her aunt, just to ask advice." Sandra smiled, as if that pleased her.

Ward, who'd sat down at the kitchen table on

his sister's left, kept his eyes on her and per-spired as if he was scared of what she might say next. Ward was strange, but today he was stranger than usual. Mary Mary-Sue, who sat to the right, sipping coffee, was at ease. Not happy — the lines in her face all ran down hill — but not nervous.

Ms. Psychologist Sandra considered a forkful of potatoes. "Kim told me she was having night-mares." She looked me in the eye as if she knew I wanted to ask more. "About running from a naked man in a dream, and sometimes he caught her and she woke up terrified. In the dream she was small and helpless. She screamed and screamed, but nobody came to help."

I shivered. The hair on my arms stood on end. And Ward's sister had kept this to herself? "So what did you advise Kim to do?" I asked, trying to keep my voice even.

"I told her to try to remember what might have happened in real life to trigger those dreams." I noticed Ward swallowed as if that spooked him. Well, of course. This was why he had been upset all along. "I gave her a book," his sister said, "called *The Courage to Heal*. I told her she could call me any time she needed to talk. And I suggested she go to a counselor on a professional basis, rather than just talk infor-mally with her aunt."

"And do you know if she did?"

In my mind's eye I saw those papers Eileen's father had given me, the papers sent to Eileen from the False Memory Syndrome Foundation. Those papers talked about false memories of childhood abuse. Why those? Why sent to Kim's twin? There must be a connection.

Sandra sighed. "All of a sudden Kim didn't want to talk about her dreams or anything connected with them. She said that whatever she did was her business. That was just before she disappeared. So I don't know if she went to see somebody and they scared her by encouraging her to face more than she felt able to face, or what. She could have gone to someone in Asheville. I wouldn't have heard about that." Sandra looked me straight in the eye again. Why did I feel like that was a challenge?

Mary Mary-Sue was mopping a tear from her cheek with a crumpled paper napkin. "If she needed help, why didn't she come to me?" she asked angrily. On the kitchen table, propped between the salt and pepper, I noticed a card with a red rose on it and one large word, CONGRATULATIONS! It was so out of place, I almost laughed.

Why hadn't Kim gone to Mary Mary-Sue? That was a good question. Nobody answered. Ward got up, went over to the electric coffee-maker on the counter, and poured himself another cup. He didn't ask if anybody else wanted any.

If Kim went to a psychologist without telling her parents, where did she get the money to pay for it? John Baylor, perhaps?

"Did you tell Kim what you thought the dreams meant?" I asked Ward's sister.

"I told her they probably meant Kim should get some professional help," she repeated, and while she kept her face and voice smooth, I sensed that was an effort — that she didn't like being the one to answer questions. "I told Kim it might have to do with something that had happened when she was a small child, even before she was adopted. And then I told her what I always tell kids. Wherever we start, we can make our own luck. We seize the moment to change. We rewrite life."

I agreed with that, but somehow the way she said it put me off — as if it were the Declaration of Independence and the Gettysburg Address rolled into one.

Mary Mary-Sue glared at Sandra. "You never told me anything about my own daughter being scared to death," she accused loudly.

I thought: *Mary Mary-Sue looks like she could kill!* Behind her, on the counter, a large block of wood with slits cut in it housed an impressive collection of knives. They all had black handles. The knife that stabbed Eileen had a black handle. But every slot in the block was full. And certainly Mary Mary-Sue wouldn't leave those knives sitting out if . . . And besides, she had no reason. I hate distrusting everyone.

"Kim didn't call me when she was driven to run away," Ms. Counselor said, frowning. "And I think we were friends. I think she trusted me.

231

And she didn't call me the day her sister, Eileen, was killed. So I don't believe she came back to take part in that meeting with Eileen and poor little Lucy Baylor. If she had seen the murder or just come back to find the body, she would have called. And I was in my office all day that Monday. She would have been so terribly upset. She would have called."

"But why would she have come to meet with Lucy?" I asked. "And if she did come and found Eileen's body, maybe she was too scared to do anything but hide."

"And why," Mary Mary-Sue asked Sandra, "why, back at the beginning before everything got crazy, didn't you even suggest that Kim should talk about her nightmares and her fears with me? Me, her mother!" Mary Mary-Sue's voice rose. "And now she's gone! And we don't know if Kim's leaving had to do with night-mares! Or if more terrible things began to happen to her after she left! You don't know how it feels, Sandra. You don't have children! You don't understand!" If she were acting the part of the distraught mother, she was doing a good job.

Ms. Counselor sat straight and glared back. "Listen, you have no idea what happened to that girl before she was two and a half years old. She wasn't yours before that. Obviously something dreadful did happen." Her voice accused.

Mary Mary-Sue flinched. "She's my daughter as much as if I'd given birth."

"And now," Sandra said, standing up, "you also need to admit that somebody is helping that girl hide. If she cashed a check, the SBI could find her. But there may be another way to find her." Sandra paused as if she expected us to ask what but then went on before we could. "If Kim went to a therapist in Asheville, that person may know where she is. I've asked around a little bit, but reputable therapists have to honor requests for confidentiality. And I haven't been able to find out anything on my own. That's why I told what I knew to the police."

Yes. Somebody must be helping Kim hide.

"So I've told the police that Kim was probably visiting a therapist who may know where she is. And I figured I ought to tell you, too."

Ward sat there poker-faced. Hiding anger? Hey, that congratulations card was for Ward and Mary Mary-Sue. They have the same anniversary date as Ted and I. They were about to celebrate their wedding anniversary. So were we. I'd almost forgotten. It was not likely to be a happy anniversary for my cousin.

"I thank you for your help, Sandra," Mary Mary-Sue said. Her tone said, "Now, get out."

Sandra announced she had to get to work.

"What therapist would Kim have been likely to go to see?" I asked quickly before Sandra got away. "Did you recommend someone?"

Sandra growled, "I wouldn't know. I've done all I can. Look in the yellow pages." She stalked out.

Mary Mary-Sue cupped her face in her hands and leaned forward on her elbows, as if her head was too heavy. "Why do we all get mad at each other just when we need each other so much? What are we going to do next?"

She was already so upset that what I said next could hardly make it worse. No point in beating around the bush.

"Mary Mary-Sue," I said, "the gossips are saying that you were so disturbed by Kim's being attracted to Abner that you persuaded her to ask John Baylor for the money to get out of the area. And then something backfired."

"No!" she cried out and burst into loud wrenching sobs. Ward went over and put his arm around her. If things got bad enough, apparently he did react. Mary Mary-Sue pulled herself together enough to force out words. "All I want is for Kim to come home safe and sound, no matter what boy she likes or doesn't like."

I was half inclined to believe her. I was half inclined not to. I leaned over and squeezed her hand. I said, "I'll pray for that." She looked so desolate that I gave her a kiss on the cheek. "We don't know what the truth is in all this. We don't know why Kim left."

Because it was always possible that even Sandra was lying, though I couldn't think why. *Quicksand* Sandra Redmon. Read that *Quicksand* Sandra *Red man.* I pictured an Indian sinking in quicksand, complete with feather headdress. I'd remember her last name that way.

I pictured Kim next to the Indian, struggling in quicksand up to her chin. Bad image. I tried to forget that.

"I'll get back to you if I find anything out, and you do the same with me," I said to Mary Mary-Sue, and left Ward to comfort her. I walked slowly down the hall, past the grand-father clock which had been stopped for thirty years, past the open door to Mary Mary-Sue's home office. The senator's picture waved eagerly at me. He didn't mean it. My feet dragged. I had the feeling there was something more I should do there. I opened the front screen door and went out on the porch. I stood and looked out over the far mountains. They were still hazy and vague, but the geranium blooms in the flower bed along the edge of the porch were vivid white and an unusual vivid red. Past their prime, though. Some of the lower blossoms on the flower heads were brown and hanging.

At the edge of the lawn, a row of sunflowers hung their heads from the weight of the seeds beginning to form in the center. The yellow petals around the edges were shriveling.

Maybe finding out what happened is like that, I thought. Maybe what you expect to find has to wither before the right seeds grow. That was a nice thought because it would mean that my nothing-fits feeling could be fruitful. But I didn't even know what I had expected to find.

The screen door opened behind me. It was

Mary Mary-Sue. Her eyes were red, but she had presence again.

"I pushed her too hard," she said. We both knew she meant Kim. "I was so upset that she cared about that boy. She was so smart. She had so much to look forward to. I could see her marrying him and throwing her life away. So when she couldn't seem to hear what I said, I just kept saying it louder. I couldn't stop. So she stopped trusting me. That's what it was." She leaned on the white porch rail as if she was tired.

I looked up into my cousin's face lined with misery. Her mouth twisted. "Not that Abner was so bad compared to what he came from. Maybe he'd stopped drinking — Kim said he had. It's possible. But what he came from didn't give him much chance." She shook her head emphatically. "His father is a drunk. His sister is retarded. His mother is a worn-out old mountain woman. She's given up."

Mary Mary-Sue took a deep breath, like a singer in the middle of a long phrase. As if she had to get this all out without interruption. "What kind of kids would Kim have," she demanded, "with a family like that? What kind of life?"

Mary Mary-Sue came to a full stop as if she were in the wrong song. She stared at me as if she'd forgotten I was there. She shook her head slowly this time, then her voice went bitter. "I wasn't smart." Long pause. "I pushed Kim too hard and I lost her. That's what I did, Peaches."

Another deep breath, then words in a rush. "And it wasn't Kim who was afraid of Abner — it was me. And so she didn't trust me. I couldn't bring myself to say that. Now I've told you the truth."

I hoped so.

Chapter

23

10:30 A.M., Friday, September 1

By the time Ted and I started home, the fog was just wispy white veils here and there and the sun sparkled on the twisty green roadsides. Even the high cliff-like walls of the main highway glistened, still fog-damp in the bright sunshine. Rather fetching. I felt saddened in one way and yet encouraged in another as I told Ted what had happened with Mary Mary-Sue and company.

"There must be a connection," Ted said, "between the fact that, on the one hand, Kim was advised to find herself a therapist who could help her sort out nightmares of abuse, and, on the other hand, the fact that her twin sister had sent off for some material pointing out the pitfalls of searching for lost memories."

"Maybe," I said, "a real parent who put those

kids up for adoption is desperate to keep whatever happened secret and is afraid it will come out somehow."

"So why kill Eileen?" Ted asked. "Or why kill Kim, if this was mistaken identity?"

"Because they were going to tell?" I asked. "Or on the other hand, maybe there is some way someone could get revenge or otherwise profit by having some horror from the past come out. Maybe Eileen wanted to prevent that. So she was killed. But those are wild guesses."

"And yet, as you said before," Ted remarked, "this could simply be related to Eileen's interest in the law. There's been a lot of legal action related to false memory. I've seen stories here and there. Cases where people said they'd been abused, repressed it for years, and then sued the family members when the 'memory' was recovered. And now some patients are suing their therapists for leading them astray — making them 'believe' things that never happened. And then the therapists sue the patients for defaming them. It's a legal can of worms. Maybe that interested Eileen."

"I could go see Eileen's father and mother," I said. "I think we need to know more about her to find Kim. Could you come, too?"

"Maybe tomorrow," he said. "I have a class this afternoon. In fact, I need to take off as soon as we get home. And if I were you, I'd take a nap. You should take care of yourself. I need you, too, you know."

We arrived home to find Fern standing by the front door. "Good luck," Ted said and kissed me. He escaped, the lucky dog. Never mind, sometimes Fern was helpful.

Fern wore a black cotton dress — stylish this year, I knew, but still rather citified for the mountains — and earrings made out of black quartz. Not a good choice. They made her face look drawn, as if she hadn't slept.

"I'm glad to see you're better," she said. Then she held her head high as she made an announcement. "Peaches, I've got it all set up for us to visit the Cherokee woman who knows about the mark of" — she hesitated — "the mark of difference, and Mike says she has it in her hand. Mike found out that Kim went to visit this Anna Littledeer on Friday, the nineteenth of August." Of course I remembered Mike, the man we met at Malaprop's, the radio-announcer type who was half Cherokee.

"Anna Littledeer remembered the date because it was her late husband's birthday. Wasn't that lucky? And," Fern said triumphantly, "that's the same day Kim disappeared!" Fern waited for me to applaud. I obliged. I was impressed. Fern was talented at inspiring people to help her. Or bullying. Whichever worked.

"And when are we to meet this Anna Littledeer?" Hey, an image made that easy to remember: me *an' a little deer.*

"Oh, two o'clock or three," Fern announced. "We've got plenty of time for lunch. I'd be

240

happy with a peanut-butter sandwich." She smiled sweetly as if that were a concession, that she really hoped for more. She sighed as if today was likely to disappoint. And yet she was pleased about the Cherokee thing, I was sure of that.

And if Anna Littledeer was the last person who had seen Kim, this woman could have some clue as to where she went.

"You're wonderful!" I told Fern.

I led the way into the kitchen and pulled out the peanut butter and jam. I was hungry, which is always a sign I'm in good shape. No return of hallucinations, thank goodness. The phone on the kitchen table rang.

"Peaches," said Pop, "Cousin Georgianna is here, and she's brought you the book and is waiting for you. You're late."

"I'm late for what?" I asked.

"I told you she was coming by today for lunch, and you said you'd come. You said you hadn't seen Georgianna in a while and you were really looking forward to it. And you aren't here!" He was in high dudgeon. "And Georgianna has been nice enough to bring the book about false memory and murder."

Now, I may be vague, but I knew I'd never said I'd come for lunch. I would have written that down. "I have to go somewhere with Fern," I told Pop, then I realized that actually we had time to stop by. And furthermore, even aside from the book, Cousin Georgianna knows more about our family tree than anybody else. And the twins should fit on the family tree. Except we had no idea where. But the tree must have a gap, right? "Can I bring Fern?" I asked.

Pop said there was plenty of chicken soup, and that did sound better than peanut butter, which was all I had in the house. I screwed the top back on the jar.

We set off through the bright sunshine. I drove because I was feeling fine. The day was suddenly brilliant. The trees glistened. But I noticed Fern drooped. Why, after working out our Indian expedition? And being invited to lunch for something better than peanut butter?

We took Webb Cove Road, which began citified but turned to winding dirt as we went up toward Town Mountain Road. We were almost to Pop's when I noticed that something felt wrong. First I felt uneasy. Why? Could someone be following us? This was a curvy road, with overhanging trees and thick woods on both sides. A car behind would be easy to miss. But I couldn't see a soul. Then I felt that something was missing. That's what was wrong. Then I knew. My pocketbook was missing. I asked Fern to look on the backseat. Not there. I sighed. "We have to go back and get my pocketbook," I said. "Dern. But wait. I'd better get it after lunch."

So we drove on to Pop's and hurried in past Georgianna's brown Ford.

Pop and Georgianna must have heard us drive

242

up. She was already pushing his wheelchair toward his place at the head of the dining-room table. Pop's dining room has glass doors on one wall just as the living room does, and looks out over the garden and the mountains beyond. I sat on his left because I like to look out. Georgianna sat next to me. Fern headed to Pop's right.

Fern dresses for moods, but Georgianna dresses for stories. Last time I saw her, she had been reading a story about the Southwest to a group of young children. So she'd been wearing a dress with Navaho designs, lots of orange and brown and tan. Today she wore a dress with a swirly surrealist design and question-mark earrings — silver like her steel glasses. As always, she looked wise, plump, and cheerfully eccentric.

She sat down and gave us a big smile. "It's good to see you, Fern, and *you* ask the most interesting questions, Peaches!"

Exactly what question did Pop tell her I'd asked? Something that interested him. He glowed with self-importance.

"Actually, there were two reasons I wanted to talk to you, Georgianna," I said. "Because you're expert at two things: how to find the right book and who in our family is related to whom and how. I need you to help me with our family tree."

"Yes, I know," she said as she fingered one of the lace table mats my mother had always saved for special occasions. Pop had obviously told Anna, his housekeeper, to pull out all the stops.

First, Anna brought us salad: green for us, tomato aspic for Pop who says he feels like a cow when he chews lettuce. Georgianna had pulled a piece of paper and pen out of her great pouch of a pocketbook. "Let's do family first. Where shall we start?" she asked.

So I explained that, since Kim and Eileen were probably related to our family, we needed to find a twin-shaped hole in the tree. I didn't know how to do that. Perhaps she might.

"If I were placing a child with family," Georgianna said, "I'd pick the closest kin I could. I guess that's very southern-mountain of me. But if the family is related to us, it's southern-mountain. Let's start with Mary Mary-Sue and work back. Or, no, let's start with her great-grandparents and work forward, which will give us close cousins.

"Mary Mary-Sue's great-grandfather Jeeter Jones married your great-grandmother Bessie Smith's sister, Ellie Smith, you know." Actually I did know, but was fuzzy on details of who gave birth to whom after that.

"Jeeter and his wife, Ellie, were herb gatherers," Georgianna said. "They farmed some, too, but she could doctor with herbs like yarrow and black cohosh. Mary Mary-Sue had an herbal recipe book of hers, but she gave it to the museum in Mars Hill." I'd heard and half forgotten. How Georgianna keeps all that stuff in her head, I'll never know. Of course I took notes between bites of lunch.

"They had four kids," Georgianna said. "A son, Bill, went to Texas and didn't write back. Just as well, he had a mean mouth. A daughter, Brenda, was skinny as a stick and never had kids. Then there was Lincoln, born in 1898. He drank quite a bit. But the youngest son, Joe, was a real blessing. He was Mary Mary-Sue's grandfather, born in 1899." She paused and ate a small roll.

"Somebody in there must have been a Unionist to name a boy Lincoln," Fern remarked. Yes, some of our mountain folks were.

"Joe Jones was a well-known preacher, great at revivals," Georgianna went on happily. "They did say he carried the smallpox with him to one town, and the people in the next town said the folks over there couldn't tell the Holy Spirit from a temperature."

"Silly gossip," Pop said. He should talk.

Luckily, Georgianna was making a diagram while she explained. She laid a piece of white paper out flat on the table, next to her plate and sketched a family tree with those long hands with the knots at the joints.

I was busy trying to put the family tree into a poem. That was the only way I would ever be able to keep it in mind. I wanted it at my beck and call in case I came across some fact that helped me place the twins on the tree. My effort was clumsy but fast.

Jeeter G. Jones, born in '79,
Picked herbs to make his friends feel fine.
His wife, Ellie,
Brewed herb cures smelly.

I remembered the yarrow tea my own grandmother brewed to treat a cold. It smelled bit-
terish. But on with the poem:
I even put in the kids who were not known to
have had children. You could never be sure.

Son Bill, the pill, vamoosed to Texas.
Slender Brenda had no kids to vex us.
Linc the drink-er, born in 1898,
Found whiskey and beer were his fate.

A few dates kept me oriented.

But Smallpox Joe, born in 1899,
Preached like an angel and turned out fine.

Shakespeare was not going to be jealous of my
poem.
Meanwhile, Georgianna had finished her
soup and was already on to the next generation.
"Lincoln was never known to be sober, but he
managed to have a son, late in life, George, in
1948. George was a mechanic and even more
religious than his uncle. So was George's wife.
They had two boys, Hal and John Charles. Hal
was a contractor in Madison County, but before
he could manage to have children, he drank too

much beer, fell off a roof, and was killed. The other son, John Charles, disappeared about twenty years ago after a fight with his father. He read too much. He had me send off for historical stuff, like the works of Samuel Pepys who lived in the 1600s." She pronounced that "Peeps." I pictured a long-ago man peeping through the knothole in a fence. But wait, I told myself, I didn't have to remember him! And Georgianna the librarian thought a kid could read too much! It must have addled his head.

"That was an unlucky branch of the family," I said. I could hardly take notes fast enough to keep up with their disasters.

"Smallpox Joe Jones was luckier with his kids than Lincoln was," Georgianna said. "Joe and his wife, Mary-Sue, had two sons. Charles moved to Florida and died there childless, but stayed in touch. Joe's other son, Joe, Jr., born in 1922, was Mary Mary-Sue's father." My head swam with names. I looked at the diagram, then versified.

Smallpox Joe and his wife, Mary-Sue,
Had Joe Junior in 1922.
Joe was pa to Mary Mary-Sue,
Who adopted Kim, who vanished into the
    blue.

Smallpox's brother Linc the Drinker,
Produced Saint George who liked to tinker.
George begat Hal, who died full of beer,
Also John C., who did disappear.

"Look here at the chart," I said to Georgianna. "In Mary Mary-Sue's family the youngest descendant, at least by adoption, of her grandfather, and the youngest descendant of her great uncle have *both* vanished. That's spooky."

"Like there was some curse on that family branch!" cried Fern, entranced. Pop's eyes sparkled with hope.

I had enough to deal with without those two dreaming up a curse. I tried to divert them. "Sometimes people just go off." I turned to Georgianna. "There was something about Ward's father vanishing, too, wasn't there?"

She sipped her soup and considered. "Ward Jenkins, our Ward's father, was a reckless man," she said. "He took incredible chances. He bought shares in a gold mine in Mexico with the food and rent money. Of course there was no gold. And then his wife, Bessie, slept with a tourist from Raleigh, and Ward's father left her in a rage. He was no loss, if you ask me." Georgianna made a face. "He was the worst tempered and most prejudiced man I ever met. We heard through the grapevine he had a new wife and two kids. I feel sorry for them. He lost touch."

"Ward is not related to us!" Pop explained loudly.

Georgianna ignored Pop. "Ward's mother, Bessie Gordon, was so mad she took back her maiden name, which, of course, Ward uses still.

But his father did send back money through some lawyer in Texas. So he and his new wife must have had money to live on. Maybe she was rich."

"The new kids weren't twins?"

Georgianna patted my hand. "You never give up, Peaches!" she said.

"Ward's relatives will not get us anyplace but bored," Pop complained, which meant he wanted to change the subject. "In fact, his mother is dead. She got so fat she exploded."

"A heart attack," said Georgianna, who prefers facts.

The next course was chocolate ice cream and lime-ginger cookies, which diverted us all. I needed a break after sorting relatives. The smooth coldness of the ice cream and the spice of the cookies perked me up.

"I have a copy of our whole family genealogy for you," Georgianna said, handing me a big sheaf of papers. "It doesn't have details, but it may be helpful if the relative or relatives you're looking for aren't close." My hunch still said they were.

"Now, I want to know about false memory and murder!" Pop cried as we drank our coffee. At least he seemed to have put the family curse out of his mind.

Georgianna pulled a book out of her big bag. "This is an overview on how memory works," she said, "but the part about false memory should particularly interest you because it talks about a case right here in the mountains." She waved her hand to indicate the view of blue-green peaks out the dining-room window.

"This is *Memory's Ghost* by Philip J. Hilts." Georgianna began flipping the pages. "Here you are," she said, "a murder case in Union Mills, North Carolina, which Mr. Hilts himself covered as a reporter. Four men were convicted of murder and rape because of eyewitness testimony. The only catch was that the star witness against them didn't remember a thing until a psychologist hypnotized him and told him he would be able to see what happened the night of the crime." Georgianna raised both eyebrows as if to say, *What do you think of that?*

Fern shrugged. She still looked drawn and even drab in her funeral black dress. So unlike Fern.

"But then, he did remember?" I asked.

"Then he remembered that he had seen a rake, and a rake handle was involved in the crime. At the trial that point was crucial because the rake hadn't been mentioned in the newspaper, so the man who remembered the rake must have been there when the crime was committed, right?"

"That sounds logical," I agreed. Fern nodded.

"Wrong! Luckily there was a videotape of the hypnotic session, and the reporter discovered that at one point the witness said he grabbed something. The psychologist asked him what he grabbed and then asked, 'Was it a rake?' The witness said it might have been. And nobody noticed that the 'enhanced-memory' rake was suggested first by the psychologist, not the witness."

Fern scowled. "So you're talking about one careless psychologist. Why make that a federal case?"

"We're interested in false memory, Fern," I said, "because just before she was killed, Eileen sent off for all sorts of material from something called the False Memory Syndrome Foundation. And . . ."

Before I could say another word, Fern stiffened as if someone had given her an electric shock. She choked on her soup. "That's this awful group." She glared accusingly at me, as if I harbored traitors. "They try to convince people they haven't been abused. They try to convince judges not to let the memory of a witness for perfectly unspeakable acts be accepted in court." She hissed "unspeakable."

"But the more unspeakable the acts, the more you'd like to be sure you convict the right person." I sounded surprised. I was nonplussed.

Fern turned to Georgianna, as if she were guilty, too. "Those people are trying to intimidate the very ones who are helping women to know why things go wrong for them." She threw her arms wide to suggest how many things went wrong. "Why women are bulimic or have nightmares or whatever. That foundation tries to intimidate people who are making wonderful discoveries, not just about child abuse, but about helping people remember they were kidnapped by space aliens, for example. And that's why they are maladjusted. Or that they were ritually abused to initiate them into a satanic cult. And made to forget all about it at the same time."

I sighed. Fern couldn't resist believing anything dramatic. I should have shut up.

"Fern," I said, "I read about the people who learned to 'remember' those things. And the FBI got into the act and did a study that could not find any evidence to support 'recovered' memories of widespread satanic cult abuse or cannibalism."

"Oh, they are very clever, these cults," she said. "They know how to dispose of the bones."

Bones! Nothing fazed Fern.

Pop was smiling broadly. He liked this better than the family tree.

"But look," I tried to reason, "you need some sort of real proof for something you might remember from the time you were a little kid, don't you?"

"Real proof? And where would you get any evidence," Fern cried, "for something that happened years ago in the strictest secrecy? Where?" Fern almost choked. I'd really upset her. "I have a friend who . . ." she said, but I stopped her and took a deep breath.

"What's important is not whether you agree with this stuff. What's important is why Eileen had it."

"It says here," continued Georgianna, flipping a page of the Hilts book, "that experiments show that under hypnosis people try to please, and if they don't know an answer, they make it up. And if the question gives a hint, they are likely to follow that hint. And afterward, what they 'remember' can seem very vivid, even if it never happened at all."

"That's ridiculous," said Fern, and suddenly I remembered that those two always went at it. If one said "black," the other said "white." Now that's the sort of thing I do remember.

Georgianna was still explaining her book. "And furthermore," she said, "the same kind of memory inspired by suggestion can happen with just ordinary questioning, if the person is suggestible." She gave Fern an appraising look. Yes, Fern is suggestible.

Fern jumped up. "We have to go," she said angrily. Actually, if I was going back to my house for my pocketbook, she was right.

I hugged Georgianna, took the book, and said, "Thanks a million!"

"You don't have to go," Pop announced. He wanted more fireworks.

"We do," I said, "and I may bring you dramatic news of where Kim is. Cross your fingers."

Of course Fern said she'd drive, so we didn't need to go back to the house for my pocketbook. She had hers, complete with driver's license. But the thought of Fern driving all the

253

way to the Cherokee woman's house was more than I could stand. I didn't say so, but she got the idea. "I have never had an accident," she said huffily. "Except once, and that was on the Santa Monica Freeway, where the traffic is wild." I remembered hearing that her car had been totaled.

"I won't be but a minute. Wait here," I suggested when we reached my house. I hurried to the front door, turned the key, and stepped inside.

After the bright sun my eyes took a second to adjust. I gasped and raised my arm to try to grab the big stick that a shadowy form held high. Someone was ready to hit me over the head. Fear took my breath away. Scared to the bone, I couldn't even scream.

Chapter

24

Friday, 1:30 P.M.

I grabbed the arm that held the big stick raised high and twisted hard.

"Cousin Peaches, don't!" cried a shrill voice. "It's only me!" I could see the big stick was really the poker from my fireplace.

"Only you with a deadly weapon," I told her. But how could Janet the Planet be deadly? I was amazed to see her standing there. She was amazed, too. Her mouth was open.

I had let go, and she had lowered the poker. "I was so scared," she said. "I was terrified. I was sure you were the killer, and I'm here all by myself." She said it as if she were the victim, as if I ought to cry for her.

"What on earth are you doing in my house?" I demanded. "Which I left all locked up just a little while ago? Who invited you in?"

255

"I had to talk to you," she said, "and I rode my bike over, and then just as I got here, this car went by slowly like it was casing the place. And of course the person saw me and then speeded up and went on. And I got behind a tree to see if the car would come back when it couldn't see me, and it did come back and went by even slower, and I was so scared I climbed in the bathroom window. And then I was really terrified because I realized that climbing inside a house where dreadful things could happen was the worst thing I could have done. But I was also scared to climb back out."

And, I thought, *you just loved being part of the drama. I bet you began to rehearse the story for your friends right while you trembled!*

My heart sank. I'd been so careful to lock everything up and keep it that way. But this morning when I took a bath, I'd opened the window to let the steam out so I could see in the mirror to do my face, and obviously I'd forgotten to lock the window! I groaned. I am not to be trusted.

"And it was so lucky that window was open, Cousin Peaches, because here you are, and I have something to tell you!"

"You tried to hit me over the head because you thought I was the person from the car?" I asked.

"Oh, yes," she said. "I thought the person had come back as soon as the coast looked clear to put poison in your tea again or set the house on fire or wait to kill you when you came home. I locked the bathroom window."

I grabbed my pocketbook off its hook near the door and put it over my shoulder. Immediately my shoulder felt right.

"And why did you come here to begin with?" I asked. I didn't suggest we sit down. Fern was waiting in the car, and we still needed to hurry.

Janet may have been too keyed up to sit anyway. She trembled with importance. "She had a diary," she said. "Kim had a diary. She told me years ago, and I forgot about it. When we were little kids. And then there was this movie advertised on TV, *Diary of a Mad Housewife*, and I thought diary, wow, and I remembered. And she hid the diary, and she told me where."

"But wasn't that years ago?"

"But don't you see?" Janet went on. "Kim told things in the diary that could help now. She told about hiding places." I must have looked skeptical. "Not behind trees," she scoffed. "No, no. Like, there's an old falling-down cabin in the woods behind her house. Well, anybody could find her there. But she said there were other places, near her grandmother's house. One was there."

"You mean Mary Mary-Sue's mother?" I asked.

"Yes, yes, and her aunts. Wherever she went to visit, she found places. It was kind of a game. She liked to pretend they were houses where

257

her real family lived, and she could go there and read or whatever. Even if it was only a kind of half cave under a big rock. She told me all about it."

Here in the mountains we still have so many woods, often backing right up to houses, with paths leading off for hunters or ginseng gatherers or whatever.

"She could go way off and not get lost," Janet said. "Her father taught her how not to get lost in the woods and all that — how to tell north by which side of a tree the moss is on. He knows that kind of thing."

"You mean Ward?" I asked. So he had an interesting side I didn't know much about.

"And she wrote about those places in her diary. She told me that."

This was probably a red herring. Would Kim really go to the trouble to get John Baylor to put money in a bank account and then go hide in the woods? Would all that kid stuff about hiding places mean anything to a girl of seventeen? I had some hiding places myself, but only as a little kid. Still, I told myself, leave no stone unturned.

"Where did she keep the diary?" I asked.

"She said it was in a hollow tree somewhere near her house."

I all but groaned. In a hollow tree ten years ago! If it still existed, it would be part of some squirrel's nest.

Someone began to pound on the door. Fern.

The door latches automatically when I shut it, or she would have marched right in.

"I have an appointment," I said to Janet. "I'm going to give you a ride home. Put your bike in the car trunk. When you get home, lock the doors and call the police and tell them what you told me." I doubted they would put much stock in her story, but you never know.

"No," she said, "we have a right to look first. And anyway, they'll think I'm being silly. You know they will. And Mom will be home. I'll be okay. Swear you won't tell anybody about this until we look."

Bam bam bam. Fern was getting upset. It was getting late. "Tell your mother what's happened, and I'll call you when I get back," I said.

Bam bam. I opened the door. Fern rushed in like a dark shadow and stared in surprise at Janet the Planet, who still had the poker clasped absentmindedly in one hand.

"We have to give Janet a ride home," I explained. "She found a window unlocked and thought she was guarding the house."

That didn't satisfy Fern for a minute. She turned to Janet. "Is that all?"

Janet said, "It's all I want to talk about right now." And Fern never got another word out of Janet about what happened.

As soon as we dropped Janet and her bike off, I tried to smooth things over. I told Fern that Janet had come to tell me a secret, which I could probably tell Fern later.

"You don't trust me!" she said. Yes, there was a little of that.

"If you know that Janet can't count on what I tell *her*, then how can you count on what I tell *you?*" I asked.

Fern shrugged. "People with big thumbs like yours and deep lines in their hands can be very stubborn," she said. "You know I'm always a big help when we do things together."

I laughed, which was a mistake. "Maybe Janet figures," I said, "that people with hands like Amelia Earhart's may not be the best copilots." That was not tactful.

Chapter

25

That Afternoon

Fern was quiet as we drove along. She told me the way, but not with good cheer. We followed a main road, then a smaller one into open country.

She pointed out a weathered wood house with a relaxed, slightly shaggy lawn and a few purple phlox by the white front door. Rows of vegetables ran down the side of the lawn across from a driveway. I recognized the curly darkness of kale and something taller, maybe bush beans. "That must be it," Fern said. "That's how Mike described it. Now, remember, be low-key — he said to do that. Begin with the weather or something like that."

What had I expected? A tepee? No. Maybe beadwork on the mailbox? No, but something to make me aware this was an Indian woman's house. The windows, two on each side of the door, were like the windows on any house. The only remarkable thing was the view. Across the road from the house, I could see ripple after ripple of mountains against a vivid blue sky. The sun shone. The air smelled good.

Fern knocked a forthright *bam bam bam.* If we were supposed to begin low-key, a *tap tap tap* would have seemed better. But Fern was still annoyed. I could tell by her jerkiness, however slight.

A small boy of about six, with short black hair, a faded red T-shirt, and jeans, opened the door. He stood there waiting without expression. I looked at Fern. *Her* friend Mike had sent us here, with directions on how to act. Fern looked at me. *So you know it all — so you talk,* her eyes said.

"Hi," I tried. "I'm Peaches Dann, and this is Fern Allen. We've come to see Anna Littledeer. A friend of hers said she might be nice enough to help us."

The boy said, "Come in," without expression, turned, walked toward a plump, dark woman in a tan knit shirt and brown slacks, and nodded to us. Then he disappeared out a back door. *We make him uneasy,* I thought.

But Anna Littledeer's eyes were alive and friendly. Her voice was warm. She was not young, though I couldn't judge her age. Her face was still smooth except for wrinkles around the eyes. I was sure this woman would have been kind to Kim. And told her what?

I introduced us again and explained that Mike had sent us. She confirmed that she was Anna, led us to two worn overstuffed chairs, and invited us to sit down. She sat down in a straight chair with a seat woven from pale wood splits.

On the wall behind her were photographs, several group portraits of dark-haired, dark-eyed mothers, fathers, and children. Anna's descendants, I thought, and maybe nieces and nephews. Proudly displayed. No other pictures. No ancestors in headdresses. Just family. Somehow the pictures went with the warmth in her eyes.

"We had a lovely ride," I said. "It's a beautiful day." I noticed a partly woven basket hanging on a hook, one of those with designs of darker and lighter oak splits. "What a lovely basket," I said. "Is that your work?"

"Yes," she said. "An old traditional pattern. I'm a basket weaver." Anna sat totally still.

"We understand you have an unusual line in your hands," Fern said, fidgeting in her chair. Even her voice was slightly jerky. Hey, wait a minute — Fern had said we should follow Mike's suggestion to start off low-key and impersonal. But Fern couldn't do it.

Nevertheless, Anna held out her hands, and there it was, the mark of — what were we calling it now? — the mark of difference, crossing her broad, smoothly marked right palm.

"We're looking for a girl with one horizontal line like that in her hand," Fern said. "We have to find her. Mike told us she came here." Her tone of voice was like stamping her foot. What on earth was with Fern? She should have done better than that. Unfortunately, I couldn't reach to nudge her without being seen.

Something closed down behind Anna's eyes, just when I'd begun to feel she really could help us. Her face became inscrutable, like the boy's had been. This was a woman who knew character. I felt it. And one of the last to see Kim. I wanted to grab Fern by the scruff of the neck and throw her out the door.

I looked her straight in the eye. "Fern, I want you to come outside for a minute." When she opened her mouth to object, I gave her my best triple-whammy look, got up, went over, took her by the arm, and led her out — more like dragged. I know about outrageous people, like Pop. Kinship gives you practice dealing with family quirks. I don't usually get drastic. "You catch more flies with honey than you do with vinegar," my grandmother used to say. But sometimes I can tell that honey is not going to work. And Fern was about to louse things up.

"Look," I said outside the door, "something is eating you, Fern, and I don't have time to hear about it now. But you are antagonizing that woman, and I intend to do this alone. Now, you go sit in the car and shut up." Luckily she was so mad she stalked off instead of arguing.

I went back inside, where Anna still sat quietly in her chair, eyes expressionless. A fly buzzed against a window pane. I made myself remember her warmth. I glanced at the family photos. "I truly need your help," I said, "because my young cousin Kim Gordon is in terrible danger. You care about young people; I can tell. Please help me."

Her eyes became warm again. She leaned toward me, reached out, and touched my hand. "How can I help?"

I told her as briefly as I could how Kim had disappeared, how her twin sister had been killed, possibly because someone thought she was Kim. I said, "I think Kim was trying to find out who she was, where she came from. And she may have thought that unusual line — the one in your hand and hers — was a clue to that. She may have been afraid it showed a weakness and hoped you could tell her that wasn't so. And one of the last people we think she came to see was you."

She nodded. "She and her sister came to look for me in Cherokee. Someone gave them my address. I enjoy all people of goodwill, not just my own people. That is known."

"Did the sister come with Kim to this house?"

Anna shook her head no. "Kim came alone."

"Did she do or say anything that could give us a clue where she went?" I asked hopefully.

Anna Littledeer sat so still, it was like a talent. As if the force inside her grew because she did not let it leak out.

"I will tell you how we talked," Anna said. "Come have a cup of coffee. I just made a pot."

She led me into the kitchen, a plain room with an electric stove and a refrigerator, vintage from 1970, and only a seed-company calendar on the wall. She indicated I should sit down at the white enamel table, which must have been an antique of sorts.

She poured me a cup of coffee in a mug with a picture of Mickey Mouse on it. Must have belonged to the boy. A grandson, I figured. She sat down at the table with me.

"Kim told me that she understood I knew the meaning of a certain line in her hand. That I had it, too." Anna held out her free hand, beautifully marked with steady lines, no chains, no worry lines.

"The girl was unhappy, confused. She wanted to find the right path. I took her out with me to pick beans." To pick beans? That stopped me.

"We did ordinary things," she continued. "It was peaceful here. She stayed a while."

Anna and I became quiet, drinking the good, rich coffee. I sensed I should let her tell the story in her own time.

Finally she resumed talking. "There was a hummingbird, hanging on its wings, drinking from a flower. I told her how the white man comes to us to ask about the eagle. The white man wants this symbol for himself, wants to soar. And we admire the eagle. But we also admire the dragonfly — or the hummingbird, which spends the whole day seeking beauty. A symbol of joy. All things give us meaning."

I waited again, sipping my coffee.

"Kim stayed until the evening. She helped snap beans and make corn bread. We ate together."

Yes, I thought, *Kim must have felt accepted.* What this woman told her would have guided her. I waited.

"At sunset she came with us outdoors to burn cedar. I told her how we burn red cedar at sunrise and say thanks for the new day. And then at sunset we burn cedar, and as the smoke rises, we say thank you for the day again. We admit what we didn't do well that day. We put that behind us so the next day is new and we can try to grow in spirit again."

"I like that idea," I said, "to start each day fresh and ready to grow. It doesn't seem like an idea that would encourage Kim to run away."

Anna took the empty mugs and put them in the sink. She seemed to be waiting for me to say something.

"You said she came to find out about the line in your hand, which was also in her hand. Mike said that line could indicate a healer's hand."

"Do you mind if I work while we talk?" Anna asked. She brought a half-finished basket and, from a corner, a bucket with wet strips of wood inside. The wet wood was pliable in her broad smooth hands. "My brother, who has the same line, is what you might call a healer. We speak of a provoker. He provokes a sick person to heal himself and change his life. Mike had heard that this line we both have in our hands is one sign that a child may be able to be trained to be a provoker, and that is true."

She began to weave a pale strip into the basket design. "Those who teach look for an anomaly. This line is often found in the hand of a slow child. But this line in the hand of a child who is healthy and of sound mind, not retarded, may show the right child for training. The child who is unusual. Just as those who train may choose a child who is blind or deaf. And then, if the temperament is right, with self-control, a sense of balance, and other things, then they can train the child to have special powers."

"And you told Kim she had these special powers? Or at least she could learn to have them?"

"No," Anna said, "that would require years of training from the time she was a child. But I told her she could look within herself and find some kind of gift. And grow with that gift to help her people."

I thought of all the family pictures in the next room. Yes, Anna would think in terms of helping your own and of growing larger from that to help others as she was trying to help me. Pop would approve. But for Kim, who was seeking to find where she came from, how would that sit?

"And what did Kim say?" I asked.

"She did not say anything except to thank me. Then she left. She had an old car."

"A blue Ford?"

"Yes."

I sighed. I was glad Fern wasn't there. Fern could not have stood not to demand to know more. But I suspected that Anna would never ask to know more than someone like Kim was ready to tell. She was willing to let the details go.

"Is there anything else that happened that could help me find her?" I asked to be sure.

Anna began to weave a row of black slats into the basket design. "Kim drove away to the left," she said. "Don't be afraid. She will grow."

She might if she lived.

Anna wove another row of blond wood, then spoke again. "There was one other thing that might help you," she said. "There were several large cardboard boxes in her car. I did not see markings on them."

"What size and shape?" I asked.

"Square. Maybe two feet by two feet. I'm not sure."

"And suitcases?" I asked.

"Yes, there was a suitcase. I don't know where she went, except she started to the left."

Chapter

26

September 1, 4:30 P.M.

So Kim had driven out of the driveway the same way we had driven in. But in fact, she could have gone in any direction unseen by Anna once she got out to the main road.

I got in the car, where Fern sat stonily silent, and pulled my car key out of my pocketbook. Out floated a piece of green paper, folded over. The outside was an ad for a sale. Now where had I seen that? Oh, yes, a tall, bony man had given me that while I was very busy at my book signing and said, "Read this later when you have time." At the very book signing that had resulted in our trip today! So I was curious. His note might be important. I opened it and found squarish upright handwriting:

Ms. Dann,

I enjoyed your talk about your book and even the part about how computers can help a weak-kneed memory. But you should warn folks about the pitfalls of computer memory. It can be misleading to say the least because it lacks human judgment. I enclose a poem which has been batting about the Internet:

Spellbound

I have a spelling checker
It came with my PC;
It plainly marks for my revue
Mistakes I cannot sea.
I've run this poem threw it,
I'm sure your please too no,
Its letter perfect in it's weigh,
My checker tolled me sew.

Nothing there to help find Kim, but I handed the poem to Fern in hopes that she would at least smile. Instead she exploded. "Is false memory all you think about?" she yelled.

What? Oh, I suppose you could call that false memory. In a way.

"You don't respect my opinion on any subject," Fern cried out. The tendons in her neck stood out. "And you're using me!" she accused. "I am the one who has found most of the clues and arranged this meeting, and you don't even pretend to trust me. Do you?"

271

"I don't trust anybody I know in every situation," I said cautiously. "I didn't trust you not to upset that woman so much that she wouldn't talk." I heard a faraway rumble of thunder, like the afternoon sky clearing its throat. Often this kind of thunder came without rain. In fact the sun was still shining.

"And you weasel around," Fern said. "You haven't answered my question. Do you trust me or don't you?" She turned in her seat, leaned over, and looked at me as straight in the eye as you can with somebody who is driving a car and doesn't intend to hit a tree.

We passed some cattle in a field, staring at us stolidly. "I don't think you are deliberately dishonest, Fern," I said. Well, I hoped not. "But you did twist that Mark of Murder business."

"Oh, that!" she said with a shrug. "That was just to help Kim. I explained about that. You're still weaseling. I'm not sure I trust you."

"That's your right," I said as we passed small houses with children playing in yards.

Fern's whole body kind of percolated with annoyance. She went back to stony-faced until we reached an area with steak houses and gas stations, and I stopped for gas. After I filled the car and paid, I got back in and turned to Fern. She looked dried out, as if all the juices in her body were leaking away. "Something is wrong. You're getting madder than you need to get."

She burst into tears. Water streamed down her face and got her black dress wet. Her quartz earrings were like black teardrops. "It's Friday," she choked when she could catch her breath.

"What's wrong with this Friday?"

"Today Richard married another woman." I was ashamed. She'd told me he was going to do that, hadn't she? And I forgot. I hadn't believed that Fern really cared. Old one-track mind here had not even taken the hint of the widow's outfit. I put my arm around her black shoulders and let her cry, after which she became herself again. I could hardly believe the change. "I needed that," she said firmly. "Richard's a bastard. I'm going to forget him!"

I told her how sorry I was that she'd been upset and started to turn the key in the ignition. "You look bushed," she said, blowing her nose. "Let me drive."

I looked in the rearview mirror. She was right. I was the one who looked totally drained. I realized I was tired, and I had been in the hospital the day before, hadn't I? And Fern looked full of energy. Renewed by tears. She was certainly prone to quick changes!

When Fern absolutely promised not to drive too fast, I took her up on her offer, which seemed to cheer her even more.

"So what did you find out?" she asked as we started off again. This was the nosy Fern I knew!

"I don't know," I said, leaning back in my seat. "I found out that Kim had some boxes, not too large, and a suitcase in her car when she left Anna Littledeer's."

"Ready to travel!" Fern cried.

"Anna couldn't tell what was in the boxes," I said. "I liked Anna. And I found out what your Mark of Murder means to a Cherokee healer." I told her briefly. "And I have a feeling that I found out something more, but I'm not sure what yet." Another faint rumble.

"In other words you don't want to tell me."

"I'd be happy to tell you if I knew myself," I said. "Something about the way Kim acted in that house has a meaning. I'm not sure what."

"But you didn't push that woman to tell you any more than you've told me."

"No," I said, "I didn't believe it would do me any good to push Anna Littledeer to tell me any more."

"That woman knows something," Fern said as she swerved past a slow-moving tractor. "She's hiding something. I could tell it right away. And you're being naive, Peaches. We don't have time to be naive. And furthermore, someone is following us. I got a glimpse when we went around that curve. And I also saw that same brown car on our way over here. Someone knows we have been to see that woman and can go and ask her the things we didn't ask. Maybe we should go back."

I shivered and began to watch in the outside rearview mirror. The small car stayed just far enough behind us so it was hard to see. Impossible to see the driver clearly. Other cars were closer, but the brown car managed always to be just a few cars behind.

"Slow down," I said, "and see if the car will pass you." She eased up on the gas. A blue Camero and a white Ford passed. The brown car slowed down when we did. Whether Fern slowed down or speeded up, the car stayed the same distance behind. I didn't like that. My heart beat faster, but I didn't think we ought to turn around. "If we went back," I told Fern, "whoever is following would be twice as sure that there's something to learn from Anna." I prayed I had not put Anna in any kind of danger. Not to mention us.

"All right," I said, "no point in wasting time. At least we can find out a few people who are *not* following us." I pulled out my electronic organizer and looked up John Baylor's office number. I punched it in on the car phone. I had to bully my way past the secretary to reach John — she first said he was out. I told John I needed to know who would inherit Eileen's trust fund. He said, in effect, that it was none of my business.

I called Mary Mary-Sue, who was out, but I got Ward. He said he didn't even try to keep track of his wife. I tried Eileen's father's number, but the line was busy.

I reached Ward's sister, Sandra Redmon, at home. "I was just coming in the door," she said, "quickly, to get away from the manure smell. Never marry a man who may decide in midlife that he's an organic farmer!"

I tried Eileen's father again. As soon as he recognized my voice, George Stackhouse began to talk so fast I could hardly understand. "I tried to call. We have amazing news! Alice got a letter! Another one." Alice. His wife.

"Try to be calm," I said. "It's hard to hear you on the car phone. I'm getting static." Also a large truck was lumbering past.

"Andrew Frank wrote us again." Yes. Alice's sister Susan's husband. Did that mean that now his name was cleared? That he was out of prison? I wondered what was shocking enough to make George Stackhouse's voice tremble so. He took a deep breath and pronounced: "My wife's sister, Susan, was the mother of twins!"

Twins. I tried to digest that. Like Eileen and Kim! So what if —

"Don't you see what that means?" he cried. "Andrew's father arranged for them to be adopted. And Andrew wanted to give them the chance to grow up without knowing what happened to their real mother and father. That's what the letter said. To have a normal, happy life. His father found a place for them with relatives. That's what Andrew said."

So was Alice Stackhouse Eileen's aunt? And Kim's aunt? But wait! My head spun. I'd been sure Eileen and Kim were related to us. Could we be related to Alice Stackhouse? My head began to ache. I was too tired to think straight, and very annoyed at that.

Next to me, Fern was all quivering eyebrows and head shakes, indicating I should tell her what was going on. Her black quartz earrings vibrated with tension. I ignored her and listened hard.

"Andrew said he didn't want to know who the twins were placed with, in case he was tempted to get in touch. And of course he didn't know our Eileen was a twin, though she wrote him a letter in prison. She was such a great girl." His voice broke.

"And you think . . ."

"Yes, yes! There's more! Andrew said he could tell us now because he's so sure his name will be cleared. The twins were two and a half when their mother was killed. Two and a half. Just like Eileen when we got her. We've lost Eileen." He let out a sob. "But we still have Kim. If we can find her." I felt tears in my eyes.

"There was one other odd thing," George Stackhouse was saying. "Andrew mentioned writing us a letter about the twins before. Last week. But we didn't get any other letter. And this is all so strange. Could someone be stealing our mail? I have to find that damned Baylor. And for God's sake, don't tell anybody about this until I know what's true."

So murder could explain Kim's nightmares. Had Kim seen it or just experienced the terror when her mother was dead and then her father was taken away? She'd been just at the edge of the age when children remember. That came back to me from the false-memory stuff; memory begins at about two and a half but sometimes later. And if Kim had seen someone kill her mother . . . I shuddered. There was such a lump in my throat, I could hardly speak. Just as well.

"I'm trying to reach that damn John Baylor," Eileen's father was saying. "His secretary swears he's out." I looked at the car clock: 4:55.

"I bet he's not out," I said. "Keep trying. I just talked to him. And can I come and talk to you and Alice in an hour?" I wanted to look at Alice's hand. Could she have the Mark of Murder?

"Don't come tonight," he said. "I'll be out tracking down John Baylor until I find him and get answers. And Alice is sedated. She's asleep."

"Time matters," I said. "Call me back after you talk to John." I gave him my car and home numbers. Then I tried John myself. His firm has several in lines, so I wouldn't prevent Eileen's father from getting through. Bullying John's secretary didn't work this time. She said he really had left. She didn't know where he'd gone. I felt totally frustrated, unsure what to do next.

The car that had been following us had disappeared briefly. Now it reappeared just at the edge of sight, with several other cars and a mobile home in between. That car was still after us, just more carefully.

"Why is time crucial?" Fern demanded. "What's going on? What in God's name was all that?"

I said, "Eileen's father is furious with John Baylor and needed to blow off steam." I could tell she didn't believe that was all. I would rather have told her the whole truth because Fern is sharp. She can be helpful. But I honored Eileen's father's request.

Thank goodness Ted was home. I needed to thrash this out with someone. Had I been on the wrong track? Were the twins not related to our family? Or what?

And this Andrew, I thought, the father of the twins, was much too idealistic for his own good. He hid his troubles from his sister for so many years, and allowed his twins to be lost to him in order to protect them from the truth. If he'd been our blood relative, we'd have probably nicknamed him one of the Too-Noble Franks. Were Kim and Eileen proud like he was? Keeping secrets for some idealistic reason? Secrets that could be lethal? And where was Kim?

Chapter

27

6:00 P.M.

I dropped Fern off at her motel, thanked her for driving, and drove myself toward home. When I was almost there, the car phone rang. What now?

Pop was stern. "Peaches, you are getting lazy. Out joyriding, and I don't suppose you've found Kim yet."

"None of us has found her yet," I said. He tended to be even more outrageous than usual at the end of the day, when he was tired. I made up my mind not to get upset.

"By now she's probably dead," he said. "That's what happens when you dawdle. Or take LSD and get as nutty as a fruitcake. I think we need to put up a sign in the lost and found." He didn't say what lost and found. "It will say, 'Lost: two bodies and one mind.'"

"Eileen isn't lost, and Kim isn't dead that we know of," I said testily as I pulled into my driveway. But Pop wasn't even listening.

He repeated himself and began to chuckle. " 'Lost: two bodies and one mind,' and I bet you've also lost your glasses."

After a whole day with Fern, that call from Pop was the last straw. For the first time in my life, I hung up on my father. I never said I was perfect.

Chapter

28

6:15 P.M.

I arrived home to find Ted in the bedroom singing "Oh, What a Beautiful Morning." It was evening and Ted hardly ever sings.

He stood near the bathroom door, pulling off his shirt, which muffled the song. As he came out the other side, he said, "Good news, my father's out of the hospital." I gave him a happy hug, and he added, "Let's go out to dinner tonight. You need a break." There was a twinkle in his eye as if that were funny.

"I have some surprising news," I said. I sat down on the edge of the bed near the bathroom door and told him about the latest on the twins.

He stopped undressing and stood completely still. "And so, what's happening now may be tied up with the past." He frowned. "But not at all like we'd thought. Still, this may be a clue the police need. They presumably know things from John Baylor that we don't." He gave me a thumbs-up sign. "Maybe they'll clear this up, find Kim, and you can concentrate on promoting your book."

I was for that.

"I'm going to take a shower and get ready." He grinned as if there were some other secret I should have guessed. So? Even my tired brain knew that's what Ted likes to do. Take a nice long shower. His favorite way to relax, next to doing crossword puzzles.

I was exhausted, so I lay down on the bed for a short nap. My white shirtwaist blouse and navy skirt would have to do for dinner. I needed a snooze. In fact, with Ted's watery rendition of "You Are My Sunshine" for a lullaby, I went out like a light. Overload.

I dreamed that Ward Gordon was trying to tell me something important, but he was speaking in Cherokee and I couldn't understand. A beeper was warning me of a truck backing up. The truck was full of puzzle pieces — hundreds of thousands — and the truck dumped them all right on top of me. For some reason that was funny. I began to put the pieces together, but a faceless person in a blood-red robe led me off into a huge, empty building, where I was lost and scared. I heard a loud crack. I sat up alarmed before I was entirely awake or even clear what scared me.

For a moment my thoughts centered on

Ward. Something had made him very nervous when I was at his house. I knew I needed to puzzle out what. My mind refocused on the strange noise and on Ted, who was out of the shower and dressed.

"Was that a gunshot?" he demanded. He ran toward the front of the house. I thought I heard a car driving away. I pulled my shoes on and ran down the hall, through the living room and out the front door. Good grief, it was raining. Some wind, too.

At first I didn't see anybody. No limb blown down from a tree, nothing to account for the noise. And no noise anymore except a steady patter of rain. My car was parked in the driveway to the left of the house, with Ted's car in front of it. The road was empty, shiny, and wet. The trees across the way moved in the light wind. Ted, who had walked out into the middle of the lawn and was already wringing wet, gave a yell and pointed to my car.

I did a double take because I was sitting in the car. That's what it looked like. In my white shirtwaist blouse, short brown hair. Except I was leaning forward, slumped over the steering wheel. My stomach turned over. (Not the one in the car, the one in me!) I ran closer, at the same time looking this way and that. Was this some practical joke?

"The back window," Ted called out. He was closer to the car than I was. "Someone fired a shot through the back window of the car." His voice was low with shock. He dripped with rain. He opened the car door just as I came alongside. And there inside was my look-alike with blood on the back of her head. I felt amazed, then numb.

"It's Gertrude," I said. "Dear God, it's poor, dull Cousin Gertrude."

He was feeling for a pulse in her wrist. He said, "She's dead." I searched the car with my eyes in that supercharged way that makes you see twice as fast in emergencies. Nothing extra there but Gertrude's big, blue pocketbook with the shoulder strap, lying on the passenger seat. Gertrude sold gifts — coy music boxes, statuettes, things you never wanted but felt compelled to buy — so her pocketbook was big enough to hold the catalog. And I found myself wondering which family members I had actually heard say they'd like to shoot Gertrude for making whoever-it-was buy a china kid-by-an-outhouse and a china cat-with-a-guitar, all out of family loyalty. But they were joking! And now Gertrude really had been shot. I felt queasy.

"You get in the house," Ted ordered.

Yes. His tone of voice made the truth hit me. Someone must have meant to kill me! Not Gertrude. Who must have rung the doorbell while Ted was singing in the shower and I was asleep. I remembered the beeps in my dream. I felt sicker. She probably got in my car to get out of the blowing rain. So maybe someone thought she was me. Because she had hair cut like mine and a white shirtwaist blouse like I was wearing. I shuddered. But why didn't she have a car? How did she get here? Who was so upset with me that he wanted to shoot me in the head? Blood ran down the back of Gertrude's head and stained the white blouse.

We went inside. While Ted called the police, I went in the bathroom and lost my lunch. I hadn't liked Gertrude. Why was I almost more upset than I'd been for Eileen? I felt hollow. I rinsed out my mouth and thought about that as I washed my face, dried the rain out of my hair, and put on dry clothes. I was upset because this could have been me, dead in the driveway. I pushed that thought away.

I wished the policeman I had known best on the Asheville force hadn't moved to Philadelphia. The police who came and questioned us for hours were not too sympathetic. "In fact," said one detective with sandy hair, "if you ever wanted to take a trip to Hawaii, now would be a good time."

Actually, I'd always wanted to go to Kathmandu. Now I was tempted. Or I could go visit Eve in Hong Kong. I'd like that. Any change would be nice. And good for my health.

Chapter

29

Later That Evening

"I made a dinner reservation at Richmond Hill," Ted said as casually as if he did that every night. As lightly as if it were the natural place to go after the police asked you ten thousand questions, including how many people would like to do you in.

"I just called the inn back to change the dinner reservation to nine and they had a last-minute room cancellation. So we have a room to spend the night in," he said. "Nobody would expect us to be there."

Yes, I'd enjoy feeling safe, and he was right, no one would guess we'd be there. Richmond Hill is one of the most elegant places in Asheville. A Victorian mansion which once belonged to a former congressman and ambassador who had lots of cash to build it with zing, it's restored and endowed with a good chef. What a place to recuperate! Not where college professors take their wives just every day. And suddenly I felt roaringly glad to be alive. And to be with Ted. I put my arms around him and kissed him hard.

"Not now," he said. "At Richmond Hill."

We threw some clothes in a bag and put out food for the cat. "And put on that pretty dress with the big flowers on it," Ted said. "If we're going out, we might as well enjoy it!" Yes. Life has to go on in spite of tragedy. Maybe *because of* tragedy.

Police were still going over the yard, but they could do that without us. We looked around carefully to be sure nobody was lurking, ready to follow, and set out for Richmond Hill. In Ted's car, naturally — the police had impounded mine as a crime scene. I didn't know if I'd be able to drive it again, anyway. The moon was almost full, the rain had stopped, and the trees along the road were lovely in the moonlight plus the moving lights from the car. I am alive, I told myself. I am lucky to be alive. I was sorry I hadn't answered the door for poor Gertrude, but I couldn't change that.

I decided to call Pop on Ted's car phone to tell him what happened. He'd be furious to hear it secondhand. Of course, he might be asleep, but sometimes he napped during the day and was awake at night. "How are you?" I asked as I pondered how to tell him about Gertrude without upsetting him too much. Meanwhile, we turned onto the main road and speeded up.

"Your cousin Janet just called here in a white-hot lather, wanting to know where you are," Pop announced. He sounded as if I should be ashamed of myself. "She says you're not home and she has something you want to see," he accused. He paused a long time, waiting for me to say something that would be a hint. He couldn't stand the silence and went on. "She found whatever it is by herself, and it has what you want to know. She wouldn't tell me what it was. I was rather annoyed." I could tell that was an understatement. You betcha! Pop gave me Janet's number, and I pulled a pencil from my shoulder bag and wrote it down just as Ted swerved around a large truck. My writing looked drunk, but never mind.

"What did Janet find?" Pop demanded. If Pop couldn't worm anything out of Janet, she was truly talented.

A convertible with the top down passed by us with music from the forties blaring from the tape deck or whatever. A white-haired couple sat close, and the wind whipped their hair. I sighed. They were glad to be alive, too, alive with someone to love.

"Pop," I said, "if Janet won't tell you what she found, I can't until she says I can." He hung up on me. Well, I had hung up first on him over that lost-and-found business, but this was getting out of hand. I tried to call back, but his line was busy. It did give me an excuse not to tell him about Gertrude yet. I could go over and tell him in person first thing in the morning.

I dialed Janet's number. Ah, modern technology. Janet answered on the first ring. She said, "Just a minute," by which I gathered she went to a phone where she wouldn't be overheard.

"I found the diary!" Her voice trembled with excitement. "It really *was* out in a hollow tree, but in a plastic bag. So it's not ruined. And it tells where Kim used to hide."

What a strange mixture this murder business seemed to involve — kids' foolishness, like hiding a diary, plus insanity or greed or fear or whatever motivated the killer.

The convertible in front of us was weaving unsteadily. Even love can be dangerous.

And Janet was oblivious to the danger. Teens believe they are invulnerable and immortal. I should have known she'd throw caution to the wind and go look for that diary herself. So, thank God, whoever it was with the gun had followed me and not Janet. At least, thank God from Janet's point of view.

"You went to look for the diary as soon as I left you at home?" I asked.

Silence. She knew she'd promised to wait for me.

Ted shook his head and frowned at her foolishness.

"Are your family all there, Janet?" I asked.

"Yes," she said, "but I can sneak out. We can go search in those places."

"Now listen to me carefully," I said. "Someone has probably just tried to kill me." I told her about Cousin Gertrude. Ted's frown deepened.

Janet drew in her breath sharply. "They must really want to kill Kim," she groaned, "if they killed you for just trying to get in the way." And yet, *had* I been in the way? Not really. What did the killer think I knew?

"Janet, you must be careful, too," I said firmly. "Now, tell me what the diary says, and I'll take notes so two of us will know. And you stay in that house with the doors locked. Did you tell your mother you might be in danger?" Long silence. "Janet, you've got to tell her," I said.

Ted swerved around the wavery convertible. Good.

"There are three hiding places," Janet said, "I mean, in addition to that old cabin by her house. She'd know her mother would look there." Janet spoke faster and faster. "And you know where Cousin Toto Small lives? Off in the woods, a pretty long way behind his house, there's a cave. Some of the college students were studying that place because there were Indian arrowheads and stuff like that buried there."

"I suppose," I said, "the Indians used the cave when they were caught in bad weather, out hunting. I read about that dig in the paper about

291

five years or so ago. But everything got taken out, I think, and there's only a cave there now. Right?"

"Maybe a few ghosts of the folks the Indians scalped." She laughed. I could see that idea appealed to Janet's imagination. She gave me directions to get there, and I wrote them down.

"Now, the second hiding place Kim mentions is where Cousin Martin lives," Janet said. "And you know where that is — on the edge of the Pisgah National Forest. That's the Cousin Martin who shot his sister and has warts on his nose."

"Near the Pisgah Forest? Cousin Martin? I remember his warts and some accident, but not where he lives." But Ted was nodding. He knew where. "Would you mind giving the directions to Ted?" I asked. "He's the navigator in this family."

Besides, Ted had taken Cousin Martin home once when his car broke down or something. I handed my husband the phone.

"A cave?" Ted repeated. So Kim had had a thing for caves. Actually, once when I was a kid, a friend and I found a very small cave and played in it. We were lucky it didn't cave in and bury us forever. But I had felt secret and safe, in the womb of the earth.

"And a cabin that hunters used now and then," Ted said after a while. That didn't sound as promising as a cave, but how could you second-guess a scared kid?

Ted handed me the phone back, and I thanked Janet and promised we'd get together the next day. "Don't tell anyone what you know," I said firmly before saying goodbye. "You could be in real danger."

Ted turned off the main road and started up a long, winding hill. We were getting closer to the inn. I didn't believe the smart young woman I knew Kim to be would hang around the place where her twin had been killed. She would be far gone by now. I was sure of that. I was glad to be going to a relatively safe place myself, safe and luxurious.

As we came to a Richmond Hill sign and turned into an even more winding drive, I told Ted, "You're getting extravagant in your old age."

He laughed his great warm laugh. "Don't you know what day this is? Women are supposed to remember these things. Men are supposed to be the ones who forget!"

First I said Saturday. Then suddenly it hit me. "Oh, Ted, this is our anniversary! And I even had a hint today. Because Mary Mary-Sue had an anniversary card! And I knew it was soon. But it's today! And I was so busy trying to find Kim that I forgot!"

"You were distracted," he said, "by a gunshot."

"But you remembered this was our day. You were going to surprise me." Not that I'm hard to surprise, with my memory. "You are the most wonderful man in the universe," I purred.

293

"I won't forget that!" he said. I could see in the moonlight that he was smiling, a pleased smile.

We came to the inn at the top of the hill, with lighted arches of a porch nearly all around the peaks of roof. We found a parking place on the side of the building in a well-lighted place. Which I was glad of. I still intended to watch my back. We walked past a black Victorian-looking buggy or some such. It was sitting, apparently permanently under what I remember my grandmother calling a porte cochere — a roofed-over, getting-in-the-car-or-whatever place.

We hurried around a wide porch with high-backed rockers on it — I guess Ted was as hungry as I — and through the front door into a cool, wood-paneled room with portraits of a boy in a sailor suit on one wall and a pretty woman on the other. On a small table with two chairs drawn up was a half-finished chess game. It was as if we had managed to go back in the past. The safe past. We asked permission to leave our rather small bags at the desk and go straight in to dinner before we went upstairs to our room.

The thick Persian carpet muffled our footsteps. The maître d' led us through two dining rooms into a third and seated us at a table with a bud vase of flowers and a small globe-in-a-chimney oil lamp. And in the lamplight Ted looked so distinguished with his white hair and strong features that I almost burst with gratitude. I was alive, and he was part of my good life.

Another table of diners was just leaving. Four men with Yankee accents and salesmen's laughs. We then had the room to ourselves — the advantage of dining late. Through the large-paned windows I could see more tables with glimmering oil lamps out on a narrow, enclosed dining porch. In the flickering light it was hard to see who was out there. Whoever it was, they seemed to be leaving. In the distance I heard a phone ring and thought, *It can't be Pop. He'd hung up before he learned where we'd be. Good! Served him right!* I was so hungry I quickly forgot Pop and glued my eyes to the menu.

"Have something you'd never have at home," Ted suggested. "After all, we're celebrating how, since knowing you, my life has never, ever been dull. Also, after a day like today, you need sustenance."

"And moral support," I said, "for which I thank you. You pick the wine, and let's drink to a calmer future." I should have known better.

The menu diverted me. I think poets write the best ones. Reading is almost as delicious as eating. Would this menu just say, "Mixed salad"? Never. Instead: "Vine-ripened beefsteak tomatoes, Bermuda red onions, sweet European cucumbers, and Holland peppers atop Lolla Rosa lettuce and Belgian endive, highlighted by a wild-honey-and-orange vinaigrette."

So I ordered that international salad and also

mint-crusted ribs of lamb with a fig compote and equally poetic description. Ted had pan-seared duckling with red and gold sun-dried cherries simmered in port with green pepper-corns.

Could anything go wrong in this lap of luxury? We had a waiter and a waitress hovering over us and even asking permission to remove plates as we finished a course. Downright formal.

"This is stepping into the past," I told our blond waitress, who looked like a college student with a summer job. "I feel like this place should have a ghost."

That stirred her up. "Some people think it does! Sometimes there's creaking on the front stairs when nobody is going up or down." She took a small brush and began to brush every single crumb from the table. "Of course there's bound to be creaking in an old house like this, but it's fun to think it might be a ghost."

I imagined the ghost: the Victorian lady in the front-room portrait, floating down the stairs. I was so tired that the delicious burgundy gave me a buzz and by the time we got to ordering dessert, I had no worries. I felt as if I lived in the age of the ornately carved sideboard behind us with the red mottled-marble top and a gleaming silver tea service sitting on it. Sherlock Holmes would appear to join us for liqueurs or possibly port when we finished our crème brûlée.

Holmes forgot to join us, so we floated back

to the desk, where a helpful young man explained that our bags were already in our room on the third floor. He led us up the creaking stairs, stopping at the first landing where I admired the splendid brass chandelier and noticed the hall and doors leading off into mystery.

The young man explained that on this floor several of the rooms were named for the late ambassador's family members. He pointed to an arched doorway and said that just beyond it were an ice machine and a refrigerator with complimentary sodas. Sherlock Holmes never enjoyed an ice machine.

One more upward flight led us to a cheerful sitting area with couch and chairs, and just off that area our guide opened the John Ehle room. That was ours. All the rooms on this floor were named for mountain-area writers, he explained. We were near the Carl Sandburg room, the Wilma Dykeman room, and the Gail Godwin room (the O. Henry and Sidney Lanier rooms were on the floor below).

"Well," I said, "if my book sells well, maybe someone will name a room for me."

"Unless they forget," Ted answered, and explained to our guide, with a wink, that I had a book out called *How to Survive Without a Memory.* The young man showed us where to find soap, towels, and John Ehle books, such as *The Winter People,* to read then left. I certainly did *not* intend to read.

Ted put his arms around me. I kissed him and

said, "There's nobody I'd rather be married to for a whole year."

He hugged me tight and said, "The best is yet to come." And I agreed.

Chapter

30

Late That Night

I lay in the dark, feeling happy and loved, and thought about Kim. Seventeen. Just growing up. Hadn't she been a happy child? She'd looked as if she enjoyed life. Sometimes she didn't walk, she danced. Oh, now and then, she'd be moody, but what child isn't? She even seemed to have a good time with Ward, who took her camping. That was the one thing he seemed to be good at — well, that and hunting. Ward. There was something I needed to remember about Ward. I couldn't think what.

But back to Kim: Fern had said Kim was upset because, when she started school, a bully teased her about being adopted. Told her she didn't fit in. But there had never been any secret that Kim was adopted. In fact, Mary Mary-Sue liked to tell how excited they'd been when they chose her to join the family and what a beautiful toddler Kim was. Dressed Kim up like a princess for the first reunions she came to. And Kim was always a good-looking kid.

But Fern had said that two years ago, when Kim heard the rumor that her birth parents were from our family, she was upset. And then that business of having the same unusual line which was common in our family made her feel sure she was related by blood. You might think she'd be glad to be among blood kin. But Fern said it was why she became moodier. That she must have asked herself why her own people would go to such lengths to keep her roots from her. Who were the ones who knew? She must have wondered if her real parents were dead. Or disgraced and disowned. Every reunion must have made her wonder. And search each face. Did she have relatives there? Did Fern exaggerate?

Janet the Planet agreed that Kim was moody. And I guess those questions about my family would have upset me. But would questions about her roots have made Kim hide? No.

And in fact, Kim had found a twin. And told no one. Why? And perhaps she'd been in love. At least she'd wanted to help Abner stop drinking. Or so he'd said, and somehow I'd believed him. She could be off hiding with him. But I believed Abner's fear for her. And where was Abner now?

So why had John Baylor told us that Kim was

running away from Abner? Did John believe it? Or was John even possibly the killer? But he'd been in his office when someone was following me. My trusty car phone had told me so.

Maybe he got his wife, Maureen, to follow me. But she seemed too goody-goody, always looking after sick relatives. And how about Kim's aunt, Ward's sister, Quicksand Sandra? But I'd checked via car phone, and Sandra was at home, smelling the manure, at the time I was followed. And she certainly seemed concerned about Kim.

Quicksand Sandra, Kim's adoptive aunt, said Kim's dreams showed she'd been abused. She was having nightmares. And yet Kim *did* seem like a happy kid. Except she played practical jokes. Was famous for it. Was that an outlet for hidden anger?

And why did Kim's newfound twin, Eileen, send off for stuff to read about false memory? Could the nature of memory — when it was real, when it was not real — be so important to Eileen that she died because of it?

And if the so-called Mark of Murder was just a ploy to find close relatives, why did Kim go to see the Cherokee woman about it? And why was the woman so sure Kim was basically okay, that she was going to grow? And who would benefit if Kim and her sister both died?

That last question was most pertinent. Only John Baylor, and probably the police, would know that. And they weren't telling.

Most important of all, where would a girl like Kim go and why? How far would her five hundred dollars in cash take her? When I'd talked to John Baylor, he claimed that Kim hadn't dipped into the bank account yet. I guess the police checked on that. So without much money, where could she be? We might help her if we knew that. I tossed and turned and got nowhere. I thought, *So, okay, I can't figure this out awake. I'll try sleep-think! At least, I won't toss around and maybe wake Ted.*

I carefully relaxed from the tip of my toes to the top of my head. Relaxed each part of me, even my fingers, one by one.

The next I knew, a dream woke me up. All I could remember was a joker from a deck of cards. The joker was laughing. He made me uncomfortable. Like he was laughing at me. Kim gambled? Was that it? If so, ten thousand dollars — even if she could get at it — might not go far. The clock with glowing numbers on the night table said 12:30. I drifted back to sleep. Perhaps the strange bed was making me restless. Or did I hear a noise of some sort? I woke up from another strange dream. A woman who looked like Kim was actually a Cherokee. She was weaving a basket, that's how I knew. The clock said 12:45. *Now, this is ridiculous,* I told myself. Waking up every fifteen minutes. Ted was sleeping peacefully. I reached out and touched him very gently so as not to wake him up. I made myself relax again.

The third time I woke up, the clock said 1:05. No dream this time. What woke me up? A noise? Maybe outside? I was thirsty. Maybe that was it. I got out of bed and headed for the bathroom for a drink of water. I tripped over my overnight bag. Damn. I stood still, scared I'd wake Ted. He continued to breathe evenly. And as I stood there, I realized I knew. I knew where Kim would be.

I knew the ten thousand dollars was the ultimate practical joke, a prank to throw people off. When Kim visited the Cherokee woman, she knew where she'd go. That's why she had the boxes in the car. They were supplies. Food. I bet she had a sleeping bag in the trunk of the car.

She'd gone to the cave where long ago she'd found the Indian arrowheads. She'd gone to meditate and find herself. Those boxes in her car were camping stuff. And when she heard about her sister being killed, if she did, she was afraid to come out of hiding. I was so awake I couldn't sleep, but I couldn't really do anything until morning, could I? If I called the police in the middle of the night, they would just think I was crazy. And of course I might be wrong about where Kim went.

Did I hear a creaking noise? I laughed. I remembered the "ghost." I was hearing the ghost! Or was it the house settling?

No point in getting back in bed. I felt wired, full of knowledge I couldn't act on yet. Or should we set out now, in the middle of the night? I went over and looked out the window. A garden far below was indistinct in the moonlight. Say, out in the hall was a little sitting alcove. With all these books by John Ehle handy, I bet there was a reading light. I could slip out and read. That would calm me down.

But I'd forgotten to bring a bathrobe. Never mind. I slipped on my dress and shoes; forget underwear. I could see the books on my bedside stand. I couldn't see the names, but I took several. I quietly opened the door. The hall lights were turned down low, but yes, there was a reading lamp. I settled down in a comfortable overstuffed chair and turned the light on. I opened *The Winter People*. What had I eaten that was salty? I was thirsty again.

I thought of the refrigerator with cold drinks in it. That's what I wanted. I would read my book with a cold drink in hand and briefly lose myself and forget my fear about Kim. Forget the tragedy of Cousin Gertrude, which was my fault in a way. Forget everything until the morning.

I put the book down on the couch beside me and set off down the narrow stairs to the second floor. The inn was deeply silent. Except the stairs creaking. But that was me, not a ghost. The next level down was dimly lit by the chandelier. Shadows in the corners. I could imagine seeing a ghost here. I turned under the arch to the room where the young man had said I'd find the refrigerator. A small room with an almost square, white refrigerator and an ice machine.

Nothing else. I opened the refrigerator door and reached in for a Pepsi.

That's when I felt something cold poke me in the back, and a voice hissed, "Don't make a sound or I'll shoot you. Keep your eyes forward."

Chapter

31

Immediately Afterward

"Now, walk out of here and to the right, eyes front," the voice whispered. "We're going down the back stairs. They're new, and they don't creak."

I don't argue with guns. So this must be the killer. Someone I hadn't heard whisper — the voice was not immediately familiar. Someone who knew I was at Richmond Hill that night — but nobody did.

I walked along the dimly lit corridor to the back stairs as slowly as I dared. I prayed someone might hear a noise, peek out a door, and call the police. Unlikely.

"Hurry up," the voice whispered. It was still hard to tell whose.

I did not hurry up. I wanted to make the person speak again.

The gun prodded my back. "Get going!"

We'd come to the back stairs. I went faster. I didn't want to be pushed down the stairs. If this voice was Mary Mary-Sue's, I'd recognize it, even disguised, wouldn't I? Would I recognize Ward's? I thought so.

My stomach turned over sharply. Tonight! Tonight was their wedding anniversary! The same day as ours. I almost stumbled but caught myself. Did they come to celebrate at Richmond Hill? And see Ted and me? Was one of them the killer — who had watched for a chance?

No, I didn't believe it. At least not Mary Mary-Sue. And did Ward have enough ambition to kill?

This couldn't be John Baylor with a gun in my back, could it? Even his whisper would be pompous. Could it be Maureen? But no, she had a broad southern accent. And I'd certainly know Fern, wouldn't I? Maybe Cousin Elvira had gone berserk. I wasn't sure I'd know her whisper. Could it be Eileen's father? But why?

At the bottom of the stairs, the voice whispered, "That way to the porch."

Of course. Whoever this was must have been having dinner on the porch when Ted and I came in! I'd seen the motion of somebody leaving without seeing clearly enough to recognize them. I almost groaned out loud. I hadn't really been watching my back, had I? It seemed such a long shot that the killer would have been having dinner on the porch of Richmond Hill at nine o'clock at night and leaving just as we arrived. So add something to the description — the killer was an opportunist. He took his chances as they came up. He played it by ear. And to come to this place at this hour, he must feel some kind of pressure, some reason to hurry. Or else he was crazy or more likely both. Or she. I couldn't rule that out.

We crossed a hallway, which must lead into the front room near the reception desk. I prayed someone would hear us. The killer pushed the gun extra hard and hurried me through toward the outside porch.

He needed to act fast. Why? Oh, Lord. He'd heard about the diary. I should have known. Janet just had to tell somebody. She couldn't keep it bottled up inside. The killer knew. Why on earth hadn't Janet told her mother? Get the need to tell out of her system that way? Or maybe her mother was the killer. That was too far-fetched. But who?

My mind raced. The killer must not know what was in that diary — how to get to Kim. Just that I knew where Kim might be. Or why kidnap me? So Janet talked to the killer after she told me the places where Kim might hide. Which meant after 8:45 or so. But this was all so complicated. Almost impossible. Maybe there was some entirely different explanation for the gun in my back.

The light was dim on the enclosed porch where the gun pushed me. But dimly, I could see a reflection of the person behind me in a glass window. I must be seeing wrong. I saw a squarish head. Above a black shirt and pants, the body almost disappeared. But this was bizarre. The person had a paper bag over the head, with eyes and mouth cut out, like a Halloween mask. I couldn't even tell whether it was a man or a woman.

We must be passing the very table where whoever it was had eaten dinner. I pictured a paper-bag head shoveling in food. I almost laughed. No time for hysteria.

On the way out the killer would have to use one hand to open the door at the end of the enclosed dining porch. Maybe I could catch him off balance. Hit the gun from the other hand. But he merely told me to push the door open. It was taped so the door had not latched.

But if some person having dinner at Richmond Hill, who therefore knew where I was, learned in some unlikely way that Janet had read me the diary, why didn't that person go after Janet? Because she was safe in the bosom of her family? Because that person was someone close to Janet? We threaded our way along the outside porch in back of the upright rockers, past the buggy in the porte cochere.

I wished Ted would wake up and notice I was gone, but he was a sound sleeper. We passed our car, and there, right next to it, my captor stopped next to a dark station wagon. The gun stayed firmly in my back. "Open the back door of the car," the killer said. "Hand me that rope on the seat." I opened the door and leaned inside, and as I did I managed to worm my foot out of one shoe and give it a light little kick away from the car. At least someone might know later that I'd been carried off in a car. Or at least from the place where cars were parked.

Now, I thought, *he'll have to use one hand to tie me up. That will give me an advantage.* But maybe it was a she. Did the figure in the moonlight seem more rounded than a man? I still couldn't be sure.

"Put your hands in the loop," I was told, and sure enough, at the end of the rope was a loop with what must be a slipknot. "Hurry up."

I slipped my hands in the loop — together, palm to palm, as if I were praying. And of course, in my head I was praying like crazy to get away. My captor kept the gun firmly in my back but pulled the knot tight and then circled the rope around me. My captor had only one free hand, but I had none. The hand that bound me was large. Could have been a woman's or a man's. I suspected now that it was a woman, but definitely not anybody whose hands I could remember.

In the bright moonlight a ring flashed. I'd seen that ring. I couldn't think where. Definitely a woman's ring.

Now that my arms were bound to my body like a chicken trussed to roast, she made me lie down on the floor in the back of the car, and she bound my feet together. I should have fought sooner. On the other hand, if I had, I might be dead. "If you should yell," she whispered, "you know I can just lean back and shoot you."

Yes, I did. So I lay and racked my brain. Where had I seen the ring? And somewhere in the back of my mind the word "anniversary" began to blink like a neon light. There was something I needed to remember about Mary Mary-Sue's anniversary. Something more than that it was the same day as mine.

Yes, something she had told me. Like a lightning bolt, the answer hit me. I knew who my captor was. I wasn't sure how that could help me, but it cheered me up. If I'd figured that out, maybe I could come up with what to do next. But I'd better do it quick, while I was still alive.

Chapter

32

Saturday, September 2

The car floor was cramped, and with my hands and feet tied, I couldn't move into a comfortable position. The ropes cut. But at least I was alive. I could feel the motion of the car but see nothing except the roof and occasional tree branches and streetlight glow as I looked up at the car windows.

The woman in the front seat had an anniversary the same day Mary Mary-Sue did, which meant the same date I did. I saw her suddenly on Mary Mary-Sue's picture collage, with Mary Mary-Sue hugging the woman in her wedding gown. Pointed out to me because that was the day Mary Mary-Sue first knew she could never have a child, first knew on her own wedding anniversary. Because she and Sandra were married on the same date, five years apart.

That's why Quicksand Sandra and her husband had been leaving Richmond Hill just as Ted and I were arriving. She heard us or caught a glimpse of us, but that still didn't explain how she knew about the diary. Someone must have called her up. Called her at Richmond Hill? Good grief, I'd heard the phone ring! Someone had known exactly where to find Quicksand Sandra.

"Now," she said, no longer bothering to whisper, "I know the three places Kim is most likely to be hiding. The three she listed in her diary. Some people might think she'd never revert to childhood like that, but I knew her well, and that stupid girl would! And you know, too. What do you think is the most likely place for her to be?"

Her dry voice made me certain. The woman in the front seat was definitely Ward's sister, Sandra. But why? What motive did she have?

I started to say I didn't think Kim was in any of those hiding places, even though I had intended to look. Would that throw this woman off? But if she agreed, she'd then feel free to shoot me as no more use to her. "I'd bet she's in the cave in Pisgah National Forest," I said, not adding the one near my cousin with the warts on his nose. Actually, I thought Kim was least likely to be at that cave. If we had to look in several places, maybe someone would find us before it was too late. I wished I could see Quicksand Sandra's face, could get some clue of

313

a possible tack to take to stay alive.

"I don't think Kim is there, Peaches," she said coldly. "Tourists sometimes go there. My informant mentioned that. I think you're lying to throw me off. I'm sure you would love to take me on a goose chase, but I'm not that naive. Try again. And speak louder."

Informant? Yes, there had to be one. What friend or relative had Janet told? And why would this person tell Quicksand Sandra? Tell her quickly, so that she could tape the porch-door open as she left Richmond Hill after dinner in order to get back in.

"I really don't know where Kim would be," I said, hoping Sandra wouldn't dispatch me in a rage.

Fortunately or unfortunately, this woman was smart as a whip. Murderous perhaps, but smart. "Kim was interested in Indians, wasn't she? Georgianna at the library told me that. And Kim had found some Indian arrowheads in the Madison County cave. I bet she's there. I know the general area where that is, but not how to get there. You're going to tell me that."

"I sort of half know how to get there," I said. That was true. I needed the written directions to be sure.

"You better know exactly," she snapped, "and if you don't tell me, I'll have to shoot you, and maybe I'll go back and shoot your husband so he won't guide the police to that girl before I get to her. Oh, I could find out

314

how to get there with no trouble in the morning, but the morning may be too late."

If Sandra knew the first part of the way to get there, I might be able to figure out the last. I get places by being lucky and a good guesser, more than by remembering how. Also, I ask. But you can't do that in the wee hours of the morning. But did I want to find the way? I wanted to stay alive. I prayed Kim wasn't in that cave.

We drove down a long, fairly straight road with some traffic. I saw car lights in flashes, brightening our windows. My wrists and ankles hurt. Sandra wouldn't care.

I tried to call up the directions to the cave in my mind. After an extremely winding road — the name escaped me — we should turn left onto a dirt road next to a big barn with a white-water rafting sign on it. Or was the turn right? I didn't know. Then, after that turn, whichever way, a driveway angled sharply off the road on the left (I hoped), and when it seemed to end at an old deserted cabin, the time had come to turn the car sharp left again and go up an old trail road by a stream. The trail passed the cave.

And who beside me did Janet Planet tell about the cave? Someone she trusted. Someone who cared about Kim. Lucy Baylor? I saw the picture of the three of them in Kim's room. Kim and Janet and Lucy, laughing together a few years back. Three happy-looking kids. My intuition said Lucy. Janet would trust Lucy never to tell. I would myself. Lucy cared about Kim and wasn't too trusting of anyone else. Not even her parents. What did she tell me? "My mother listens on the phone." Good Lord. Maybe her mother had listened tonight. And maybe Lucy didn't know her mother was home. Or was so fascinated with the news that she forgot about her mother.

But why would Lucy's mother call and tell Quicksand Sandra? They'd been friends when they were young. Were they close again?

If Maureen heard about that diary, why didn't she tell her husband, John, instead of Quicksand Sandra? Maybe she did! And if John Baylor wasn't the killer's accomplice and if his wife, Maureen, told him about this case, maybe he'd set out for this place in the middle of the night, too. Maybe he'd save me. Yeah, and Santa Claus was real.

The car began to turn this way and that. There were no more street lights, only tree limbs against the full moon. We were on the winding road, getting close.

I'd figured John was not the killer. Because I thought it was the killer who had followed us back from visiting Anna Littledeer, but I'd called John on my car phone then and reached him at the office. I'd also reached Sandra, who definitely seemed to have lethal intentions. Did she have an assistant? Was there a conspiracy?

This was all too complicated. Still, I could verify some things.

"Today is your anniversary, and it's my anniversary, too," I said loudly, so Sandra could hear over the seat between us. "You had dinner at Richmond Hill just like we did, didn't you? Very elegant," I said a little bitterly. The elegance would not help me now.

No answer from the front seat. "You were at Richmond Hill," I repeated. "We were late. And you were leaving as we came in." Talk about lousy, rotten luck.

Sandra laughed a bitter laugh. At last I had gotten a rise. "Thirty years with a loser," she said. "A loser who takes me out to a place where he can trade lettuce and cabbage for dinner. An amateur farmer. Well, I didn't deserve to be a loser myself. While that girl Kim was going to have everything."

What? What was the connection? Why was Kim going to have everything? I was confused.

Like a flash from left field, the false-memory thing lit up my mind and came thunderingly clear. This woman hated Kim. This woman hated Kim so much she had wanted to destroy her mind. To fill it with nightmares, with terrible memories.

I should have kept my mouth shut, but I was electrified.

"You were Kim's therapist," I said. I should have said "fake therapist." "You never sent her to anyone else. You deliberately played on her nightmares. You knew about the ways in which suggestion could fake vivid memories, terrible memories. You knew that people could do that by mistake. So you did it on purpose! And her memories scared her, so she kept them secret."

"Kim was a fool," she said. "I could make her believe almost anything."

My God, she must be crazy. Where was the borderline between obsessive hate and sheer madness? She must have crossed it. I was in the car with a madwoman.

"All right," she said, "we've reached the big barn on Hill Road. I can read the white-water rafting sign on the side of the barn in the moonlight. I know the place is somewhere around here, but I don't know where. Which way do we turn now?"

"I could tell better," I said, "if I could see." I kept my voice calm. It wouldn't help if she killed me. "We turn into a dirt road." I had a feeling that was so. I had used a memory device for the directions, but it was a pencil and a piece of paper now back on the bedside table at Richmond Hill.

I felt the car turn and then begin to bump slightly. So we must be on dirt. I had guessed right about that. My mind was still racing. Eileen had suspected that Kim's memories were wrong. Was that it? And wanted to show Kim how that could be?

"Now which way?" Sandra demanded.

"Look for a very sharp turn into a driveway on the . . ." I hesitated.

"Speak up," Sandra said sharply. Pressure

doesn't help. I made a blind guess. "On the right."

We drove along for quite a way, and the road got bumpier and bumpier. Must be badly rutted. No lights reflected off the car windows here. No sounds except a faraway dog barking. Please let Kim be far away.

"You're deliberately taking me the wrong way." Sandra's voice was raised in fury.

"No," I gasped. "I'm just no good at getting places. If it wasn't on the right that we were supposed to turn, then it was left." That followed!

"You are an idiot," she sneered. But she must have found a driveway where she could turn the car around, and soon we were heading back, too fast for the bumps. She was probably desperate to find the place before Ted woke up and began to guess where I might be. I hoped. Please let him have nightmares, wake up, and call the police. Not likely.

A fair way back down the road, Sandra turned sharply left. She must have found the drive. My heart sank. We must be almost to the cave.

"This can't be the way," she said. "It's ending at some shack. Damn it, you're no good to me at all." She stopped the car with a jolt, turned sharply, and I half expected her to shoot.

"No!" I cried out. "This is the way. There's a wood-road. It must be overgrown. It starts near the shed."

I heard her door slam as she got out of the car to look. The ropes were cutting into my hands and feet. They were knotted so tightly that wiggling didn't loosen them.

She got back in the car and headed up a rough track with huge bumps, as if we were going over fallen branches. Finally we stopped and to our right I could see a high bluff, with one tall pine tree on top against the sky and a bright star near the tip. This must be the place. My heart lurched. *Please hide, Kim, if you're here,* I said inside my head. Then I prayed. *Please wake up Ted and call the police. Since I've been shot at, so to speak, they'll believe I've been kidnapped. They will. They will! Please God, make them believe it. Make them come quickly.*

Sandra stopped, got out, and opened the door by my head. I could hear a creek burbling. She double-checked the rope around my arms, then went around the car, opened the other door, and untied my feet. They were numb, and I wiggled them to get the circulation back. I managed to stand up by the car. The creek was downhill from us. Water for anyone who hid in the cave.

"I probably won't need you now," Sandra said. "So if you let out one peep, I'll shoot you in the head." She was taking me in the cave to kill me there and hide my body. I understood that now. Naturally she didn't trust me to be silent. She found a scarf on the backseat and stuffed it in my mouth. It was wooly and dry, and I almost gagged.

From the car's backseat she took another rope with a noose at the end. Not like the first rope

— this one looked like a clothesline. Yes, she'd done this on the spur of the moment. Improvised.

"Walk in front of me," she ordered and poked the gun in my back. I was so cold with fear I almost couldn't walk. I had a shoe on one foot but not on the other, which didn't help at all. But the gun inspired me.

The ground was uneven, but the moon was bright. Even without Sandra's flashlight, I could see. We walked toward a black hole in the side of the cliff. As we came close, the cliff obscured the moonlight. The beam of Sandra's flashlight made a stab in the darkness. Not toward the ground, but toward the back of the cave.

I had to go forward by feel. The ground was loose and slippery.

"Hurry up," Sandra whispered crossly. How far inside would she figure I needed to be before she could hide my body safely? But she wouldn't shoot till she found Kim, or would she?

I managed to get my bound hands up to my face. She must be paying more attention to the cave than to me. I got a finger hooked through the scarf in my mouth and pulled. The scarf came out and fell at my feet. If she put it back, it would be gritty.

She poked me with the gun. "Keep going." Her voice echoed in the cave. Bits of mica glimmered in her moving flashlight beam.

I walked a little way farther in before I spoke.

"If you kill me here, and then someone admits to telling you about this place and my dead body is found here, that will make a connection with you," I said quickly. I tried to sound threatening. My feet slipped on the slanting floor of the cave, but I managed not to fall. Having one foot unshod actually helped me grip.

Sandra hit me on the back of my head, furious that I'd ungagged myself, no doubt. "Shut up," she said. "I can kill you here and take your body somewhere else." I was slightly dizzy. At least carrying my body would be more work for her.

The flashlight revealed a roundish room with the floor sloping up and two dark entrances to something more beyond. It was cool, almost chilly as we went deeper into the hillside. No trash to suggest Kim was in this cave. I prayed she wasn't. I prayed that if Sandra went through one of the openings ahead, Kim would be through the other or not here at all.

But when Sandra poked me through the opening, it became clear that both openings led to the same room. And there were boxes, cans, a sleeping bag on the floor. Finally the flashlight revealed Kim, standing against the rocky cave wall. She wore jeans and a wrinkled shirt, and her hair was disheveled. She must have woken up when she heard our footsteps. Her eyes were wide with fear. Behind the flashlight we'd be indistinct, an unknown menace.

"Who's there?" Kim demanded as if we were trespassing.

"Go stand by Kim," Sandra said to me. "And I want you both to understand that, if either of you tries to bolt, one of you will be shot and killed, possibly both."

"Aunt Sandra!" Kim gasped. "But what . . . ? But why . . . ? You have a gun!" A wave of fear rocked her slight body, and something in her hand flashed as she moved it behind her.

"Damned right! And I'm a good shot," Sandra said. "My father used to take me hunting. Before he dumped me. Before he got his new family, instead of us."

"Us." That would be Sandra and Ward. What had Pop said about Ward? I wracked my brain. Something related to cannibal tadpoles. Something about how he hated the world because his father disinherited him. That same ugliness was plainly in Sandra.

I went and stood close to Kim. She was cold and trembling but tin-soldier straight. I couldn't hug her with my hands bound, but I said, "Hold on."

"Be quiet," Sandra commanded. She was carrying the clothesline with the slipknot loop at the end in her left hand, the gun in the right. "Hold out your hands," she said to Kim. She tightened the slipknot over Kim's hands, wound the rope round and round her, then managed to make a knot with one hand. "Now turn around," she said and pulled a kitchen knife out of Kim's back jeans pocket. Kim hadn't been able to hide it properly. I was sick with disappointment to see us lose this un-expected chance.

"Both of you go out in front of me," Sandra barked.

The footing was difficult. Several times I slipped and caught myself, and once I fell on the slanting floor. I was terrified Sandra would shoot, but she merely said, "Don't be a clown." She let me struggle back to my feet and go on. A skinned knee hurt, but I was alive. Kim moved in silence, but she was more surefooted than I. She was barefoot, and by now she probably knew every inch of this cave. I prayed there'd be some way for us to trick Sandra. What did Fern say? There was contradiction in Kim. She liked to plan ahead, but she took chances.

We came out into the bright night, and Sandra herded us toward the car. I didn't dare try to bolt because if she missed me, she'd shoot Kim. "You're the one, aren't you?" Kim said to Sandra. "You killed Eileen. You killed my sister. For no good reason."

I heard a crack like a whip. It was Sandra's hand against Kim's cheek, a slap so hard Kim's head snapped back. Kim seemed to go into shock.

At the car Sandra undid Kim's hands. "You do exactly what I say, or you'll be dead, too," she said. "You lie down in the back," she ordered me, pointing at the car. "Now you tie her feet and do it good," she ordered Kim.

And Kim did it, though her hands were

shaking so, she had trouble tying knots. Sandra pushed me onto the car floor. She made Kim lie on the backseat and tied her hands first, then her feet. Then she was able to put her gun in her pocket and inspect our bonds and tighten them. A very methodical lady.

I didn't yell for help. Neither did Kim. Do not antagonize a madwoman.

It was still dark, but light was beginning to streak the sky as Sandra drove out to the road and turned back the way we'd come.

I listened desperately for the sound of a car because we had at least a small chance someone would find us here. Where would Quicksand Sandra take us next? To a place where our bodies would not be found. I understood that.

Chapter

33

Half an Hour Later

I knew, without being able to see much, that Sandra was taking back roads. I could tell by how curvy the roads were and how up and down the hills. The sky was now dark gray-blue. The moon had vanished. Probably about five o'clock, I told myself. I'd left my watch somewhere. Back at Richmond Hill.

With an effort I managed to sit up, however awkwardly, and work at the knots that held Kim's hands. Sandra had tied my hands in front of me, by the grace of God. Kim's hands were tied behind her back. Her back was toward me. Still, my work with the knots was slow because I could hardly move my own bound hands.

When I couldn't stand my awkward crouch anymore, I lay back and tried to talk to Sandra in the front seat. I threw out thoughts to see if she'd react.

"Maureen Baylor told you about Kim's diary, didn't she?" No answer. "Because she overheard Janet tell Lucy. What made her tell you?" No answer. I needed to say something that would make her annoyed enough to respond, but not annoyed enough to be crazy. "It was blackmail, wasn't it? You were blackmailing Lucy's mother."

"She owed me a debt," Sandra said.

Blackmail! My crazy guess was right. But Maureen was so goody-goody! And if Sandra was admitting blackmail, certainly she intended to kill us quick. Awkwardly, I managed to sit up again and go back to work on Kim's bonds. Her face was pressed into the backseat, muffling a frightened sob.

"Maureen is a fool," Sandra said. "And John Baylor is a prig. If he knew that Maureen was pregnant when he married her — if he knew that Lucy was another man's child — he'd divorce Maureen first thing. I know about Lucy because when Maureen got knocked up, she was such a fool that she told me."

"You were good friends," I said, trying not to sound contemptuous.

Kim whispered, "What a friend!" She clenched her hands. She was mad. In my experience mad is safer than scared stiff.

"Maureen seems so sweet and helpful, loving all her relatives. Well, let me tell you, she's scared silly she'll lose that big, fancy house and all her antiques. She'll do anything it takes to keep her goodies."

"So you made her shadow us," I said. "In case we managed to find Kim's trail. Because you had to get to Kim first. And everyone assumed Maureen was nursing the sick, as usual. But," I guessed, "she wouldn't kill people for you. You had to do that." And of course Maureen must have a car phone just as I did. She could alert Sandra to take action. Modern technology!

"Maureen's too lily-livered to kill." Sandra's voice vibrated with anger.

At the word "kill," Kim began to tremble again. She was so young to face death! The morning light had grown; I could see how slender Kim was. No grown-up curves yet. But there was steel in her, too. I could feel it.

"So Maureen would eavesdrop on Lucy and spy on her husband!"

"I demanded it!" Sandra spit that out.

The car turned sharply, and I guessed this was a driveway. Sandra drove into something like a garage — I could see the rough-finished side walls. The car came to a stop. Sandra got out and opened the back car door. Alas, with all my effort, I had hardly loosened Kim's bonds at all. Sandra inspected our wrists. It was light enough to see quite well by now. She noticed the slight loosening around Kim's wrists and bound the rope tighter.

Sandra went over to the side of the shed and took a knife off a shelf.

"You're going to kill us!" Kim cried out in terror. "You have to tell us why, Aunt Sandra? Why?"

But Sandra ignored her and merely cut the ropes off our feet. She pointed the gun at us. "March! And you hurry up," she said to Kim, who was moving as slowly as possible. "I don't have all day. Arthur will be awake soon."

We must be at their farm, I realized. In a drive-in building with boxes along one wall and a few shelves. Oh, yes, I remembered Arthur had some sort of a cooperative marketing scheme with other local organic farmers. On our left was a big metal door. Sandra opened it and waved the gun for us to go inside. If I tried to dive for the gun, she might shoot me or Kim or both of us. And if I screamed, she'd shoot. With hands bound, I wouldn't have much chance.

"Have fun," she said with a leer and waved with the hand that didn't hold the gun. Waved so that I saw her palm. I followed Fern's training. Even while I wracked my brains for a way to escape, I checked the lines in her hand.

I almost gasped. Her hand was marked like Eileen's, just as I'd seen it in the picture I took of her poor dead hands. Sandra had that same rare marking, which even Fern had seen only once.

Where I had two horizontal lines, heart line

and head line, and Kim had only one, the mark of difference, Eileen and Sandra had three lines across. Those lines had been clearly marked and balanced in Eileen's hand. In Sandra's hand they were uneven. They were ugly, which fit.

"Hurry up," Sandra commanded, pointing the gun at my head. We stepped into cold. This was a walk-in refrigerator. Large. Before I could decide what to do next, the door clanged shut and wrapped us in total darkness. Only the doorknob glowed. I heard an odd little click. Instinctively I grabbed the door handle and pushed. It was locked. Don't refrigerators have safety doors? Where had I read that? But I could guess what the click was. Sandra had locked the door from the outside, with a padlock maybe.

I touched Kim and said, "We're going to get out of here." She leaned against me, and I could feel the wetness of her tears.

"I can fight," she said. "But how can we get out? How?"

"We'll be ready in case she comes back," I told Kim firmly. "Then you scream and divert her, and I'll try to get the gun. But before we even scream for help, we have to get our hands untied."

Because Sandra might come back and kill us. Sandra, who must be related to Kim and Eileen by blood, not just as Kim's adoptive father's sister. How did that fit in? The odds against two unrelated hands having that rare mark must be tremendous. I did not say that. Not yet. Kim had enough to be depressed about.

"She's going to leave us here," Kim cried. "She's going to leave us here to freeze to death. What are we going to do?"

"We are not going to give up," I said firmly. "That will kill us. Turn around and let me work at your ropes." I reached out and felt for her shaking hands. "You've got to be still," I said. "Tell me about Eileen."

"Eileen was so great! And if she hadn't met me . . ."

"You don't know that," I said. "Because you don't know why Sandra wants to kill you and me. Or why she killed Eileen." In the dark it was hard to get anywhere with the knots, especially with my own hands tied.

"But I was so happy to find Eileen!" Kim cried.

"And when did you find her?" I must stay sharp, cold or not.

"Right after I cut my hair!" she said. "I cut it short during that hot spell at the end of July. Boy, I'd love some of that hot now! And then people began to tell me they'd seen me in places where I couldn't have been. And I thought: there's someone else like me. And I found her. I just bumped into her in Asheville one day. At the Old Europe Bakery, because we both loved sweets." Kim choked back a sob.

"You must be still," I said. "Undoing these knots may be a matter of life and death. And why didn't you tell your mother or even John Baylor about your sister? Or tell Fern? Or your father? Why keep this wonderful news a secret? Why?"

"Because something was wrong," Kim said. "Something bad. Or why did they keep it a secret from us? Even though I'd heard that I, at least, was adopted by relatives. Although my adoptive parents didn't seem to believe that. I was so confused." As she talked, my groping fingers pulled the top knot loose. Though Kim's hands were still thoroughly bound, the other knots would be easier. There would be longer rope ends to work with. Good!

"I was confused," Kim said, "because, you see, my aunt Sandra had been telling me I'd been abused as a little kid. I even began to kind of remember it, after she hypnotized me and helped me to . . . to 'remember' that my father did it. The whole thing seemed so real and terrible."

I went hot with anger and started to speak out, but I knew I mustn't interrupt.

"But I began not to trust Sandra. And I was right!" Ah, smart girl!

Then Kim became excited. She sat up straighter. "Maybe someone will go to that cave and find the things I wrote about Sandra." There was hope and fear in her voice. "And then they'll come look here."

She was clutching at slim hope. "What did you write?" I asked.

"In school we were reading *The Diary of Anne Frank*, and I thought that when you went off to a place when you were afraid, it would help to write down what happened and how you felt. So I took paper and I wrote about everything that scared me and how Aunt Sandra seemed to be trying to make me believe ugly things that maybe weren't true." She began to shake. "Why does she want to hurt me? My own aunt. No. Not my own."

"So you and Eileen were afraid." I tried to get back on that track.

"I was sure something was wrong, but who could I trust? And I wanted us to find out what was wrong before we told how we'd found each other. And Eileen agreed to that. In fact, at first, it was kind of fun. Having a secret together. And trying to find out things."

"All right," I said firmly, "Eileen was on your side, right? She wanted you to be okay."

"Oh, yes," Kim sobbed.

"She helped you find out that the line across your hand was not a mark of bad luck, right?"

"Yes, I told her how Fern's old book called it the Mark of Murder. I was scared it was bad luck. Eileen found the Cherokee woman who knew about the good meaning of that line. Eileen was smart. She even encouraged me to go off in the woods to think. If that was right for me."

The second knot came undone. I was encouraged. Maybe we'd outwit Quicksand Sandra yet.

"Why would Sandra want to kill Eileen or you or both? Do you have any idea?" I asked.

"I think it had to do with my father," Kim said. "But I don't know how." She was shaking less, even in this cold, concentrating on the why of Sandra.

"You mean she killed Eileen because of something to do with Ward?" That amazed me.

"No, my real father. Eileen found out who he was."

I caught my breath. She'd kept so much a secret. And maybe her intuition not to tell was right. "Who?" I demanded.

"The man in prison, Andrew Frank!" she cried. "And our mother is dead. It's so terrible. I found out Andrew Frank is our father the day our family had that reunion at your father's house. I was in the cave place, trying to think things out," she said in a parched voice, "all by myself."

I wished my hands were free to hug her. "When did Eileen find out? How did you hear?"

"Not all at once," Kim said, and I could feel her straining to be clear, to explain it right. "You see, Eileen's adoptive mother got a letter from a man who said he had married her sister. Eileen's mom hadn't heard from the sister in years. The man's name was Andrew Frank. Eileen told me about that because it was so interesting and sad — but we didn't know it had anything to do with us. Andrew Frank was in prison in California for killing his wife."

Yes, I knew that. But some other germ of knowledge at the back of my mind stirred. I knew it was important, but I couldn't reach it. The blackness in my mind stayed as total as the blackness all around us.

"Eileen's father told me about the brother-in-law," I said.

"Andrew Frank wrote that he was innocent," Kim continued, "and that someone else had confessed to the murder! And Eileen had been so excited because she wanted to be a lawyer and she thought maybe she could help with figuring out how to set him free. Because someone else confessing isn't enough. There are things to work out. That first letter came just before I went off to think. And like I say, we didn't know that it affected us."

Would they have been safer if they knew?

"So when another letter came from the prison," she said, "and Eileen's adoptive father was off at work, Eileen figured he wouldn't mind if she opened it. And the letter swore George Stackhouse to secrecy first, then Andrew Frank said he had twin daughters somewhere but he didn't know where. His wife's father had worked out the adoption of the twins with relatives. And this Andrew Frank . . . must have been our real father, don't you think? I mean, we were twins and Eileen's adoptive mother was his wife's sister, and that's certainly a relative!"

What a shock for Eileen to read that letter!

"But this Andrew Frank in prison said he didn't even want to look for the twins until he'd cleared his name. He didn't want us to be tainted with the idea that our father killed our mother. That he was just going to write this one letter and then not mention it again until his name was clear. He cared that much about us!" Kim was shaking again. I almost gave up on the knots. I mustn't.

"Eileen didn't leave the letter she found for her adoptive father," Kim went on, "because she figured it was about her. It was her business — our business."

"And how did Eileen tell you about it?" I asked. "Because by then you were off in the cave, right?"

"There was this little store down the road from the cave place, with milk and bread and canned things, and a pay phone and a news-paper stand outside. And I went there after dark. And I called Eileen, and she told me. And then Eileen said to call her again and we'd get together and she'd show me the letter. But she didn't know how to get to where I was. I didn't tell anybody, not even her. The next day there were a lot of people at the store, so I waited an-other day, until the coast was clear. And then there was this newspaper in the rack in front of the store. I saw the picture and the headline. And Eileen was dead." Kim let out a sob. "And I was scared."

"You were right to be scared," I said. "But

how would all that make Sandra want to kill us?" I needed to know as much as I could about Sandra.

"I don't know," she said. "Except she had such a thing about proving to me that my real father had abused me — that he was a bad man. And then I found out he was maybe about to get out of prison. And Sandra must have killed Eileen. And Sandra is going to kill us." She began to sob again.

Outside the refrigerator I heard a noise. Someone moving around. I prayed it wasn't Sandra, coming before we were loose. But the footsteps went away. Maybe I should have screamed. I shuddered to think we could have missed a friend.

"I'd heard maybe I was related to my mother, I mean Mary Mary-Sue, and now I guess I'm not," Kim said. "I fight with my mother but I love her."

Once again that germ of an idea stirred in my mind. From something Kim had said? But what? "Listen," I said, "the mark of difference makes me think you are related to us. I want you to be, and you will be in our hearts, no matter what."

As I said that, the last stubborn knot holding Kim's hands broke loose.

"Thank God," I said. "Now undo my hands, and we'll be in business." I was numb with cold, as if my hands were shot with Novocaine. She must be numb, too, but she began to work on my knots. Much easier with two hands loose.

I thought of the relatives rhyme and recited it to Kim. I went over it again, beginning with the part about the children of Jeeter Jones, Mary Mary-Sue's great-grandfather.

Son Bill, the pill, vamoosed to Texas.
Slender Brenda had no kids to vex us.
Linc the drink-er, born in 1898,
Found whiskey and beer were his fate.
But Smallpox Joe, born in 1899,
Preached like an angel and turned out fine.

Smallpox Joe and his wife, Mary-Sue,
Had Joe Junior in 1922.
Joe was pa to Mary Mary-Sue,
Who adopted Kim, who vanished into the
blue.

Smallpox's brother Linc the Drinker,
Produced Saint George who liked to tinker.
George begat Hal, who died full of beer,
Also John C., who did disappear.

I thought about the line about Bill, who vamoosed to Texas. "Your mother came from Texas to begin with," I said. "That could give a connection through Bill, but he disappeared back at the turn of the century."

Some thought went right on trying to force its way into my mind. Some association was trying to goose my Swiss-cheese memory with the holes in it. I went back to the poem, to the line about John C., who disappeared. Wasn't Mary Mary-Sue from the same generation as John C.? Yes, he was the right age to be Kim's father.

Hey! The thing tickling my mind was *The Diary of Anne Frank.* Kim said she'd read it. So? Lots of kids did. The story had made me cry when I was younger. But why did it come back to me now?

I found myself thinking about a crossword puzzle. What? When I might freeze or be shot if Sandra came back? The things that pop into my mind are as amazing as the things that don't.

I saw Ted doing a crossword puzzle just the Sunday before. And he said, "I need a famous diary writer. Samuel Pepys doesn't fit." And suddenly it came to me with a crash. The seed of knowledge bloomed. John C. was the right age to be Kim's father but with the wrong name. He was an oddball, fascinated with diaries. He'd made Georgianna send off for Samuel Pepys. He'd said he had resigned from our family. Made a big thing of it. So he took a new name related to the last diary anyone would ever suspect, Anne Frank's. Andrew Frank. Hey, was I crazy, or did that puzzle piece fit?

The idea was so wild that I didn't say it. Not yet. And besides I was diverted. I felt the rope around my wrists come loose. Kim was fast. Time to act fast.

"Let's do what Eileen would want us to do," I said. "Let's outwit Quicksand Sandra. Let's go over every inch of this room. We need to know if there is anything in here we can use as a weapon, or maybe to pry open the door. You crawl and feel to the left, and I'll go to the right around the edge of the room."

In the brief moment when the door had been open, I'd noticed that the center of this space was bare. I had a feeling I'd seen some shelves or some such to the right. I got down on my knees and began to search along the edge. Oh, how lovely to have hands loose, however numb. The tile floor was icy against my knees. I shivered even more in my thin dress. I came to an obstruction, the leg of something. Yes, there were wooden shelves. I felt along the lowest shelf. Bottles of something. Probably fruit juice, by the shape — short and squat. Yes, I could hit Sandra over the head with a bottle if I had to. On the second shelf I touched large crocks, but they were empty. And on the third shelf was only a basket of what felt and smelled like apples. Early apples. The fourth shelf was empty, I thought. But then, over in the back corner, I felt something. Wow! A pair of kitchen shears. I felt the points. Not sharp enough to stab Sandra, but we could use them some way. I put them in my pocket.

And still my mind was worrying at the problem of Sandra. She must be related to Kim. That unusual triple line in Eileen's hand and in Sandra's must prove it. And their relationship must be part of the reason Sandra wanted to kill the twins. And somehow, in some way, I bet this had to do with money. Not that I could see how yet. But people kill for love or hate or money.

I had gone only a little way beyond the shelves when I met Kim. Which is to say, we bumped into each other. She was icy, too. Quietly, I told Kim about the shelves, the bottles, and the scissors. I didn't tell her about my speculation yet. I could be dead wrong.

She'd found a box of lettuce and two burlap sacks. We put the sacks around our shivering shoulders.

I heard a car drive off. Sandra? Or maybe her husband, Arthur? With him gone, Sandra might feel freer to kill us and bury us somewhere. I felt my way to the bottles of juice and clutched one, ready to bean Sandra if she opened the door. The bottle was so cold, it almost stuck to my fingers. Could the cold alone kill us? How fast?

I felt around the door. No crack where the scissors could pry. So what could we do?

"We need to huddle together," I told Kim. I remembered an old lady I knew who had lived through a blizzard with no heat for three days by staying under a quilt curled up with a cat. We had no quilt, only two burlap bags. I put my arms around Kim. She felt so young and scared.

"Do you know how to tap out an SOS?" I asked. Perhaps you had to be my age to have learned that in Scouts. I told her how to do three quick taps, then three slow taps, then three quick taps for the international distress signal.

341

I handed her the scissors. "You take the first turn," I said. "If we keep tapping, anybody who comes near this place will hear us and know that dots and dashes aren't natural noises for a walk-in fridge to make."

Metal on metal made good loud noise. I prayed like crazy for someone to come near enough to hear it.

We took turns tapping. I strained my ears. No sound of life except ours. Ted should be awake by now, but Sandra was the last person he was likely to connect with my disappearance. The only clue he'd have was one shoe in the parking lot. He might check out the cave. He'd see that Kim had been there. So maybe all the members of the family would be questioned. That was just barely possible, so Sandra wouldn't dare keep us here too long, would she? Maybe even now she was out digging our graves in the woods.

Then there was the sound of a car driving up.

My hand was growing tired, but I kept tapping. "Now, remember," I told Kim, "if you are our blood relative — a member of our family — you inherit not giving up. You inherit being so damned determined that nobody ought to try to get the best of you if he's in his right mind."

My hand ached from tapping. "It's your turn," I said to Kim. She took the scissors and began SOS, SOS.

And then, through the taps, I thought I heard footsteps. I reached out and held her hand silent. Yes, definitely footsteps. "Okay, keep tapping," I said and went to get two bottles of the juice that could be a weapon. "Now, remember," I whispered, "if it's Sandra, you stand flat against the wall so you're hard to see and then scream and divert her, and I'll hit her over the head." That wouldn't be easy. Maybe I should throw the juice at her and hit her in the solar plexus. Then grab her gun arm while she was off balance.

The light suddenly went on, and the door began to open. Kim flattened against the wall. I raised the juice bottle. But this wasn't Sandra.

"Good Lord," said Ward. "What on earth are you doing here, Peaches? Are you all right? Kim! Thank God I found you!"

He looked from one of us to the other. He did not look dangerous. Kim started forward and then hesitated. I lowered the juice and started toward the door. That was a mistake.

Chapter

34

Immediately Afterward

A voice behind him said, "Get out of the way, Ward! I'm looking out for our interests here." It was his sister, Sandra, holding the gun again. Like it had grown attached to the end of her arm. She wore overalls, an old plaid shirt, and boots like a good farm wife. Or maybe like somebody who was looking forward to a difficult burying job. Behind her a rake and shovel hung on the wall. Her brown eyes glittered. "We'll make our own luck. I wish our father were here to see this," she crowed, "and know that he could disown us, could do everything for his other children, and even grandchildren, but we'll come out on top! Because I do know how to seize the moment."

His other children? My head whirled. What a tangle! Eileen and Kim's mother was a kid from the Texas family of Sandra's father, Ward's reckless father. From his second nesting, so to speak.

Kim froze with her back to the wall inside the walk-in door. Good. The least exposed position. I froze because Ward wasn't moving, and I was half behind him. Besides, I needed a moment to think what to do next.

What had Pop said about Ward? That if he were a tadpole, he would eat his father? No. A salamander. Pop said Ward was angry because his father left his mother and never saw his mountain kids again. Disowned them. And now Ward stood rigid in his plaid shirt and jeans as he listened to his sister's rage. So was Ward our friend or not?

"Sandra," Ward said in that drawl of his, "don't do anything that will get us in trouble." Oh, what an optimist! It was too late for Sandra to be not guilty. She'd as good as told us she'd killed Eileen.

"Ward," she said like a schoolteacher, "you're a fool. We're the children of a millionaire — old Ward T. Jenkins, known as Mr. Got-Rocks. He may have been a moralistic old coot, but he still struck oil in his Texas farm and got filthy rich. Which he didn't deserve. And he left all that money to those two girls when his wife dies. And she's in a nursing home right now. We deserve that money. We have a right." Good grief! So this *was* over money. As well as anger. Anger with deep roots.

"I don't care about money!" Kim cried. "I just want to be alive!"

Sandra pinned Kim with her eyes. "Shut up."

"How do you know how our father left his money?" Ward asked, ignoring Kim. "How do you know how much?"

For a moment I'd hoped Ward might help us, that he might be fond enough of Kim, having helped raise her. But now he seemed interested in how much he could get.

"I have a captive spy!" Sandra was saying. "Maureen Baylor, who used to work in John Baylor's office. She still has a key. She knows the combination to the safe. John Baylor made out our father's will. He knows about the wife in the nursing home — pays for her care since our father died. Maureen says we won't get a cent. Because our mother cheated on our saintly father. Because they hated each other." Sandra's eyes pulsed with fury. "That's not fair. It's not our fault."

Ward stayed cool. He seemed almost bemused. Neither good luck nor bad raised his hackles. I wanted to scream, *You won't get away with this!* But I knew my best bet was to be as invisible as possible until I made a move.

"And if both kids died, all the money would come to us?" Ward asked. He fingered his ear as if he might have heard wrong.

"We could sue for it. And with the ones he left it to both gone, I think we'd win. At least our part." Her eyes flashed. "I've spent my life dreaming of this: of showing the old coot he couldn't disown us. I wish he were here now to watch!"

Ward rubbed the back of his neck as if he were thinking. "It might not be easy to hide two bodies," he said.

Kim cried out, "Daddy, don't let her kill me!"

But Sandra didn't seem to hear either one of them. "The kids' mother is dead: our sainted father's new daughter. After he left us. And he disinherited Alice Stackhouse, too, his other daughter, when she married a Cuban. That's what Maureen says. Her Cuban husband may be dead and replaced, but the will stands. We have a chance to get the old man's money, damn him." She shook. Her wedge of black bangs vibrated. Her hands clenched.

I thought: *She's obsessed. Trapped in rage. Blind to danger.* Or was she simply sure she had some way to get away with murder?

"Look, Sis," Ward drawled, "before you do anything, I want to show you something."

What on earth? He walked over to her nonchalantly, relaxed as always. He stood next to her, reached in his pocket, and appeared to pull out something. My eyes and Sandra's were both riveted on it. Was this the moment for me to act?

But before I could do anything, Ward had reached with lightning speed and grabbed the gun. Sandra was surprisingly strong. The gun wavered up and down in their two hands.

I should have grabbed the shovel, but right beside me was that bottle of juice. I grabbed the bottle, ran around, and hit Sandra over the head, hard. The gun went off as the bottle broke. Tomato juice ran down like blood. She fell to the floor, and Ward fell with her. The gun went off again. She lay still. He got up slowly and shook himself. He seemed dazed.

"Is she gone?" I asked. It pays to be sure. I knelt down on the dusty floor beside Sandra and felt her pulse. Nothing. "Yes," I said, "she's gone."

Ward said, "I'm sorry," as if Sandra could hear him. Or maybe he meant he was sorry she had terrorized us. Or both. He still seemed dazed. "She could be strange," he said in a choked voice. "She killed my puppy because it chewed her shoe." He shook his head in wonder. "But I couldn't believe . . . I couldn't believe she'd kill a person . . . or kidnap . . ."

My eyes began to sort out tomato juice and blood. Blood oozed from Sandra's neck. There was a hole beneath her chin. A bullet must have gone straight up under her chin into her head.

Ward was staring at her, too. "She'd been acting so tense," he said, "that I came over. To satisfy myself that she was not . . . And I looked around, just on a hunch. And I heard you tapping . . ." He shook his head "no" again.

Then he turned away from Sandra, head bowed, and Kim ran over to him. She threw her arms around him. "You saved us!"

Ward held her tight. "You're my kid," he said, "even if you do have another father, too."

Kim burst into tears. I felt like crying myself. With relief.

Chapter

35

Two Months Later

I'd told Pop it wasn't appropriate to give a coming-out party for a man released from prison. Naturally, Pop hadn't listened.

He'd ordered Allie — still his favorite sitter because she'd do anything he asked — to send out all the invitations to the party honoring Andrew Frank, Kim's father, who had indeed been born John Charles Jones. I discovered Pop's whole plot only when an invitation came to us by mail.

I rushed to Pop's house to learn more, but before I could say one word, he gave me that cunning smile that means he thinks he's finally won an argument. "Sit down," he said, patting the place beside him at his table. I sat.

"We never would have found Kim alive," he said, "if it hadn't been for Aunt Nancy." He nodded toward the fishpond out the window where his sister had drowned. Good grief, he was still trying to prove, nearly three months later, that he had picked the right place for our family reunion. He said, "Nancy and Fern turned everyone's attention to preventing murder."

Had he forgotten about Eileen and Gertrude? Not enough.

"And isn't it amazing," he said, "that a woman like Gertrude, who was totally without flair and style, should have died for vanity — walking to lose weight and getting in your car to stay dry."

I opened my mouth to say it would be nice to speak well of the dead, but he put his hand on my arm as if to say "wait."

"You will enjoy this party," he said. "I am going to present Ted and Ward with medals on this great occasion."

They did deserve medals, I'll say that. Especially from Pop's point of view.

You see, when Ted woke up in the room at Richmond Hill and found me gone, and then found one abandoned shoe that shouted "kidnapped," he called the police. Before he did anything further, he also called Mary Mary-Sue and Pop, just to be sure they didn't know where I could be. So Pop was in on all the suspense. Which made Ted a superhero, even aside from the fact that he talked to the Richmond Hill staff and found out that Sandra and Arthur had been there for dinner. Ted had guessed one of them might be the villain. He and the police arrived at Sandra's farm not too long after Ward saved us.

What did I know? Everybody accepted Pop's invitation to the coming-out party. Except for John Baylor. "He has his hands full," Pop told us as we waited in Pop's spruced-up living room for the first guests. "Don't you admire the way John's sticking by Maureen and Lucy?"

I did. I wouldn't have expected it of stuffy John, even after he found out he wasn't Lucy's father. After Maureen's arrest as an accessory, he'd found her the best possible trial lawyer, and their strategy, I heard, would be to paint her as a victim of Sandra's madness.

"As a family," Pop said, "we are superbly loyal. Heredity is a marvelous thing."

I thought about Kim's heredity and even mine. "Heredity," I said, "is like Russian roulette. What comes down to you can make you rejoice or work like a dog to get around. Or both. Heredity is a challenge, that's what."

Pop was not listening. He was looking eagerly at the door because the first guests were arriving: Kim with both her fathers, one of whom was also an uncle, and with her mother, who was also a cousin. They were all dressed up, Kim in lacy green cotton and Mary Mary-Sue in red, white, and blue, left over perhaps from a rally. Ward even had on a suit, and so did Andrew. They looked quite happy to be connected.

Andrew was living temporarily with Ward, Mary Mary-Sue, and Kim. Well, after all, he was Mary Mary-Sue's cousin as well as Kim's father. I found myself thinking of a silly song about relationships. Something like, "I am my own grandfather." At least Kim's family wasn't that complicated.

Andrew was good-looking in an interesting way. Pale and slender with a high forehead and dreamy, wide eyes, like a baby's. His face was creased by downward suffering lines, more intriguing than depressing. I could imagine him writing poetry. The kind that's hard to understand and chock full of lofty ideas nobody can live up to.

Perhaps it was interesting for Kim to have two fathers, one to show her how to get lost in the stars, and one to show her how not to get lost in the woods. A nice balance.

"I want you to meet my first father," Kim said proudly to Pop. Kim seemed older than she had before our harrowing adventures, more mature.

Pop wheeled his chair forward. "Any father of Kim's is a friend of mine."

Andrew stuck out one long, slender hand with knots at the joints to shake Pop's. Not like Kim's hand at all. Hers must have come from some grandparent or such. "I've needed some time to myself, to decompress," he said. He had a Texas accent like George Stackhouse's, with California overtones like Fern's, a musical voice like a preacher's. "I needed to sort things out in my own mind and with Kim, here. Kim could hardly believe that, out in California, I'd met a girl whose family had roots in western North Carolina. But of course, that's how I got to know Susan because I was from the place her father came from and always talked about. She said her father had a mean streak but made the mountains sound great." He beamed at Kim. "We have so much in common," he said. "We both keep diaries." Well, thank goodness!

The next ring of the doorbell brought George Stackhouse with his wife, Alice — Kim's blood aunt who had been Eileen's adoptive mother, a large, motherly woman in baby-blue lace. More hugs all around. I'd met Alice at the service for Eileen. I told her how sorry I was about her daughter and had to work not to choke up.

Meanwhile, Fern arrived. "Of course I had to fly back for a party like this!" She handed Kim a small jeweler's box. "I think this is what you wanted," she said. "I will always help Kim any way I can." Meaning, I realized, that she already had, and we should be grateful.

"And now that I'm going to be a lawyer — going to do that for Eileen," Kim said, "I need all the help I can get." For just a moment I thought she was going to cry, but she swallowed any tears. Judging by the number of relatives who kept arriving to embrace her, she'd get plenty of moral support. I was glad Kim was aiming at law school and not marrying Abner.

Finally Pop pulled out two big tin buttons

Allie must have had made for him at that shop on Biltmore Avenue. Each one said HERO. He pinned one on Ward and one on Ted.

Some medals! We all laughed. I guess he figured females aren't heroes. None for me. Only Fern glowered. Then Mary Mary-Sue pinned an orchid on Fern "for all you did," and Fern burst into tears.

And on that happy note, Kim said, "I have something for you, Peaches. You asked me why I had an envelope on my desk marked RATTLE-SNAKE EGGS. I want you to have this and find out for yourself." She handed me the very envelope. I opened it cautiously. As I pulled out a folded paper, there was a swish, a rustle, and something jumped out at me. I swear it tried to bite me. I screamed. I stepped backward against an overstuffed chair and fell into it.

Kim nearly fell over laughing. She picked up an elastic band and a twisted wire from the floor. A trick device. "You stinker!" I said. Plainly, Kim was going to survive. She handed me another box with little gold snake earrings. "For good luck," she said. "Fern tells me snakes are a symbol for rebirth. You helped me start again."

So Pop's party turned out better than I had expected. I even had a chance to ask Fern about that very rare triple line across Eileen's and Sandra's hands. Call me morbid, but I kept wondering about that. It was a useful clue, but aside from that, what did it mean? She'd never told me.

"The old books say it means that a person can act in very different ways on different occasions," she said. "That a person might almost have two personalities." And that was certainly true of Sandra. At her school job she had seemed like a helpful guidance counselor. Then she used the LSD she took from a kid to fry my mind — and she was a killer.

"Actually, speaking of hand reading," Fern said, "I never worried about you, Peaches. The fate line, sometimes called the line of purpose, is strong and straight up the center of your hand. That means you're not likely to be done in."

"But you don't read the future!" I said.

Fern shrugged. "I don't read the future in front of John Baylor. But actually, future reading turns out to be about sixty-five percent correct. And so sometimes . . ."

I should have known Fern would believe at least part of anything marvelous. "Sixty-five percent," I said, "is not the odds I want for my life. And this is the last time I'll ever get mixed up with murder."

Ted said, "That would be nice."

"I am a memory expert," I said, "not a detective. I am a book promoter. Which certainly keeps me busy."

But on the way home I sighed. "You know, for right now, I'm tired of talking about memory," I said to Ted. "I need a little vacation from memory and false memory and the whole schmeer. I need to forget. One week of amnesia would be a nice vacation."

"And yet," Ted said, "without memory you wouldn't be a person. You are who you re-member you are. Plus the present flash of a second. Without memory you couldn't even imagine the future." He'd been reading some of my memory reference books.

"Perhaps," I said, "if memory can be molded, I could learn to remember that I was the queen of England. No, she has her own troubles. And actually, I can't think of anybody I'd rather re-member I am than me. Married to you. You do look marvelous in your medal."

The employees of Thorndike Press hope you have enjoyed this Large Print book. All our Thorndike and Wheeler Large Print titles are designed for easy reading, and all our books are made to last. Other Thorndike Press Large Print books are available at your library, through selected bookstores, or directly from us.

For information about titles, please call:

(800) 223-1244

or visit our Web site at:

www.gale.com/thorndike
www.gale.com/wheeler

To share your comments, please write:

Publisher
Thorndike Press
295 Kennedy Memorial Drive
Waterville, ME   04901